Praise for *The Last Days*

"The most important thing to say about *The Last Days* is that it works. Erudition is seldom welcome at the gates of satire, but the late Raymond Queneau's autobiographical novel of Parisian student life in the 1920s is profound, complex and instantly likable. It is also very, very funny."—Octavio Roca, *Washington Times*

"The flavor of this French novelist's wit is wise and dolorous, like that of someone slightly regretful in the face of helpless recognitions. . . . This novel, luminously rendered into English by Queneau's frequent translator Barbara Wright, demonstrates that the artifices of fiction are among the most satisfying and revealing of all life's patterns."—*New Yorker*

"Queneau writes about this Gallic wasteland with his usual deadpan alley panache, a dextrous mix of neologisms ('subyelped'), malapropisms, and outrageous images that make you laugh and cringe."—Bill Marx, *Boston Review*

"A witty novel that is a witness both to Queneau's marvelous sense of humor and his capacity for self-examination."—*Choice*

"Dazzling in its wordplay."—*Kirkus Reviews*

"The mystery that occurs to me when reading this novel is why it has not been translated into English until now. It's one of the better all-round efforts by one of the major prose fiction writers of our century."—Harvey Pekar, *San Diego Tribune*

The Last Days

Raymond Queneau

Translated by Barbara Wright
with an Introduction by Vivian Kogan

Dalkey Archive Press

Originally published as *Les Derniers jours* in 1936 by Editions Gallimard.
English translation © 1990 by Barbara Wright
Introduction © 1990 by Vivian Kogan
First hardcover edition, 1990
First paperback edition, 1991
Second paperback edition, 1996

Library of Congress Cataloging-in-Publication Data
Queneau, Raymond, 1903-1976.
    [Derniers jours. English]
    The last days / Raymond Queneau: translated by Barbara Wright;
with an introduction by Vivian Kogan.
    Translation of: Les derniers jours.
PQ2633.U43D413   1990   843'.912—dc20   90-3075
ISBN 1-56478-140-2

Dalkey Archive Press
Illinois State University
Campus Box 4241
Normal, IL 61790-4241

Printed on permanent/durable acid-free paper and bound in the United States of America.

Contents

Introduction

Vivian Kogan

THE EVENTS IN Raymond Queneau's *The Last Days* take place in the 1920s, but the novel was written more than a decade later and published in 1936. The thirties were a bleak decade, heavy with foreboding in all of Europe. There was a sense of imminent war and of economic and political instability. The population was aging. The theory of relativity was radically changing the sciences and psychoanalysis was challenging the notion of the subject in Western culture. Such a context may illuminate some of the themes and explain the title of Queneau's novel, at least in part, but it does not explain why the novel had so little initial success. A different climate reigned when the remaining copies of *The Last Days* sold out in 1951, but the novel remained unavailable until 1963. Since then the text has been reprinted more than once, and it is attracting considerable attention now that Queneau's renown is assured and his complete work has begun to appear in the Pléiade edition.

As a retrospective picture of Parisian student life in the 1920s, *The Last Days* draws upon Queneau's intimate journal (1920–1928) for many details. Vincent Tuquedenne is an intellectual adventurer who, according to Jean Piel, is the very likeness of Queneau during his student years. It should be noted that Queneau wrote four novels that constitute an autobiographical quartet of sorts. Queneau's autobiographical interest may have been prompted by his psychoanalytic treatment which began in 1933 and lasted at least six years. Aside from *The Last Days,* the quartet includes *Odile* (1937), a love story set against the backdrop of Parisian literary and political movements in the twenties and thirties, as well as perhaps Queneau's most amusing text, *Chêne et chien* (1937), a novel in verse that transposes Queneau's psychoanalysis in the second part. The last novel of the quartet is *A Hard Winter* (1939), though the resemblances with the author's past are more difficult to identify in this sober, lyrical work. In *The Last Days,* however, the resemblances are so transparent, Queneau felt, so little transposed or fictionalized, that the author refused to reprint the novel for over twenty years.

Like Queneau, Vincent Tuquedenne came to the Sorbonne in Paris to study philosophy in 1920. His parents, shopkeepers, sold their business in Normandy to retire to Paris and keep watch over their only son. Like Tuquedenne, Queneau read voraciously, the acquisition of knowledge being both a function of his intellectual curiosity and a possible way to escape the social determinism that would have led him to become a provincial school teacher or a bureaucrat. The life of the adult petit bourgeois is explicitly characterized in *The Last Days* as a form of slavery the protagonist clearly wishes to avoid. Tuquedenne seems convinced of the uselessness and sterility of studying, in contrast to the fruitfulness and pleasure of reading. Like his fictional character, Queneau was a loner, a rather timid young man, with a broad range of interests. Also like Vincent, Queneau received the first part of his diploma, a certificate of general philosophy and logic, in 1923. In 1926, he was granted his *licence* in philosophy. These similarities between Vincent and Queneau's life are noteworthy, but do not explain *The Last Days,* nor our pleasure in reading it.

A large part of the enjoyment we derive is in identifying the

series of oppositions and similarities, or "rhymes," that constitute the novel. Tolut, for example, is paired with Brabbant:
they are both old, they have drooping mustaches, they seem to
echo one another in the initial chapter regarding the oily
nature of the falling rain and their nostalgia for the good old
days, before the entire cosmos was disturbed by the cannons of
World War I. Similarly, Vincent Tuquedenne and Hublin are
good friends at first; they have long, unkempt hair and share a
common past in Le Havre.

As for the oppositions, they exist both between the genera-
tions and within them, between retired teachers who discover
they are intellectual "crooks" and "real" crooks who go straight.
There is also the paradox of Hublin, who wishes to be a seer,
yet who blinds the one-eyed man, Tormoigne. Another contrast
exists in the explanation his friends give for Hublin's sudden
departure for Brazil—as the height of adventure—and the
motive the reader, who is better informed, attributes to his
flight: to escape the police. There are also less dramatic ten-
sions between Hublin's spiritualism and Tuquedenne's love of
everyday life; between his love of everyday life and his esoteric
reading; between Vincent's taking ideas seriously and Rohel's
refusal to do so; between Alfred's infallible scientific system
and Einstein's theory of relativity; between the living "philosopher," Alfred, and the sterile teaching of philosophy in school.
The possibilities seem endless and they give readers a sense
that they can read the novel in a variety of ways. It can be seen
as the apprenticeship of several young men into a society that
is of questionable moral and intellectual integrity. It can also
be viewed as a literary interrogation regarding the nature of
knowledge, and particularly the way in which culture is handed
down from one generation to the next. It can also be summa-
rized as an investigation of the relation between the ways in
which a society is codified in texts as opposed to the experience
of individuals. Finally, and more literally, it can be described as
the fulfillment of the various destinies of the fictional characters

involved, which holds surprises even for septuagenarians. Yet, on a larger and more existential level, the destinies are predictable. The fate of old men is to die; the fate of French students who have completed their studies is to leave Paris. On this level, the novel may be said to contrast the particular fate of the individual, the accidental, as Plato might say, which is idiosyncratic and usually unknowable, to the generic fate or the essential, which is predictable.

The unique Alfred has the experience to be able to identify and predict both: he recognizes the cycles that dominate a man's life and he develops a system that can predict an individual's fate. Alfred's system deserves a closer look. His method is devised to allow him to win back exactly the amount his father lost at the races twenty years previously, including the rise in the cost of living and the accumulated interest. Alfred's calculations are based on the geographic situation of the racetrack, the orientation of the magnetic currents, the planets, and statistical research on the ninety-one elements of horse racing as a sport. The fantasy nature of the bases for such calculations are immediately apparent, for how does one quantify such information? We thus begin by thinking that Alfred must be a crank; in other words, we start out applying the conventions of the world to the fiction. We are soon surprised and delighted to find Alfred's predictions accurate, not only about the final restitution of his fortune, but also about the amorous and business adventures of the slippery Brabbant, alias Martin-Martin. Queneau plays here with the difference between expectations the reader might have and the laws operating in his literary universe.

Like so many of Queneau's protagonists, Alfred remains modest, a model for humanity. He has been likened to a Tao sage except that his ambition involves money. Yet he merely wants what the pari-mutuel, the state-run betting organization, owes him, nothing more, so he can enjoy a comfortable old age —a house in the country and a nest egg. Above all, he wants to be free to work if he wishes to and, significantly, he discovers that he does. Another way of describing Alfred's ambition is to see it as a desire for justice. Unlike the other old men of the novel, he is not agitated by remorse, ambition, nor lust, though Queneau's narrator never judges any of his characters. Alfred does not judge others either, though he watches them from the perspective of his superior knowledge and sees their foibles clearly. He realizes, for example, that Brabbant is a petty crook and that his meeting with Tolut and Brennuire was no accident, even if Brabbant had mistaken his man. Alfred is nevertheless generous with his advice to Brabbant, refusing, however, to exploit his research for commercial gain. Unlike the other members of the older generation, Alfred does not die. Nor does he leave, as the students do: he remains at his post having fulfilled his destiny and realized his desire—as did Brabbant. The difference is that Alfred alone is responsible for his success.

However exceptional Alfred may be in the fiction, the structure of pairing applies to him as well. Alfred's counterpart is Jules, a fellow waiter. The chapter attributed to Jules, although different in style from Alfred's (for he has none of Alfred's gifts), is also in the first person and constitutes an interior monologue, a situated perspective on the world with which the reader comes to identify. He provides a model of action and reflection, both on his experience and others'. This distinguishes the Alfred/Jules chapters from the others, which are generally in the third person. The external mark of this difference between the Alfred/Jules chapters and the others is that instead of a number, these chapters are entitled by the name of the character. This reflects Alfred's exceptional status and the structural role he plays: he is clearly the unifying center of the story; his narrative presence philosophically embraces all the other characters.

Similarly, the allusions to philosophers and to novelists in *The Last Days* situate Queneau's text in an intellectual tradition and a modernist literary perspective. The poets who attend Brennuire's gatherings provide references to Paul Verlaine, a symbolist poet, and allusions to Jules Laforgue, the symbolist poet who is credited with inventing free verse along with Gustave Kahn. We also find allusions to Flaubert's *Bouvard and Pécuchet;* Herman Melville's *Moby-Dick*—in which a character joins a funeral procession of someone unknown to him; Joseph Conrad's *Lord Jim,* which Queneau read in 1922; Edgar Allan Poe, who wrote about a premature burial; Sophocles' *Oedipus Rex,* as Tolut threatens to put out his eyes. Queneau even imitates the style of Proust in his wonderful pastiche on timidity. The most fully developed intertextual reference is to André Gide's *Les Caves du Vatican* (1922). Like Gide's text, Queneau's is a mixture of irony, fantasy and realism that explodes traditional attitudes toward knowledge and the fictional representation of the world. Most pertinently both novels explore moral questions in a fictionally defined way. In *The Last Days,* Hublin blinds Tormoigne in a totally unexpected action. The reader later realizes, however, during the students' drunken escapade in Le Havre, that violence is indeed the mark of Hublin's character. Such play with the levels of motivation, psychological, moral and fictional, leads us to consider the question of legitimacy or authenticity of literary texts that are presented as fabrications. These questions were especially pertinent in the first half of the twentieth century. Queneau's emphasis on the literariness of his work is reinforced not only by the allusions, but also by the neologisms, puns and rhetorical devices—even Alfred's system—all of which illustrate the primacy of the word and of invention in literature. What is important is not its superficial coincidence with the world, but its revelation of a more profound knowledge.

Furthermore, Queneau's narrative focuses on the beginning and the ending of actions, rather than their development. What is described is the initial formation of the various characters into groups (except Alfred) and their ultimate dispersal or death. The title, *The Last Days,* also evokes the notion of ending or finality. It calls to mind similar titles like Plato's *The Last Days of Socrates.* What similarities can we find between Alfred and Socrates? Philosophers both, though Alfred never goes on trial and lacks a Plato to preserve his teachings. As a result, Alfred's system, unlike Socrates' teachings, is lost to the world, which is seen as advancing in a morass of subjectivism and relativity. Ironically enough today, more than sixty years after Alfred's calculations, theoretical physicists are talking about a so-called super-unified theory or theory of everything (T.O.E.), a masterful set of equations that would embrace both quantum mechanics and relativity. A T.O.E. would permit new understanding of every basic process in nature, from the death of stars to the birth of the universe. But would it be capable of predicting the outcome of a horse race? or of my own enterprise?

The Last Days of Pompeii? This would suggest that the kind of life Queneau describes in the novel, as representative of a larger society on a profound level, was threatened with extinction by an apocalypse of some sort: war? the fragmentation of knowledge? The latter is best illustrated by Tolut's bad conscience. Though he had led an honorable life and had devoted himself to transmitting the knowledge of his time to a generation of students, he can no longer justify the validity of his teaching. His inevitable suicide suggests the fragility of all the institutions of society. The phantom he hopes to leave behind points to the contemporary haunting of our institutions by the nagging doubts we retain about their legitimacy.

The examples I have chosen to mention are limited. But Queneau's brilliant, foresightful and satirical novel offers a wealth of other possibilities.

Dartmouth College

1

THE WEATHER WAS of the little-drops-of-water-here-and-there sort, a sort of damp, night weather. The light from the street lamps was dribbling down in pools on to the pavements. An old man was standing irresolutely at the corner of the rue Dante and the boulevard Saint-Germain, not daring to cross. A lorry brushed against his umbrella; perched on top of some packing cases, a dog barked at its moon-shaped ribs. The fellow stepped back a little, muttering into his mustache, which he wore thick and drooping. Every conceivable kind of vehicle was going by: taxis, owner-driven cars, serf-driven cars, bicycles, hippomobiles, trams. He hated them all. Not so very long before, a box tricycle had nearly run into his ribs, and ever since this brush he had enjoyed segmented breathing and increased prudence; he promised himself that one day he would suppress these death-dealing missiles in no uncertain fashion, but *which* day remained uncertain. Sometimes he imagined himself furtively puncturing the tires of those parked along the pavements; it can easily be done with a small penknife. But he never carried out this project, perhaps because of the risks, because of the possible kicks up the behind. The only thing he was still hoping for was that, on one of those lousy days that cover the cobblestones with grease, one of these instruments would turn turtle and be transformed under his eyes into muddy morsels, its horseman included. In any case it was just the right sort of weather for that. October was neither summer nor winter, neither fish, flesh nor good red herring, but if you insisted on calling it some sort of a fish it would probably be more of a sardine than a herring. That was much more like it: a sardine in oil. Wouldn't you say there was something oily about this pluviosity? He didn't like food cooked in oil; even in a vinaigrette you don't want too much oil. A second old man came and stood by his side on the curb, waiting for a gap that would enable him to cross.

They were as alike as two brothers. But they were not brothers—neither close nor distant ones. Perhaps it was their thick, drooping mustaches that made them as alike as two brothers. In the same way as the innocent eye takes all colonizable natives for multiple examples of the same invariable model, so a different sort of differently innocent eye takes all old men with thick, drooping mustaches for replicas of the same individual. It is true that, conversely, the considered opinion of one of the old men here present was that all young men look alike because of their hairless faces. Even so, it was not he who had chalked up this imprecation in the urinals: "Pull the plug on the clean-shaven mug."

He was called Monsieur Brabbant. He looked at the other, who was called Monsieur Tolut. Monsieur Tolut looked at Monsieur Brabbant. Brabbant said to Tolut:

"You'd think it was oil, wouldn't you? Personally, I don't call this weather, I call it oil."

"What d'you expect—its been like this ever since the war. The shells have played havoc with the seasons. Think back to the prewar Octobers. There was real rain, then. And the sun, where there was any sun, it was real sun. Whereas these days it's all mixed up—the dishcloths with the napkins, and Christmas with Midsummer. These days there's nothing to tell you when to wear your overcoat or when to leave it off."

"What I think, it's because of all the guns that everything has become oily like this."

"That's what I think, too. Just as well that that was the last war, otherwise we'd end up having Christmas at Midsummer, as I was just saying."

Brabbant looked at Tolut from under his brolly.

"My goodness—I rather think I know you, my dear monsieur. I believe we've already met somewhere."

The other considered the matter.

"At the Record Office, perhaps? What they call the National Archives?"

"No, certainly not. I know nothing about the Archives—all I know is the street of that name. And yet your features are by no means unfamiliar to me. I can't help wondering where I can have met you."

"At my brother-in-law's, then?"

"Your brother-in-law?"

"Yes, Brennuire, you know: he publishes art books. You may well have seen me at his place. He does a lot of entertaining: writers, painters, journalists, and even poets."

Brabbant cackled:

"Oh! poets!" he insinuated.

"Some of them are very good," retorted Tolut, offended.

Not that lyricism didn't frighten him quite a bit, but as he often met poets at his brother-in-law's he felt obliged to think well of them. However, being something of a coward, he added:

"Poets, well, naturally!"

The oleaginous drops were no longer trickling down from the black skies. Tolut shut his umbrella. Brabbant did likewise and exclaimed:

"I've got it! Now I remember you! Weren't you in the Luxembourg Gardens all this summer, sitting . . ."

"Sitting on the nursery garden side? Precisely. I remember you too. Were you not in the habit of sitting near the statue of . . ."

"Precisely," said Brabbant, extending his hand. "My name is

Brabbant. Antoine Brabbant. A veteran of 1870. I was seventeen at the battle of Bapaume."

"January the third, 1871. It was won by General Faidherbe, whom the Germans had nicknamed *couch grass* because of his tenacity."

"Ha ha! Very good. Were you there?"

"No. I am—I was—a history teacher. My name is Tolut, Monsieur Jérôme Tolut. My pupils used to call me The Lozenge."

"Kids are so stupid," said Brabbant.

"Some are intelligent. I've had some who knew all the dates in modern history by heart—the dates they have to know for their baccalaureate."

They stayed chatting at the curb.

"Look—I do believe we can cross," said Brabbant.

A lorry had just managed to get wedged between a tram and a bus.

"Let's make the most of it."

They took a few prudent steps.

"It's slippery—it's like grease. Like oil. They still haven't discovered the proper way to pave a street."

They reached the other side.

"It was in the reign of Philippe-Auguste that they started to pave the streets of Paris," said Tolut.

"Really? I'd never have thought it. I am so pleased to have made your acquaintance, dear monsieur. Seeing you every day in the Luxembourg Gardens I said to myself: 'My goodness, what can he be, that gentleman? A businessman? A magistrate? A soldier?' I must admit that I was rather inclined to opt for the latter."

"So you didn't hit on it, eh? The teaching profession! For thirty-five years, monsieur, I taught history. Ancient, modern and contemporary history, French and world history, Greek and Roman history. And geography too, monsieur, I also taught geography: France, Europe, the great world powers. I am even the author of a few modest works on the history of the French

Revolution in the Seine-Maritime, as for the last twenty years I taught at the lycée in Le Havre."

"Seine-Maritime, chief town Le Havre. Sub-prefectures Fécamp, Bolbec, Pont-Audemer, Honfleur," said Brabbant very rapidly.

Tolut stopped in his tracks, looked worried; he hesitated a moment and then started walking again, his eyes fixed on his shoelaces. His companion looked round to follow a charming young girl with his eyes, after which he executed a few stylish, twirling movements with his umbrella.

"History is really damned interesting," he exclaimed vivaciously. "It gives you a knowledge of men :.."

"And of things."

"I am absolutely delighted to have made your acquaintance, dear monsieur," Brabbant concluded.

They had come to the boulevard Saint-Michel. They walked up it towards the Luxembourg Gardens. It began to rain again, even harder. Both reopened their brollies.

"This time it's real water," said Brabbant, with some satisfaction.

"It's the gunfire that has turned all the seasons upside down. Ah! that war. We're still suffering from its effects."

"And this rain; it doesn't look as if it's ever going to stop."

"No, it doesn't look like it."

"What would you say, dear monsieur, to the idea of going and seating ourselves in front of some stimulating beverage?"

"My word: I have no objection."

"And what would you say to the Soufflet?"

"I went there as a youth; I go back an old man," Tolut declaimed.

"Oh! an old man! oh! oh! an old man!"

"Even so, I'm not exactly a child anymore!"

They went into the café with a light heart and, with a casual, sophisticated air, shut their umbrellas. There was very little room; the coats on the pegs were shedding their humidity. The place smelled of dog, of wet dog, of a wet dog who had been smoking a pipe. With some difficulty the two new arrivals found a table, between a group of young people about whose provincialism there was no doubt, and a whore. The group was making a noise to seem to be something; the woman was dreaming. The rain could be heard pelting down on the asphalt. Brabbant and Tolut made contact with the banquette, emitting little sighs of satisfaction. The woman, raising her heavy, voluptuous eyelids, weighed them up with her ruminative gaze. Then she went back to her dream. They, the young provincials, took not the slightest notice of the old men.

"I'll have a Pernod," said Brabbant.

"The same for me," said Tolut, who was not at all in the habit of drinking this beverage.

"Though it's not a patch on absinthe, of course."

"Of course not," said Tolut.

Under the influence of the warmth they had been beginning to feel drowsy. The Pernod woke them up.

"Were you in the war, dear monsieur?"

"Neither in the last one nor in the previous one, alas. But I did my duty, in my own way; I looked on my profession as a sacred mission!"

"I understand you."

"I have formed the opinions of many a young man, monsieur. I have taught them to know their fellowmen . . . the lessons of history . . . its defeats, its victories . . . chronology . . ."

These suggestions being beyond him, Brabbant tossed a few gulps of green alcohol down his throat.

"That's where our politicians fall short—they have no knowledge of history. Or of geography. You know what they say about the French?"

Brabbant looked blank. Tolut informed him of it. The definition amused them. They perceived that it didn't apply to them because even though they had both won decorations, one from the 1870 war and the other for his academic prowess, they did on the other hand possess a thorough knowledge of geography, which for the one was only normal and even as you might say necessary, but which for the other did not seem altogether obvious. Brabbant justified himself thus:

"Because of my travels, you see."

"Have you traveled much?"

"Extensively."

"I haven't traveled extensively. Almost not at all. I really would have liked . . ."

His pensive mustache leaned over the ice cube melting in his glass.

"I really would have liked to travel," he went on. "Ah, monsieur, how many ships have I seen disappearing over the horizon! And how many others returning from the Indies, from the Americas. As we used to say in the old days: the Americas. For twenty years I taught at the lycée in Le Havre. That great harbor of . . . I am speaking of the town, not of the lycée—that was more like a harbor of vice."

"Ha ha!"

"Where was I? Oh yes, Le Havre. Yes, monsieur, I have seen vessels leaving there for distant peripluses—yes yes: peripluses. Some were going to the poles, and others to the antipodes. Whereas I—I have never even set foot on the boat that goes across the estuary to Trouville. I'm too old, now, to go gadding about, or to set sail on some little cockleshell. I'm too old."

He was practically sniveling. Brabbant coughed. His companion recovered a little of his dignity.

"I have pupils who have become sailors, or who live in the colonies. Some of them have sent me postcards from all over the world. From all over the world."

After this echo, he said no more. His companion, breaking the silence, enumerated several regions in which he said he had sojourned, but he might just as well have told him that the country he knew best was a certain French colony in South

America, because of the fifteen years he sometimes believed he had spent there in a penal colony.

2

THERE WAS ALREADY quite a crowd at Monsieur Brennuire's
when Rohel entered the salon. Georges Brennuire introduced
him to his father and to some of the people there, men of the
pen and men of the brush, bearing names well known at the
Mercure de France, or at the small private presses such as
Vanier's. They were impressionist poets or symbolist painters;
they had known friends of Paul Verlaine; they still remembered
tubercular or alcoholic beings who had died in the first years
of the century, victims of rare words and of punctuation. Some
remembered Guillaume Apollinaire's first efforts. It was exactly
two years and two days since Guillaume Apollinaire had died.

J.-H. Cormois narrated a few recollections: when Guillaume
was in Germany on the banks of the Rhine, and when he used
to bury himself in the books in the department of the Biblio-
théque Nationale that was forbidden to the ordinary reader,
and when he was a gunner in Nîmes, and when he got his war
wound, and when he died of the Spanish influenza.

"The Spanish influenza!" someone sneered. "But it was the
plague! The Black Death! Quite simply. Just like in 1348!"

Rohel was most amazed; he had recognized The Lozenge's
voice. Georges had omitted to introduce him to his uncle. But
the latter, raising his eyes, immediately identified his former
pupil.

"My goodness, it's Rohel!" exclaimed Jérôme Tolut in his sour little voice. "So you're in Paris, are you. Are you studying for the entrance examination to the Ecole normale supérieure?"

"Yes, monsieur."

He was not studying for the entrance exam to the above-named college.

"That's good; that's very good. You weren't a bad pupil in my time, but I heard that your philosophy year was most disturbed, most disturbed."

Rohel had deflowered a well-born young lady on Armistice Day, which had caused quite a flutter. The whole town had been talking about it. But Rohel had dismissed it from his mind.

"Where are you? at Louis-le-Grand?"

"Yes, monsieur, at Louis-le-Grand."

He was not at Louis-le-Grand.

"That's good; that's very good," said the old teacher.

The old teacher was beginning to get on his nerves, and Brennuire's sister wasn't there. Yet he had been very much hoping to meet her. But she wasn't there. (J.-H. Cormois was recounting his memories.) He was flattered to find himself rubbing shoulders with poets whom he only knew from their printed works. He had a few vague ambitious ideas himself about literature. But none of this amused him any longer. His vanity had hibernated; what was more, it was snoring. At the moment he could see the people around him only as puppets.

The poet Sybarys Tulle had black nails and kept sticking his fingers up his nose; and he looked old, so old, so old. Benedictine worked, with him. In the old days he was wont to compare his soul to a startled doe, and his ennui to autumn rain. S.-T. Caravant, the novelist, had forgotten to do up his fly-buttons; he was chewing something with what remained of his teeth. He too would have been only too pleased to have some Benedictine, but the other man had monopolized the bottle. He couldn't get his hands on it. (J.-H. Cormois was still recounting his memories.)

Rohel was coming up against all the degrading aspects of everyday life. These vile appearances could not possibly conceal geniuses. He was no longer finding the poet's black nails amusing. And anyway, Benedictine disgusted him and made him feel sick. He drew Georges into a corner, near an artistic vase placed on a period pedestal table.

"It's not much fun."

"We'll show you some really great men," thought Georges. It was just as well that he did not answer thus, for Rohel would have retorted: "Not so great as you say; a bit moth-eaten, your great men; you'd think they were the provinces of Paris."

"It's not much fun," he murmured. "You might at least have warned me that one of my old teachers would be here."

"My uncle? Was he one of your teachers?"

"You might have known it. Never mind, it really doesn't matter. So he's your uncle, is he?"

"It hadn't occurred to me that he might have had you for a pupil. He's getting gaga, you know."

"He always has been."

Rohel was beginning to irritate Brennuire. He had hardly been six months in Paris and he was already trying to lay down the law about everything. You give him the entrée to a literary salon frequented by the best authors and he turns up his nose! He's nothing but a provincial, that's what he is.

"Don't they drink anything but *sweet* liqueurs? Doesn't your father keep any liqueur brandy?"

Indeed he does; some magnificent liqueur brandy which he doesn't offer to his guests. Georges knows where he hides it; Rohel and he move unobtrusively into the dining room and pour themselves out a glass.

"How is it your sister isn't here?"

"She never comes to these little parties. They bore her."

"How right she is. I entirely approve of her. She's most attractive, your sister is."

"You leave my sister alone."

"Give me another glass."

"That's enough. He'll notice that we've been at it."

"You've got no guts. Let me help myself. No, really, you've got no guts."

"All right. Have one more glass. But no more after that."

He himself abstained.

Rohel went back into the salon, his stomach warm and his head hot. J.-H. Cormois was coming to the end of his memories of Guillaume Apollinaire. Rohel listened with extreme interest. He was making himself very comfortable in an armchair, his legs crossed on a level with his nose. His stomach was warm and his head hot. J.-H. Cormois had come to the end of his memories of Guillaume Apollinaire.

"Obviously it's very sad that he died," said Sybarys Tulle, "and especially on a day like that. He played a worthy part in defending his country of adoption, I'll grant that too, but you'll never get me to take those ... calligrammes ... for poetry. I absolutely refuse."

"Obviously, they're just fantasies," said S.-T. Caravant.

"I humbly beg your pardon," retorted J.-H. Cormois, "but they are poems, and even great poems."

Bravo, Cormois, that's really talking! Now *there's* a sound fellow, and he understands young people, too. How could he demonstrate his fellow-feeling? By showing him where old man Brennuire hides his brandy?

The discussion on modern poetry was flagging. One side went on asserting that it was nothing but a hoax; the other side was inclined to indulgence. People were becoming restive. Benedictine often has that effect. Rohel, dared by Georges Brennuire, recited a "cubist" poem. This exhibition had a more or less good effect. While it was being commented on, J.-H. Cormois took Rohel aside. Rohel was finally able to dispense his fellow-feeling. He led him into the dining room and unsideboarded the bottle of strong alcohol.

"Monsieur Brennuire isn't very hospitable to his guests," he said. "Allow *me* to do you the honors of the house."

He filled two glasses. They drank each other's health cordially.

"Remind me of your name, will you?"

"Rohel. Armand Rohel."

"And you're a student?"

"I'm taking an arts degree."

"And you write poetry?"

"Now and then."

He smiled in a somewhat cynical and embarrassed fashion, as if he really did write poetry, and as if the fact of his writing poetry really did make him self-conscious. But he didn't; he didn't write poetry.

"I should be pleased to see your poems."

"And I—to submit them to you."

He felt very much at his ease, now. If this decent fellow wanted to see some of Rohel's poems, Rohel would produce some for him. The nice thing about alcohol is the warmth that floods up to the top of your skull and raises you up to the ceiling. Hm, here's old Brennuire.

"As you see, my dear friend, we're making ourselves at home," said Cormois.

"A recital of modern poetry must be accompanied by the imbibing of ancient alcohol," added Rohel. "And in any case it was I who invited monsieur to make himself at home."

The bloke laughed crookedly. He'd dislocate his jaw if he went on smirking like that.

"Yours is delicious, dear monsieur. It rejoices the heart of the youth of the avant-garde in the person of my modest person. O miracle: it is no longer a torch that the older generation hands on to the younger, but a bottle of Napoleon liqueur brandy. Monsieur Brennuire—in the name of cubism, futurism and dadaism, I thank you most sincerely."

Monsieur Brennuire smiled like a rodent, the corner of his lip curled back. He turned his rabbit's face to Cormois:

"I was looking for you, my dear fellow. Our friend Caravant has a question he would like to ask you."

And he whisked the great man away.

Rohel, left alone, was really beginning to enjoy himself. No, quite definitely, he was never going to grow old. He absolutely refused to grow old and to write poetry. And that was that. There was nothing to stop him having another glass. O miracle, it wasn't a torch that the older generation was handing on to the younger, but a bottle of Napoleon liqueur brandy. Precisely. Hm, here's old Brennuire replaced by young Brennuire. His dear friend Georges.

"You know, my father's furious with you. My goodness, isn't he just furious with you."

"Why? Isn't he pleased? I paid him heaps of compliments on his liqueur brandy."

"You really have got a nerve."

"And you're just a milksop. You know what I said to your father? 'Monsieur,' I said to him, 'the tallow candle that the older generation used to hand on to its successors has been advantageously replaced, by you, by a bottle of Benedictine.' That was really talking, eh? I'm sorry you didn't hear it."

"You're drunk."

"Mind your own business. And lock up your sisters. Oh, sorry, I didn't want to insinuate anything about your sister, you know. Your sister is charming. Personally, you know, I find your sister charming. Why isn't she here tonight?"

"My father told me off..."

"How right he was."

"...for bringing you here. I think he'd prefer you not to come again."

"Really? So he's kicking me out, is he? Because I recited a cubist poem! Monsieur Brennuire has kicked me out because I recited a cubist poem!"

"You'd be well advised to leave now. You're drunk, and you're going to do something silly. It wouldn't be very nice of you if you stayed."

Rohel remained silent for a few moments, and then murmured:

"Monsieur Brennuire has kicked me out because I knew a cubist poem by heart."

He evacuated the room with dignity, grabbed his hat and coat, and caused the door to vibrate behind him. Once in the street he immediately felt at his ease. There was no doubt that he would never again wipe his feet on old shitbag Brennuire's doormat. As for his dear son, he's not worth bothering about; he's irresponsible.

In the métro he found himself sitting opposite a very beautiful woman. He was in luck; she liked young men and she found the idea of going home alone extremely boring. He noticed, with a great deal of pride, that the Armistice and its anniversaries always brought him what he already dared to call good luck.

3

WHEN VINCENT TUQUEDENNE got off the Le Havre train he was shy, an individualist, an anarchist and an atheist. He didn't wear glasses although he was shortsighted, and he was letting his hair grow in order to display his opinions. All this had come to him from reading books, a lot of books, an enormous amount of books.

Having difficulty in carrying the weight of a suitcase that was too heavy for his unexercized muscles, he walked with a hesitant step towards the little hotel in the rue de Kabul, near the Gare Saint-Lazare. His parents had reserved a room for him there, because they knew Madame Sabord, the manageress, very well, and were sure that she would not allow their son to commit any infringement, however minor, of what they considered the rules of pure conduct. Madame Sabord welcomed Vincent Tuquedenne with the conventional signs of the greatest amiability and gave him the worst room in her dump, one that was dark and near the lavatory. Tuquedenne had an idea that it wasn't the one his father had reserved for him but he didn't dare protest, and acquiesced in the deceit.

He didn't stay long in his atticky little room and embarked on the Nord-Sud métro line to go to the Latin Quarter. He made a mistake in getting off at Rennes, thinking he could change there for Saint-Michel, but was nevertheless amazed that he was coping so well. He signed on for the first year arts degree course, new system. He spent his day there, contemplating with scorn the wild youth surrounding him, avid for degrees and stupidly rowdy. It wasn't very different from the new school year at the lycée in Le Havre.

Towards four o'clock he found himself in possession of a university record book and a student's card adorned with his photograph. (He didn't look bad in that photo, he thought; he really did look like a reader of Stirner and Bergson.) The Sorbonne clock informed him that it was five minutes past four; he didn't know what to do until dinner. He walked up the boulevard Saint-Michel as far as the rue Gay-Lussac, and then down it again to the Seine. After which he walked up it again as far as the rue Gay-Lussac, and then down it again to the Seine. He tried the left-hand pavement, having first trodden the right-hand one. Night fell over the town. Vincent Tuquedenne went on killing time with his heels, trampling these disastrously empty minutes that he didn't even know how to fill with white coffees. On the stroke of seven he entered the Chartier in the rue Racine, a restaurant recommended to him by his father, and there absorbed, sitting at a table on the first floor on the left as you go up, a fillet of herring in oil, an andouillette with potatoes, a dessert of almonds, raisins, nuts and figs (a *mendiant*) and a quarter of red wine. Then he went to the Place Saint-Michel, took an AI bus, and got back without difficulty to the Hôtel du Tambour, that being the name of the joint.

When he had shut the door of his room behind him, he perceived that there was no one in it but himself. He endeavored to destroy his solitude by arranging his toilet articles, his clothes, his books. He tried to get excited at the thought that he was living in the rue de Kabul and that this town is the capital of Afghanistan, but without success. All the time he was hearing the lavatory chain in action. He moved a little table under the lamp, took a brand new little notebook and sat down in front of a blank page which he scratched with his writing. Vincent Tuquedenne knew that today was a great day and that he was beginning a new period of his life. So he needed a new notebook for his journal. He wrote quite simply on the first page: *Journal from the 12th November 1920,* but on the second copied out a few more ambitious epigraphs:

Ah! there is something mysterious and somber about your character that makes me tremble: God knows what inferences you draw from so much reading!

—Stendhal.

Διχα δ'αλλων μονοψρων ειμι.

—Aeschylus.

Octave considered himself a philosopher, and profound.

—Stendhal.

Then he tried to describe this first day, but couldn't manage it. A bloody-well-too-bloody cockroach of a depression was sucking the marrow out of his skull. He had imagined, he had believed, he thought that the first day he spent in Paris or rather the first night, well! he would sleep with a woman. It wasn't like that. It wouldn't be like that unless the serving girl were to come up and ask him hypocritically whether he didn't want an ashtray, which would mean that, lovestruck, she was going to fall into his arms.

She didn't take this course.

He heard someone pulling the chain, next door. It was certainly the worst room in the hotel, and he had been cowardly enough not to dare to complain. It was true that he was only going to be there for a month and a half. He couldn't manage to put his day into prose. So he tried to put it into verse. He obtained the following result:

NOVEMBER 1920

Life is sad and ludicrous
elegant gestures of the métro workers
Kabul capital of Afghanistan
the song ceases
the clock continues
the key
No. 18
the water like a cataract the water crashing down
mille sabords! mille tambours!
shiver my timbers!
funny aren't we
and these words are so far away
come on it's too late
oh plans made in another town
what has become of you?

                              EXIT ON THE RIGHT

It was short, and not very good.

He wandered around the few square meters of his room, undressed, brushed his teeth, got into bed chastely and fell asleep, his heart devastated, his loins melancholy, and remembering that family custom demanded that he should go as soon as possible to pay his respects to his grandmother, who lived in the rue de la Convention.

The next morning he went to see Jean Hublin, a schoolmate, who rented a furnished room in the rue Galande. He found him reading a book on our dear departed who talk in the dark.

"It's a joke! Have you become a spiritist?"

"Oh no. I take it with a pinch of salt. It's awfully interesting. I found it secondhand."

"I know. Spiritism isn't serious."

"We'll talk about it some other time."

"That's right. You'll see that it's just a joke."

"That's right, we'll talk about it another time. When did you get here?"

"Yesterday, at one. I'm in a hotel in the rue de Kabul, until my parents come to live in Paris."

"Is it good, your hotel?"

"Yes. Not a student place at all. Travelers, people passing through. I wouldn't like to live in the Latin Quarter."

"Where do you eat?"

"Yesterday, at the Chartier. Today, I'll see. I shall change."

"*I* eat here. Come and look."

Behind a screen there was a little gas stove and a big saucepan. Hublin showed him its contents.

"I cook enough rice to last a week. Then I don't have to bother. From time to time I buy some fish. I eat for practically nothing, like the Japanese."

"You believe in reincarnation, then?"

"What's the connection? Well, naturally I believe in reincarnation. I'm a vegetarian on principle."

"What about the fish?"

"That's like the Japanese."

"Spiritism—I know what it is. You'll find out, it isn't serious."

"So you're in favor of serious things?"

"I'm in favor of life. Those people, they hate life. They hate everyday life."

" 'Ah, how *daily* life is!' said a poet you were in the habit of quoting to me last year."

"A very bad poet. Long live the métro, and down with reincarnation!"

"You aren't serious."

"I love life."

"What have you done since you've been in Paris?"

"What d'you expect me to have had time to do?"

"I'm asking you."

"And you, what do you do?"

"I go to Sainte-Geneviève."

"You go to church?"

"Of course not, it's a library. You'll see, you can find everything you want there. There's the Sorbonne library, too. By the way, did you choose the old or the new system?"

"The new."

"I chose the old; it's easier."

"And I, the new. It's more difficult."

"So you attach some importance to those exams?"

"No, of course not. I don't give a hoot for those exams."

"Tell me, are you still a Bergsonian?"

"I used to be under his influence. At the moment, I'm a dadaist."

"A what?"

"I'm in favor of the Dada movement."

"And you talk about being serious?"

"Of course. It's very serious."

"You certainly do love paradox!"

"I love life."

"What do you know about life?"

"Nothing. That's another paradox."

"You're too clever for me. No, though, your attitude is too facile. What haunts *me*—do you know what haunts me? It's death. Or rather, life after death. Haven't you ever gone in for table turning?"

"Have you got to that point?"

"If the afterlife could be experimentally proved, it would be an unheard-of spiritual revolution. If we were certain we were going to live after death . . . and to live again."

"Really? Do you believe that spirits live in table legs?"

"I don't know. These are questions that I put to myself."

"I've put them to myself too. The answer is in the negative."

"You're very sure of yourself."

"There's such a lot of eyewash in everything those people say. And anyway, they hate life. Have you read Nietzsche?"

"Yes. I don't like him. He went mad."

"Better a mad life than a reasonable death!"

"Oh, you know, your paradoxes don't impress me."

"Are you going to come and have lunch with me?"

"No, old man, I can't. I have to manage this way. Rice, fish."

"I thought it was because of reincarnation."

"It's because of both."

"Aren't you going to come out, either?"

"No, old man, I'm going to stay here and read."

"Ah well. Tell me, where is it, the Sainte-Geneviève library?"

"To the left of the Panthéon, when you come from the rue Soufflot."

"And it's open to the public?"

"Yes. You'll see, you can find everything you want there. You also have the right to use the Sorbonne library."

"Many thanks."

"We'll see each other on Tuesday, at Brunschvicg's class?"

"That's right. Tuesday, at Brunschvicg's class."

"Good-bye, old man."

"Good-bye, old man."

4

"I'M TRULY SORRY but I've already engaged someone. You seem intelligent and resourceful. I believe we would have got on well. But what can I do, I can't go back on my decision. I'm really very sorry."

"I'm sorry too, monsieur."

"You can always leave me your address. I may well get in touch with you one day."

"Certainly, monsieur."

"Well then, your name, first names and address?"

"Rohel, with an *h* in the middle, Armand, Collège Sully."

"Aha, Collège Sully."

"Yes, I'm a housemaster."

"Ah, a housemaster! I understand why you would like to find another situation. It is not a very amusing profession."

"Not very."

"How sorry I am that I've already engaged someone. The thing is, you came too late! Ah well, should the occasion arise, I'll write to you."

The young man stood up, bowed and disappeared. Monsieur Martin-Martin remained apparently pensive for a few moments and then called his typist.

"What did you think of him?"

"He's quite a good-looking boy."

"Ah, silk stockings!" he said, looking at the girl's legs, "it's a fashion that will go to my head. You may go."

She went out elegantly. Once again Monsieur Martin-Martin remained immobilized in his indecision for a few moments and then, taking his overcoat and bowler hat, left. It was a bit nippy, but what you might call nice weather for November. He walked as far as the boulevard Sébastopol. He caught an 8 bus and got off at the Luxembourg Gardens. A crisp little wind was chilling the benches and chairs and driving the last strollers out of the gardens. Monsieur Tolut was not of their number. Monsieur Martin-Martin left this place, slightly disgruntled, slightly chilled. Whereupon he told himself that a little grog wouldn't do him any harm. With a view to taking his medicine in the greatest comfort, he chose the Soufflet. While swallowing the Americano that Alfred had brought him, Monsieur Martin-Martin looked around him casually. This time too, he was disappointed. Alfred came up to him.

"Is monsieur looking for someone?"

"No, Alfred, thank you. It's the depths of winter already."

"A very bad winter, believe me, monsieur."

"You think it's going to be a bad winter, Alfred?"

"Yes, monsieur, because of the planets."

"That's extremely interesting."

"There's a veritable telescoping of the planets, monsieur. Believe me, we're in for a very bad winter."

"What do I owe you, Alfred?"

Monsieur Martin-Martin left him a generous tip. He returned the next day at about the same time. The cold had got colder.

"You see, monsieur, what I was telling you yesterday," said Alfred, bringing him an Americano. "And it's going to get worse."

"Do you perhaps bet on the horses, Alfred?"

"Monsieur has guessed right away."

"Of course I guessed."

"Monsieur is very clever. Although actually, I do not bet on the horses. It was a tragedy in my family, monsieur. My father ruined himself on the horses the way other people do on the girls, on the cocottes, as they used to say in those days."

"Ah, the cocottes!" sighed Monsieur Martin-Martin.

"My father ruined himself, monsieur. I would say more: he committed suicide. It was terrible. At his deathbed, I swore I would never bet on the horses. I was fifteen. So far I have kept my promise, but . . ."

"But?"

"I am secretly working on an infallible system to win at Longchamp, Vincennes, Auteuil and Enghien. And when this system has been perfected, I shall win back all the money my father lost, taking into account the rise in the cost of living, of course."

"And what do you base your system on?"

"In the first place, on the geographical situation of the racecourses and the orientation of the magnetic currents that cross them; and then on the course of the planets; and finally on statistical research bearing on the ninety-one constituent elements of the hippic sport."

"Ah! And do you think you'll have finished soon?"

"In two or three years, monsieur."

"Bring me a very black very hot small coffee," said the sourish voice of a customer who had only just sat down.

"Well! who'd have thought it!" exclaimed Monsieur Martin-Martin. "It's Monsieur Tolut!"

"I rather think I recognize you," said the latter.

"I'm Monsieur Brabbant. You remember, the battle of Bapaume, ocean voyages . . ."

"Oh, quite so, quite so. I am delighted to see you again."

"And so am I! I know so few people in Paris that it is a real pleasure to meet an acquaintance. No relations, no friends: alone in the world. Allow me, dear monsieur, to call you my dear Tolut!"

Tolut examined him with the suspicion of the old.

"Do you play billards, Monsieur Brabbant?"

"Indeed I do," replied Brabbant.

"Well then! why don't we try our strength?"

Brabbant accepted enthusiastically.

They went to the Ludo and had to wait some time until a table became free. The game began with remarks like "I haven't played for quite a time" and "I used to be very good but I'm out of practice." The ex-soldier of 1870 had to acknowledge his defeat by the officer of state education who beat him by twenty-seven points out of a hundred. They parted extremely satisfied with one another. The next day Monsieur Tolut gained another victory, and the day after that Monsieur Brabbant once again had to confess himself beaten. Three days later he found himself obliged to accept a handicap of twenty-five points, despite which he once again bit the dust that besprinkles the Ludo floor in uneven layers.

"I'll get my revenge tomorrow."

"No, my dear Brabbant . . ."

"How d'you mean, no? It was touch and go today."

"Yes, but tomorrow is Sunday, and I won't be able to come."

"Well then! I'll see you on Monday, in that case."

"I'm going to see my brother-in-law."

"Ah yes, your brother-in-law. Monsieur . . . Brennuire?"

"That is correct. Believe it or not, the other day one of my former pupils whom I met there by chance, well not properly speaking by chance seeing that he is a friend of my nephew, and my nephew invited him, well, this young man recited a cubist poem to us."

"Not possible," said Brabbant, very genuinely surprised.

"I will confess that I didn't understand a word, and neither did my great friend the famous poet Sybarys Tulle."

As the name of Sybarys Tulle didn't seem to ring a bell with Brabbant, Tolut continued:

"Sybarys Tulle, you must know him, the author of *Le Soulier d'Améthyste,* one of the founders of *Le Mercure.*"

"How I envy you, to be able to frequent men of such merit," declared Brabbant in a voice trembling with emotion.

"It is a great honor for me."

"I have the most profound admiration for Monsieur Tulle," said Brabbant, not very sure of himself.

"Have you read his poems?"

"Shall I make a confession? *Le Soulier d'Améthyste* is my bedside book. Poetry, quite simply, is my hobby."

"Would you be a poet?" asked Tolut, startled by this singular revelation.

"Not at all, not at all. But I read almost nothing but poetry. I find refreshment in it from my business, from the strain of everyday life. Not only am I interested in poetry, but also in poets, poets in person, in flesh and blood."

"Would you like to make the acquaintance of Sybarys Tulle?"

"I wouldn't make so bold . . ."

"But there's nothing easier!" Tolut screeched. "Just come next Thursday. My brother-in-law will be delighted."

"I wouldn't like to be de trop."

"But not at all! I'll mention it to him tomorrow. Nothing easier. He will certainly be delighted. Then that's all right for Monday?"

"That's all right for Monday, my dear Tolut, and thank you for your invitation."

"Not at all, not at all."

Tolut had made himself late for dinner; he nourished himself at fixed hours in a boardinghouse where unpunctuality covered one with shame and aroused the most malicious suspicions; he fled. But Brabbant left in no hurry. He dined in a mediocre restaurant, ate with relish, and then went and sat in the Soufflet. Alfred brought him a black coffee.

"Do you believe, Alfred, that people can foretell the success of something they undertake?"

"It depends on the planets, monsieur, and on statistics."

"Which ones?"

"It all depends, monsieur. If monsieur would care to give me a few details about this undertaking, I might perhaps be able to advise monsieur."

"Hm, hm! but it's not so easy."

"That's already an indication."

"I will go so far as to tell you, Alfred, that this . . . undertaking . . . must remain secret."

"A very important detail, but which is not enough. Could you tell me, for example, when it will start?"

"It's already started—a good month ago."

"What day?"

"Alas, I don't remember."

"And you don't remember what time?"

"It must have been at around six."

"In the morning?"

"In the evening."

Alfred looked at the ceiling.

"Must remain secret. Started on an unknown day, at around eighteen hours."

He took a notebook out of his pocket, each page of which was covered in figures and bore multiple traces of fingerprints. Alfred turned over its pages with his right index finger, dampened with saliva.

"I can only give you a rough answer," he explained. "I haven't got the day, you see."

"That'll still be something," said Brabbant.

"Well then, it's very easy. I have a ready reckoner here, what you might call logarithmic tables. Let's have a look. Ah, here we are!"

He smiled.

"Was monsieur born on an odd day of the month?"

"A first."

"And an odd month?"

"How do you mean?"

"In January? in March? in May?"

"You've got it."

"Monsieur was born on the first of May?"

"Precisely."

"Well then! There are nine chances out of ten that what you are undertaking will succeed."

And he added:

"But not in the way you think."

Brabbant left, pensive, and wearing a bowler hat.

5

15 November	Coffee	1.-
	Lunch	5.90
	Tobacco	1.-
	Fusees	0.20
	Métro	1.-
	Dinner	6.30
	Newspaper	0.15
16 November	Coffee	1.50
	Lunch	5.30
	Fusees	0.20
	Métro	1.-
	Dinner	5.50
	Newspaper	0.15
17 November	Coffee	1.-
	Shave	1.-
	L'Ordre naturel	0.25
	Lunch	4.65
	Tobacco	1.-
	Fusees	0.20
	Métro	1.-
	Dinner	5.15
	Newspaper	0.15

18 November	Coffee	1.-
	Lunch	5.90
	Fusees	0.20
	Métro	1.-
	Dinner	5. exactly
	Newspaper	0.15
19 November	Coffee	1.-
	Shave	1.-
	Lunch	4.75
	Tobacco	1.-
	Fusees	0.20
	Métro	1.-
	Dinner	6.05
	Newspaper	0.15
20 November	Coffee	1.-
	Lunch	5.30
	Le Libertaire	0.20
	Fusees	0.20
	Métro	1.-
	Dinner	5.90
	Newspaper	0.15

This was how Vincent Tuquedenne lived.

Walking down the boulevard Saint-Michel one day, as he was passing the Source he bumped into some young people who were just going to have a drink in this famous café.

"Here's the great man!" they exclaimed.

Vincent then recognized Muraut and Ponsec, accompanied by two persons unknown. Muraut introduced his companions:

"Wullmar, PCN, Brennuire, a colleague of yours."

And, pointing to him:

"Tuquedenne, a chap who's read everything. Now at the Sorbonne."

"I rather think I've seen you at Brunschvicg's lectures," said Brennuire.

"That's possible. I'm doing philo(sophie) géné(rale)."

"I recognize you because of your hair."

"You really ought to get it cut," said Ponsec. "Makes it look dirty."

Tuquedenne didn't answer.

"Coming with us, then?" Muraut suggested. "We're going to have a *demi.*"

He and Ponsec had been among the most recalcitrant dunces in the Le Havre lycée. They had been awarded a pass in the baccalaureate like a sort of Croix de Guerre, because of the heroic deaths of their genitors. They now counted on studying medicine for many years and prolonging their stay in the Latin Quarter until an advanced age.

All five went into the back room and sat down.

Two chaps were playing billiards; badly.

"Well, old man, where are you living?" asked Muraut.

"Rue de Kabul."

"Rue de Kabul?"

"It's near the Gare Saint-Lazare."

"Funny idea to hang out there," said Ponsec. "*We* live in the rue Gay-Lussac."

"There's bags of brothels near the Gare Saint-Lazare," said Brennuire.

"There's certainly no shortage," Tuquedenne confirmed, although he would have been incapable of coming up with a single address.

"Do you know Rohel? He's doing philo(sophie) too."

"I've never met him at the Sorbonne."

"He doesn't have a lot of time to go there. He's a *pion.*"

"He's from Le Havre too," said Ponsec, who was possessed of local pride.

"And Hublin—what's become of him?" asked Muraut.

"He's become a spiritist," replied Tuquedenne. "He eats

nothing but rice and advocates chastity."

The others guffawed.

"Is he the chap with all the thatch who was with you?" asked Brennuire.

"Got to be," said Muraut.

"I spotted them both," said Brennuire.

Once again the compatriots slapped their thighs. As for Wullmar, he didn't condescend to laugh and remained silent. Brennuire continued:

"Are you a spiritist too?"

"Far from it."

"He's a Bergsonian," said Muraut.

"When you're doing philo(sophie), it's preferable not to have any personal opinions," Brennuire remarked.

"Don't you have any?" Tuquedenne asked him, amazed.

"I have those of the professors, which is more advisable."

"For me, they don't count for much."

"They count in the exams."

"Brennuire's right," Muraut put in. "Personal ideas, they're what fail you."

"Especially in PCN," Vincent retorted.

"He thinks it's only imbeciles who do PCN," said Wullmar, closely examining his *demi.* "He gives me a pain with his philo(sophie)."

Tuquedenne smiled. It was better to take this as a joke.

The others began to talk broads. Muraut had just dropped a kid who worked at the stationer's on the corner of the rue Saint-Jacques and the rue Soufflot. She was chasing him, but there was nothing doing, he didn't want a concubine. As for Ponsec, he had a hell of a thing about a mulattress who was studying medicine, it plagued him night and day. However long it took him he was determined he'd have her one day. Brennuire disapproved of these student amours, and was all for ancillary ones. He made no secret of the fact that every evening he had it off with Papa's maid. Wullmar sang the praises of the houses of tolerance. Whereupon Muraut, who was very laical, remarked that churches ought to be called houses of intolerance. Brennuire, while calling him an "homais," accused him of having pinched that quip from somewhere or other. Wullmar then claimed that he had one day made eyes at a Sister of Charity. These uninhibited remarks continued for a time and then they parted, the PCNs one way, Brennuire another, and Tuquedenne in a third direction.

Vincent was in low spirits when he left them. He reproached himself: firstly, for having spoken ironically about his best friend, which was despicable; secondly, for not having given Wullmar hell, which was cowardly; and thirdly, for the others' sexual adventures.

All day long he pondered over this sorry observation: that he was a virgin and a coward. That evening, when he went down into the métro he was not yet in despair, but when he met Hublin the next day he was still a virgin and a coward.

"I saw Muraut and Ponsec yesterday. What cretins they are, always talking about skirts. They want to make out that they're already medical students. It's painful to listen to them."

"Muraut isn't a bad sort."

"There was a friend of Rohel's with them, who's taking a degree. He boasts of not having any personal opinions. He's the typical Parisian arriviste, you can see that."

Tuquedenne saw that Hublin wasn't paying any attention to his gripes, so he shut up. They walked for some time in silence.

"If you're really a Bergsonian," Hublin said suddenly, "you ought to be a spiritist."

"That's possible, but I'm not really a Bergsonian."

"Well, what I meant was that you ought to take an interest in psychical research. You can't neglect that side of psychology. If the survival of the soul for even a few days could be proved, that would already be an enormous result."

"I don't give a damn. What interests me is life, life on this earth. All the rest's just the ravings of madmen, as Nietzsche says."

"Then you think I'm mad? And Nietzsche—wasn't he mad?"

They had reached the corner of the boulevard Saint-Germain and the rue Saint-Jacques when two pimps wearing caps and blue raincoats passed them and turned round. One said: "What a couple of clowns, eh, with their badly cut hair."

The other said:

"It's a disgusting sight."

Then they went their way, guffawing.

Tuquedenne and Hublin continued their discussion. But when Tuquedenne got home he was no less prostrated than on the previous day. He started to plot some murders, and wondered whether Hublin was even more cowardly than he. But Hublin too was dreaming of vengeance and, as he believed that thoughts materialize, he was trying to compensate for the noxiousness of his own thoughts by emitting pastel-colored astral shapes.

On the 17th of the month of December Vincent Tuquedenne drank a coffee, that was one franc, lunched for the sum of five francs thirty, bought a packet of tobacco for one franc and a box of fusee-matches for zero francs twenty centimes, took the métro twice, that was one franc, dined for the sum of six francs ten centimes and bought *le Journal*. This last expense amounted to zero francs fifteen centimes.

On the 18th he departed for Le Havre, for it was the vacation, and furthermore his parents were moving house. As of the 1st of January they were going to live in the rue de la Convention with grandmother Tuquedenne because of the crisis. On the day of their departure he went to look at the sea one last time; he tried to smoke a pipe but the persistent rain put it out. In the train, the passengers were talking of Landru. He spent the week after Christmas at the Hôtel du Tambour, but because of the presence of his parents Madame Sabord gave him a good room. It was a boring week with furnishing preoccupations and family outings. They moved in at the end of the year and lost no time in settling down into new habits.

Alfred

THAT GENTLEMAN—it would be of no interest to tell you exactly how long he has been coming here. The main thing is that he does come, and every time he comes he talks to me and we have a chat; he's interested in what I say to him, and I look as if I'm interested in what he says to me, even though he never tells me what he does, what he is, where he comes from, where he's going, or what profession he follows. I have a lot of customers, old and young, men and women, fat ones and thin ones, civilians and soldiers. At the beginning of the year there's a slight change, some students leave, others arrive, old men die, young men age. When January comes around, it's what you might call always the same ones who come to my tables. This year there are several groups of young men who regularly meet at them. Some concern themselves with politics, others are interested in literature, some talk sports and women to you; it's always like that, every year; whatever happens, every species is represented. Even during the war it was like that. That's why I go in for statistics. That's what they're like this year? Well then, next year it will be just the same. There will be some who will talk about literary things and others about political things and others about sporting whats-its and all of them about sex, not counting the ones who have long hair and think no end of themselves and not counting the ones who don't say much and who make you wonder what sorts of subjects they're studying and what's in their heads, but after all that's none of my business. And then there are the old men, the ones who've been coming for dozens of years and who've inevitably acquired their own habits. And then there are the women, too. Some of them are little bits of skirt brought here by their men friends; they're licensed and don't do much trade, my goodness. If I were a woman who'd fallen on hard times and into prostitution, I certainly wouldn't wear down my high heels in the Latin Quarter, there's not enough money in it. They're nice to me; they have to be, they stay here for whole days over a *bock;* that doesn't come to much of a tip in the end. If everyone was like that we wouldn't pick up a great deal in our day's work; all the more so in that everyone in the Quarter tends to be like that. The time that gets wasted in a café like this, it's unbelievable.

This year there's something I find odd. None of these young people has started a review yet. I do believe that this is the first time. The reviews I've seen started! But I tell myself that these things don't happen in the Quarter anymore and that the young people who have kept up with the times, the young people who know what's what, don't come around here at all anymore and prefer the more remote districts. Well, that's their business; to see reviews being started or not to see reviews being started, it makes no odds to me as you can well imagine.

To come back to that gentleman, he started coming here at the beginning of last year, at the beginning of the academic year, that is. I count by academic years of course; in October they arrive and then in July they depart. So it was round about October that he started coming. Last year, he never came. Sometimes he came alone, and sometimes with another gentleman much like himself. They're both elderly gentlemen, and speak well. I have the impression that they didn't meet by chance but that he wanted it to happen. He—that's the first one I was speaking of. He's called Monsieur Brabbant. The other one's called Monsieur Tolut. Well! it's an impression I have, but I think Monsieur Brabbant wanted to make the acquaintance of Monsieur Tolut. And why? It's none of my business, of course, yet I remember one day this winter Monsieur Brabbant asked me whether I thought his undertaking would succeed, and I asked him what sort of undertaking it was; then he told me that it was a secret. I took my notebook out of my pocket and told him that there was a good chance that it would succeed, but not in the way he thought. But he hadn't told me what it was. In any case, my reply was right, and it's certain that there is a good chance that it will succeed, but not in the way he believes. I've seen them both very often since; they come at around six-thirty or seven and have an aperitif together. Before that they play billiards, after which they come here. It's the same every day. They chat, and I've found out that Monsieur Tolut is much better at billiards than Monsieur Brabbant. For a little time now there have been three of them. They're here every day; I see to it that they have their own table, they sit down, chat, and drink their Pernod. The third one is called Monsieur Brennuire. All three look as if they're old friends and yet I am well aware that it isn't even six months since they got to know one another, or at least since they got to know Monsieur Brabbant, because the other two have already known each other for quite some time, seeing that one of them is married to the sister of the other one. Personally I call them the two brothers-in-law, and the other one, what you might call the entrepreneur, I call the undertaker, because he is undertaking something. Of course this is a play on words, and not a very good one. Well then, they all three come here virtually every day and I serve them their Pernods. For their part, they chat. They discuss politics, literature, and what they'd like the weather to do, and then they also talk about Landru. They don't seem to be much interested in sports, and when they talk about women it's only to make slightly smutty jokes about them. I can understand that they aren't interested in sports, but they might talk about women in a different way. All they do is talk about them because it looks as if they're somewhat tired of the thing itself, except for Monsieur Brabbant who chases very young girls, so far as I can tell. I believe it depends on the planets. People who are born under a particular planet go hard at it with the women until an advanced age, while those who are born elsewhere, well, they get slack very young. It's the same everywhere in life; people are this way or that because of the planets and the stars. And then, statistics have to be taken into account. But naturally, statistics about horses, you can go ahead because it's printed and it's all done officially. When it's a question of knowing who is making love and how many times a week and since when, well then of course there aren't any official figures and you can only talk about it more or less at random, without any serious scientific basis. Naturally, if I wanted to, *I* could work out some statistics on that too, but I'm more particularly concerned with a different branch of the science.

Apropos of science, I've read some articles in the papers about that German who's called Einstein and his relativity. It's the fashion at the moment and it seems there's nothing in it. I heard a gentleman who claims to be in the know saying that it can't stand up in the face of the facts and that when it's eight o'clock in a station, it isn't five to eight in the train, not even if the train is traveling very fast. That was his argument. It seems that this Einstein measures the speed of time by shots fired from cannons, clocks in Manchuria and trains traveling in every direction, so you end up not knowing where you are. *My* system will be scientific, and with my system you'll be absolutely certain to win at the races. It will be based at the same time on magnetic currents, on the planets and on statistics, which means that as everything has been foreseen, you're sure to win. With my system I shall win back all the money they stole from my father, plus compound interest, and after that I shall go and live in the country unless I come back here, but that won't be of the slightest importance anymore.

To come back to Einstein, I've heard young men saying things like this: it upsets all the ideas that have been accepted up to the present. But I know that old song, and ten years from now I know very well that their younger brothers will be coming to drink their coffees feeling that their hearts are broken by some cruel girlfriend or by a great ambition, and relativity isn't going to change anything very much for them. For personally I'm a philosopher, and no one has any idea how much experience of the world an old waiter can have. Nothing upsets anything, not even a war. I spent the war here, there were the German bombers and then Big Bertha, the customers weren't the same, we had aviators and Americans and well, fundamentally it didn't make the slightest difference and as for me, I was still a waiter. And neither Einstein nor his relativity is going to change that.

To come back to the entrepreneur, I've noticed a curious thing, which is that he seems much more friendly towards Monsieur Brennuire than towards Monsieur Tolut. It may be because he hits it off more with the one than with the other, although it may be for a different reason. Well, all I see in the whole thing is that it gives me a group of new customers, very faithful and very regular ones, which makes up for the negligible tips they leave, for from that point of view these gentlemen are not particularly openhanded.

So there we are, they come, and we have some customers. We get young ones, old ones, men, women, fat ones, thin ones, civilians, soldiers. My job is to serve their drinks. What I hear, what I see, doesn't make any difference to what I think. I've already seen everything. What I hear, what I see, is none of my business. I serve their drinks and I make my calculations. In two or three years' time I shall have finished, I shall have perfected my system and I shall build up my father's fortune again. After that I shall retire to the country, unless I come back here, but that won't be of the slightest importance anymore.

7

ROHEL AND Brennuire found Wullmar sitting in front of a *demi*.

"Beer in the morning disgusts me," said Rohel.

"Cheers," said Wullmar.

And he emptied his glass.

"I'll have a cognac."

He imagined he was going to impress him, but Wullmar had been around. Brennuire ordered a white coffee.

"Well then, so you were bored rigid this morning?" Wullmar asked.

Rohel wanted to give him some idea of how it had been and attempted to paint a brilliant picture of a session at the Sorbonne, with the pack of erudite imbeciles and the little dolls who think that all you have to do is take notes, not forgetting the twitchy-faced man driveling on the rostrum. He gave it all he'd got, and more, in the way of the picturesque and the caricatural, the satirical and the lyrical. But Wullmar took refuge in an erudite mutism that made a great impression. Rohel wanted to strike up a friendship with him, but Wullmar repelled his advances with a chess-player's precision. He went off discouraged, his only consolation being the prospect of going and putting on the feed bag with boarders and day boarders.

"He hasn't been turned into a complete idiot by philo(sophie), that fellow," said Wullmar. "But you can't help wondering why he puts on such an act. It makes him look like a queer."

"I don't agree," said Brennuire. "And anyway, he's in love with Thérèse."

"That doesn't prove a thing," Wullmar retorted.

And then:

"How would you react if he was sleeping with Thérèse?"

"Swine."

"It's a question that springs to mind, even so."

Brennuire shrugged his shoulders.

"It's true," Wullmar went on. "Why are you boasting about Rohel being in love with Thérèse? In the first place, I shall ask him if it's true next time I see him, and what's more you'd be very fed up if they were sleeping together."

"*I* would? What business is it of mine?"

"I know you. You'd like to prevent your sister from making love until she's married, the poor child. As if she couldn't have a few shots at it beforehand. I'm not saying with me, because she detests me, but with that Rohel, for example. They'd make a fine couple. I can well imagine . . ."

"That's enough. I'm going."

"Good idea. Good-bye."

And, keeping his hand in his:

"Do you know that Thérèse is the only girl I've met with whom I'd like to make love?"

"You bore me."

Brennuire disengaged his hand and left with dignity.

They hadn't waited lunch for him. So he ate some tepid stew, reading the paper, and then drank a cup of coffee that smelled of dishrags.

"Not good today," he said to Mélanie, who was clearing the table at top speed.

"Should've come home on time, you didn't really think I was going to make you some fresh, whatever next?" replied the dear old servant.

She bored him too. He went and knocked on Thérèse's door. He was told "come in"; even so he went in.

"What d'you want?"

"Nothing."

"Then why are you disturbing me?"

He sat down and placed his right ankle on his left knee.

"You wouldn't have had a letter, by any chance?"

"A letter from whom?"

"From one of my friends."

"And you'd expect me to tell you if I had had one?"

"Precisely."

"You can be so stupid."

"Has he written to you, yes or no?"

"Who is supposed to have written to me?"

"I'm not going to tell you."

"Poor boy."

He stood up solemnly.

"You've no reason to be proud of yourself," Thérèse told him.

He went and shut himself in his own room to write an essay on mental dynamism, which he intended to do in three sections. He stopped at the beginning of the second, rather exhausted. Then it occurred to him that he felt like going to the Mahieu to meet a few pals from the Faculty of Law who, like him, were considering becoming assistant editors in some ministry or other, hoping thereby to lead a nice easy life dedicated, maybe, to literature.

In the boulevard Saint-Michel he came across the hirsute contingent. Perhaps he might tell them a thing or two. He suggested they should all have a drink. Hublin asked for a hot milk and Tuquedenne a white coffee. He ordered a cognac, to impress them. From deeds he went on to words.

"You know, I had a good evening the other day with Muraut and Ponsec, and some other pals you don't know. We played a

terrific practical joke on Ponsec, the one about putting someone's eye out, do you know it?"

The hirsute contingent didn't know it.

"You blindfold a chap and then get him to start walking,
with his index finger pointing in front of him. You tell him:
'You're going to put out so-and-so's eye.' In the meantime you
put some moistened bread in an egg cup. The chap sticks his
finger into it and believes he really has put a pal's eye out. We
played that trick on Ponsec. He fainted."

"With good reason," said Hublin.

"What a laugh we had. We drank a nice little white wine.
Muraut and Ponsec are good friends. Afterwards we went to
the rue Blondel. What a laugh we had."

The other two said nothing. Brennuire went on, speaking
very quickly:

"Why didn't you study medicine? I bet I know why not.
Because of the stiffs. Me too, stiffs disgust me. You know,
before they're brought into the amphitheater, they remove the
worms they have inside them."

"People ought to respect the dead," said Hublin.

"Pah! What *is* a corpse? The only thing it's good for is the
maggots!" said Brennuire.

Tuquedenne listened to him without the slightest sign of
impatience.

"What about your crackpots?" Brennuire asked him. "Are
you still reading those crackpots' literature?"

"What crackpots?"

"The dadaists."

Vincent handed him the book he had been resting his elbow
on. Brennuire opened it at random and read:

> *DADA is intangible*
> *Like imperfection*
> *There are no pretty women*
> *Any more than there are truths.*

"It's not true. There *are* pretty women!"

"Just as there are truths," said Tuquedenne.

"Well then?" Brennuire asked.

"The mask of skepticism. I'm like Descartes: *Larvatus prodeo.*"

"It's not serious," said Brennuire.

"If I took Dada seriously I shouldn't be a dadaist, and if I didn't take Dada seriously I shouldn't be a Leibnitzian."

"I'm going to see some pals at the Mahieu," Brennuire concluded in disgust. "That'll give me a rest from these acrobatics."

Tuquedenne was by no means displeased at having thus shut up a former student of the Lycée Louis-le-Grand, a chap who had spent his whole childhood in Paris.

"That was horrible, that joke," Hublin said suddenly.

"What joke?"

"The eye being put out."

"They're medical students' stories," Tuquedenne said absent-mindedly.

He asked for writing materials, and there and then drafted an outline of his philosophical system.

1. *Philosophical method consists: a) in personal research that may result either in adopting an existing system or in establishing a new one; b) in the synthesis of the result of one's research and the results obtained by other thinkers.*

2. *Philosophical systems differ only according to the point of view adopted.*

3. *Two kinds of phenomena can be identified, the one termed external (sensations, perceptions), the other termed internal (images, memories).*

4. *All phenomena are invested with two kinds of quality: duration and extension.*

5. *Time and space are merely schematic distortions of duration and extension; nevertheless it is not incorrect to consider them as a priori intuitions.*

6. *Concepts are beyond duration and extension.*

7. *Observation of internal phenomena shows that something invariant underlies duration.*

8. *Observation of external phenomena shows complex and divisible objects.*

9. *That which is constant underneath the flux of duration, the bed of the stream of internal phenomena, is substance.*

10. *That which is noncomplex and nondivisible is substance.*

11. *The substance revealed by internal intuition is identical to the substance revealed by external analysis.*

12. *The latter must not be confused with the atom, a contradictory notion.*

13. *Substance exists beyond time and space.*

14. *Substances appear.*

15. *The totality of phenomena constitutes the physical world; the totality of substances (and essences) constitutes the metaphysical world.*

16. *Perception is a prism that transforms the metaphysical world into a physical world.*

17. *Matter consists in the passage of organizations of substances through this distorting prism.*

Resistance is the individuality of substances. Force is the tendency to organization.

18. *An individual substance appears to us, then, as something infinitely active, for it contains the distorting prism within it.*

19. *Furthermore, although timeless in the metaphysical world, this substance nevertheless develops, and this development, deflected by the prism of internal perception, makes us believe in a flux of internal phenomena.*

20. *The metaphysical world is beyond categories such as time, space, causality, etc., and even that of substance.*

21. *Every problem we may put to ourselves about the metaphysical world is insoluble, by the very fact that language is governed by categories. So long as language comes between*

the problem and ourselves, it will be unintelligible to us.
    22. The metaphysical world doesn't exist, for existence is a category.
    23. If we isolate "substance" from the rest of the metaphysical world, then we do so in order to use it as a category.
    24. It is the world of substances (and essences) seen through categories that constitutes the phenomenal world.
    25. The "substance" isolated from other substances envisages the metaphysical world in an increasingly degraded form.
    26. Being-above-Being is the metaphysical world; Being-positing-non-Being is the world of substances isolating themselves; Being-non-Being is the world of phenomena.
    27. Science and religion are merely limitations of metaphysics.
    28. History is an immobile flux.

Vincent Tuquedenne couldn't remain on the level of these twenty-eight points. The spring was making him reel. He was floundering in the dark waters of erudition. He no longer read anything but bookshop catalogues, bibliographies, works of reference. He strolled aimlessly through the streets, but always the same streets. He began to write poems, such as:

THE PLASTER STATUE

Against a violet sky a rainbow
subtly reveals the seedbed
of a dream born of the twilight glow
a dream of the emasculated dead

Multicolored flares
complete their trajectory
and the cinema poster dares
us to taste adventure

To reward the harlequin's craft
foreign women bring black flowers which unfurl
on the astonishing crankshaft
that pierced the young shopgirl.

He went on studying for his philo(sophie) géné(rale) and logic exams.

8

WHEN SUMMER CAME round again, Monsieur Martin-Martin
felt his interest in women beginning to revive.

"Ah, those silk stockings!" he said, looking at his typist's legs,
"they'll go to my head."

"No more letters for today?"

"If I asked you to have dinner with me tonight, would you
accept?"

"It's my aunt's birthday tonight, monsieur. So I'm having
dinner with the family."

"I thought as much. No, mademoiselle, no more letters for
today."

Monsieur Martin-Martin sighed. He put his papers away,
tidied things up a bit and then, putting on a billycock, went
out. This was his usual hour for meeting some recent old
friends in a café in the Latin Quarter: a retired history teacher
named Tolut and his brother-in-law, the publisher of art books,
Brennuire. But he didn't go straight there today, he took a taxi
and had himself driven to the rue des Petits-Champs, number
80 *bis*. He dragged himself up to the fifth floor and stood panting outside a door that a copper plate indicated as being that of
the flat of a certain Madame Dutilleul. He rang and entered.

"What name shall I say?" the maid asked.

"Well well, have you been here long?" asked Monsieur

Martin-Martin, looking her up and down from thigh to breast.

"No, monsieur. Only a month. What name shall I say?"

"Monsieur Dutilleul."

She went away and reappeared at once.

"Madame will see you."

The visitor went into a little salon cluttered with furniture and knickknacks, rugs and cushions. An old procuress was sitting in a periwinkle-blue tapestry armchair. She smiled amiably at him, dentures in her mush and rings on her fingers.

"My dear old Louis," she said sweetly. "It's a good long time since you came to see me."

He kissed her on the forehead and sat down respectfully on a period chair.

"I've been very busy all winter. But now the time for distractions has come."

"Are they still the same?"

"Do people change at my age?"

Madame Dutilleul considered the matter.

"I've been thinking of you recently. I said to myself: 'Hm, the fine weather's back. Louis'll soon be coming to see me again.' I've been looking for something for you."

"That was nice of you."

"And I've found it."

"What is it?"

"Fifteen years old. She works for a laundress."

"Ah, a laundress! . . . That's good, a laundress . . . I've never known any laundresses . . ."

"You'll see, it'll turn out very well."

"Where is she?"

"We'll have to make an appointment. When would you like it to be?"

"As soon as possible."

"I'll try to arrange it for tomorrow."

"That's right, tomorrow . . . a laundress . . ."

He stood up and once again kissed Madame Dutilleul's

forehead.

"See you tomorrow then, my Louis," she whispered tenderly.

But he didn't linger over these vain demonstrations of cozy sentimentality, and cleared off. When he got to the Soufflet, Messieurs Brennuire and Tolut were already finishing their Pernods.

"You're late, old man," said Brennuire. "Whatever happened to you? Been visiting the girlies, eh! eh?"

"Alfred, a Pernod! And I hope you aren't going to leave me on my own! Alfred, three Pernods!"

"I was expecting you at the Ludo for a game of billiards," said Tolut. "When you didn't come I had a game with a young student."

"Did you beat him?"

"He was a very bad player, he did all the wrong things. And anyway, I wasn't on form."

"Do forgive me," said Brabbant. "I had a cousin up from the country and I had to show him the sights of Paris."

"I bet you took him to see one of our famous houses," said Brennuire. "What they sometimes call houses of *ill* fame," he added quickly, with a glance around him.

"You certainly have got a one-track mind," said Brabbant, irritated.

"Oh, my dear fellow, I didn't mean to offend you."

Brabbant drank a mouthful of poison.

"Rrah," he went, "when I think of the prewar absinthe! Every time I think about it I feel so sad. And do you think there're any fewer alcoholics, now that they've banned absinthe?"

"No," said Brennuire energetically, "certainly not."

"You know, the last time I drank absinthe was in '19, in Constantinople. That was two years ago and, well, you won't believe it, but I still have the taste in my mouth."

"You never told me you'd been to Constantinople," Tolut remarked.

"I have other surprises in store for you," Brabbant replied with a wink.

The other two laughed with the gusto that ensues from two Pernods.

"Ha, ha, ha!" went Tolut.

"Ha, ha, ha!" went Brennuire.

"Ha, ha, ha!" they both went, not understanding.

"Ha, ha, ha!" Brabbant did *not* go. "And how are the children?"

"The exams are coming up, they're working."

"I remember that your daughter is studying for her baccalaureate, her bachot, as they say, but I can never remember the name of the exam your son has got to take. It's odd."

"He's studying for the certificates in psychology, ethics and sociology, for a degree in philosophy."

"Phew. It must be terribly interesting, philosophy, psychology and all the rest of it. And difficult."

He emptied his glass, down whose sides a few drops of a cloudy liquid were trickling; a tiny piece of ice was stagnating, glinting like an imperfect emerald. Brabbant contemplated the ensemble, the drops, the glass, the sides, the ice, and said:

"It's funny to teach philosophy to kids. Philosophy is something that comes with age. When you've seen wars, shipwrecks, tortures like I have, that's when you start to philosophize. What can the philosophy of a young man of eighteen be based on, I ask you?"

"You're confusing things, my friend," Tolut put in, "you're confusing things."

"What am I confusing?"

"It's a confusion that is often to be found among people who are not *au fait* with university studies. The word 'philosophy' doesn't have the same meaning in that context. At the Sorbonne, philosophy is what they call a certain number of disciplines such as psychology, sociology, history of philosophy, and logic, which have nothing in common with what is generally called philosophy."

"How peculiar," Brabbant murmured.

"Heavens, it's already half past seven," subyelped Brennuire, looking at his watch with the second hand.

"But psychology?" Brennuire asked. "Even so, you have to have had a certain experience of men to become a psychologist?"

"Still the same confusion! Scientific psychology and psychology as it is understood by the common man are two entirely different things. It's only the first that counts in exams."

"We must go," said Brennuire, bringing some sous out of his waistcoat pocket.

"One round is mine," said Brabbant.

Tolut went off with his brother-in-law. The common-man-philosopher was left alone. Alfred approached.

"It's been a beautiful day today," he said.

"It's even been very beautiful."

"Oh yes! We can say it's been a very beautiful day."

"Tell me, Alfred, what do *you* call philosophy?"

"As it happens, monsieur, one of those young men left a philosophy treatise on a banquette one day, it was for use in the baccalaureate. So you see, it was something very serious.

"Well, monsieur! in my opinion it was a real logogriph. Not to mention that it was incomplete. For example, there wasn't a word about magnetism, or the planets, or statistics. That's surprising, isn't it? Incidentally, monsieur, perhaps I'm being rather indiscreet, but what happened to that undertaking you were telling me about in the winter?"

"It's going all right, thank you. I hope you won't be proved wrong."

"It's very unlikely that I shall be proved wrong, monsieur."

"Alfred, I have a new project. Project isn't the right word, but still, tell me, will *that* succeed?"

"Did it start today?"

"Yes."

"Is it secret?"

"Yes."

"Money?"

"No."

"I see, I see. What month were you born in?"

"May."

"Then it will soon be your birthday?"

"Don't talk about it."

Alfred consulted his little notebook.

"Nine chances out of ten. You will get what you want."

Monsieur Brabbant smiled.

"I'd like to offer you a drink."

"That isn't done here, monsieur."

"I know, I know."

"Monsieur can leave a tip."

Monsieur Brabbant smiled.

"Then it's going to succeed?"

And he thought: "A laundress, a laundress, a laundress, a laundress."

"You know what they call philosophy at the Sorbonne?" Brabbant went on. "Sociology, logic, things like that, but how to deal with life, pah! they don't talk about that."

"That's just what I was saying to monsieur."

"Here, this is for you."

He handed him two five-franc notes.

"Thank you very much, monsieur. The planets are never wrong, monsieur."

"I hope not, I hope not."

And, billycock on head, he went out jauntily.

9

His name wasn't there; so he had failed. It didn't particularly surprise him; he looked at the list with a detached air, as if he were trying to find a friend's name. The others' satisfaction or chagrin merely inspired him with contempt. He walked away with an indifferent step. A little farther on he passed a fellow in whom he thought he recognized Rohel. He hesitated, because of his shortsightedness, but the fellow came up to him.

"Well well, Tuquedenne. How are you?"

"All right, thanks. Have you passed?"

"I'm just going to look."

"I've failed," said Tuquedenne.

"What was it?"

"Philo(sophie) géné(rale) and logic."

"I took psycho(logie) and socio(logie)."

Tuquedenne retraced his steps, with Rohel. The latter consulted the lists of the candidates who had passed the oral.

"That's that. I've failed."

"In both?"

"In both. Brennuire has passed in psycho(logie)."

"That's not surprising," said Tuquedenne scornfully.

"What about Hublin? I didn't notice."

"Failed too, that's rotten."

"There are an awful lot of failures this year."

"They're trying to raise the standard. What clowns."

"What are you doing now?" Rohel asked.

"Nothing in particular."

"We could go to the Luxembourg."

Rohel had heard from Brennuire that Tuquedenne was interested in modern poetry and, as they had just been failed together, he felt prepared to be friendly. They passed a hat shop with a signed portrait of the boxer Georges Carpentier in its window.

"They'll bore us to death with that bloke," said Rohel.

"And turn people into total morons," said Tuquedenne. "Like all sports do."

"That depends," said Rohel. "What's idiotic are the championships and the hysterical interest they arouse."

"It's true," said Tuquedenne, "that *you* go in for sports."

Tuquedenne, as a child, had certainly not kicked a football more than seven times; his parents had even forbidden him to learn to ride a bicycle, considering this means of transport far too dangerous. Rohel, though, could even ride a motorbike, and in the old days had been thought of as one of the possible hopes of the Haque (Havre Athletic Club). Since he had been in Paris he had neglected his sporting possibilities, but he didn't despise them.

They crossed the Place Médicis and went into the Luxembourg Gardens.

"Where do you live?" Rohel asked.

"Rue de la Convention. You know that my parents live in Paris now."

"You won't go to Le Havre this summer?"

"No. I think I shall stay in Paris."

"*I* shall go to Le Havre," said Rohel.

"It isn't the same anymore," said Tuquedenne. "During the war it was a terrific town, with the English, the Chinese, the Indians, the Kabyles."

"And the Belgians. Not much fun, the Belgians."

"No, they don't contribute much. Do you remember when the workmen made mincemeat of the Kabyles, near the Rond-Point? and the Chinese New Year celebrations in the Place Thiers?"

"And the Armistice. Do you remember the Armistice?"

A woman passed them. Rohel looked her straight in the eyes. She met his gaze and went on. They had reached the rue d'Assas gate.

"Well, I'll leave you," said Rohel.

"I hope to see you next term," said Tuquedenne.

"I hope so too. I'm giving up the foul business of being a *pion*. I shall have more free time, so we'll be able to see each other more often. Adieu."

They shook hands cordially. Rohel about-turned. Tuquedenne slowed his pace, and then looked back: Rohel was indeed following the woman. He spied on them from a distance, curious, and concerned to be so. Rohel caught up with her and walked alongside her for a few moments. Tuquedenne saw that he was talking to her. He couldn't make out whether she was answering him. Rohel was still walking by her side. They passed the fountain, then went up the steps. At this point Tuquedenne saw that the woman was smiling. He stopped, and looked absentmindedly at the toy boats some children were sailing. The sun was beginning to go down. The Senate clock struck five. A liner capsized, and its owner could be heard caterwauling. Tuquedenne turned back towards the rue d'Assas. He was thinking vaguely, very vaguely. He was thinking flabbily. His thought was like cotton wool.

On his right, he saw the dark group made up of the croquet enthusiasts. He walked towards them, dragging his feet. Some old gentlemen were ardently devoting themselves to the subtleties of this singular game, challenging one another vigorously, arguing bitterly, raising their arms to the heavens in despair or triumph. The spectators entered into conversation, appreciating the strokes. Tuquedenne stayed there a few minutes, filling himself with scorn right up to his diaphragm at such stupid sentiments. When one particular exploit provoked cries of admiration he turned and went, his mouth full of ashes. He passed several women who didn't look at him. He overtook others, but couldn't bear the thought of them staring at his back. Weren't some of them quietly laughing at his appearance?

In the rue d'Assas he got into a bus and sat down facing an extremely pretty girl. He wouldn't have dared to do this if it hadn't been the only free seat. Naturally, this girl didn't interest him in the least. He looked at the landscape; he had the impression that the other passengers were saying to themselves: "That boy with the long hair is making eyes at the girl opposite him"; but it wasn't true, he wasn't at all making eyes at her. He looked at her. She met his gaze. He blushed horribly. It was intolerable. And the other passengers who were scrutinizing him. She got out at Montparnasse; a nondescript human being replaced her. Tuquedenne felt relieved. If his parents hadn't been expecting him he might well have got off and followed her and spoken to her. He didn't think she had taken a dislike to him. Maybe he'd meet her again another time, in the same bus, at about the same hour. What an idiot he was.

He got off at the rue d'Alésia, walked up the rue de Vouillé, and arrived home. The concierge handed him a bookshop catalogue, the kind of mail he usually received.

His parents were waiting for him in the dining room.

"Well?" his father asked him.

It was true. Vincent had forgotten all about it. He had failed.

Alfred

I HAD plainly seen in the planets that he wouldn't win. I'd heard so much about it that I finally got interested in the question. According to my calculations it was clear; he was going to be beaten. But it wouldn't have been wise for me to say so, they were too excited. They all swore that he was going to beat the American hollow and that it would be a victory for France. They all said that, the regular customers and the new ones, the fat and the thin, the civilians and the soldiers. Even serious gentlemen like Monsieur Brennuire and his friends were elated by the event, absolutely sure as they were that Carpentier was going to wallop Dempsey on account of his left and his footwork. I let them say what they liked, but I'd plainly seen that it would be a defeat, and even a defeat by *queneau-kout*. They'd never have been willing to believe it, because Carpentier was French. So I preferred to keep quiet because I'd have looked like a defeatist. There's something even more extraordinary: Jules almost bashed Ernest's face in because he made fun of Carpentier's saucepan factory. In short, everyone believed in a victory. There was a publicity balloon in the sky and the wireless was all set to announce it. In a certain sense it was something like the triumph of modern inventions. Not to mention the Bengal lights they were going to send up but which are not a modern invention, as Monsieur Tolut informed us the other day.

Well! he was beaten. He was k'no-ktout by the American. I saw some girls crying over it. People were very sad that day. Really, you might have thought we were back in the days when Charleroi was taken, but this time with no battle of the Marne in prospect. Yes, people were very sad, the regulars and the new customers, the fat and the thin, the civilians and the soldiers. It didn't affect *me*. I knew it beforehand, I'd seen it in the planets. So I wasn't sad like the rest of them. Monsieur Brabbant, for his part, was very pleased. Even so he did say that it was unfortunate and that Georges Carpentier deserved to be world champion, but fundamentally he was very pleased. And this is the reason why. The day before he'd had a word in my ear and asked me: "Who's going to win?" I say: "You won't be angry if I tell you?" He answers: "Tell me who's going to win. It's for a bet." So I tell him: "It'll be the American." He looks me straight in the eye. "Are you sure of your planets?" That's what he asks me. "I am sure of them." That's what I answer. Because of that he gives me a ten-franc tip, and today he's given me another twenty. That's why I think that fundamentally he's very pleased, even though he tells everyone who's prepared to listen that it's a great misfortune for our country. Even so there are some people who don't agree and who say that it isn't boxing that makes a nation great but great scientists, like Pasteur or Madame Curie, or even that Einstein the Germans have now that they never stop talking about. It seems there's so much algebra in his calculations that there aren't three people who can follow them. *My* calculations are just as complicated, I'm the only one who can follow them and yet I'm not particularly keen on passing for a glory of the nation. All I want is to get back from the pari-mutuel the money it won from my poor father. Only a few more years now and it'll all be finalized. And then I shall go to the races knowing what I'm doing and not blindly like my pals who bet five francs here, five francs there, and who've finally lost quite a bit by the end of the year if you add it all up. Which means that people who believe that waiters must have a nice income coming in when they're old, well! they're completely wrong because they don't realize what betting on the horses means for a waiter. What I do, I keep quiet and await my hour, and when I see the hot weather approaching in the summer I tell myself only one or two more summers like this one and I shall be ready to go, as they say. So it doesn't make me sad when I see this year's students leaving and I'm waiting for next year's lot. There are still people to serve because it's hot and that makes them want a drink, but they are only passing trade, foreign students, you don't exactly know what they're doing in France, or Parisians who don't go on holiday or who only go on holiday for a very short time and who've acquired their habits in the district. Monsieur Brabbant is one of these, like Monsieur Tolut, like Monsieur Brennuire, and like still others. Monsieur Brabbant doesn't come every single day, though. He sometimes stays away. He sometimes stays away for over a week. He has business abroad, or at least that's what he says. When Monsieur Brabbant is away the others are so bored, so bored. It's hard to see just why this is the case, yet it's quite clear that they're bored when he isn't there. If only they played manille, you could say that they need him to make up a fourth. But they never play cards. He simply holds them by the charm of his conversation, or something like that, it's like what you might call a mysterious fluid that he throws in their eyes.

As for the kind of business he does, it doesn't seem very clear. He might be a property dealer, that's a good trade, especially at the moment, there's a fine living to be got out of dealing with profiteers, the swine who get rich while other people are coming a cropper. I know very well how these things work. I was in Paris during the whole of the war and even during Big Bertha. I saw them all in Paris during the war, the profiteers, the dodgers, the soldiers on leave, the aviators, the Americans, the unfit, the old men, the widows, the nurses, the tarts. I know very well what they were like, all of them in their own line. In wartime you don't have any trouble recognizing what line people are in, believe me! In peacetime, too, but there I'm only speaking for myself. To come back to Monsieur Brabbant, he's of good appearance, he speaks even better, especially about his travels. What a lot he's traveled, Monsieur Brabbant! Whereas the others, they've hardly even gone to the seaside, and Monsieur Tolut, for example, who used to teach geography before he retired from the profession, he's never been out of France. You wouldn't believe people could teach something without ever seeing what they talk about. It's like with philosophy. I remember Monsieur Brabbant telling me one day that they teach philosophy to schoolkids. As if that were possible! You only become a philosopher with age. Take me, for example, I know plenty of philosophers who're all over seventy, and others again who hardly know how to write. To come back to Monsieur Brabbant, I don't think he's a philosopher. I have the impression that there are too many things going through his head and that he has a passion for things he's really too old for, that's easy to see from the way he eyes the legs of one of those people who come here on account of their profession. And Monsieur Tolut, he isn't a philosopher either, but not for the same reasons. He looks very gentle, he looks very calm, yes, but!—his professional conscience is troubling him, after the event: he wants to travel. I don't know whether it was Monsieur Brabbant who put the idea into his head or whether he begot it all by himself, but he wants to travel. When he hears people talking about boats, or sleeping cars, or caravans, he sighs. Yes, he sighs, old as he is. All the countries where Monsieur Brabbant says he's been, he can't wait to go there, and to the others too. Not so very long ago he was here on his own, drinking his Pernod. Monsieur Brabbant had gone and Monsieur Brennuire had said he wouldn't be coming. So Monsieur Tolut was alone; and then he asks me for the railway timetable, I give it to him, he studies it for well over half an hour until finally a customer asks for it and I'm obliged to take it out of his hands. Then I ask him whether he's going away; he gave me a queer sort of look and said that he might perhaps be going abroad. But he hasn't gone yet. He doesn't even look like going at all. Actually, do you need to have traveled in order to teach children geography? I wonder whether it isn't just an idea he's got into his head, maybe to stop himself having others.

11

IT WAS A GHASTLY SUMMER.

For four months Tuquedenne was alone in Paris. He was alone. He was alone, because the human beings he lived with didn't constitute any kind of society for him. By his side, apart from him, his parents led the diminished existence of retired state employees, deprived of all raison d'être. So Tuquedenne was alone throughout the vacation, and everyone knows that the university vacation fills four months. That year, which was the twenty-first of this century, the summer also lasted for four months, for October was exceptionally fine.

Tuquedenne had not the slightest remembrance of July. Later, this amazed him, and he tried to think what he could well have been doing during that time but never managed to remember. It always seemed to him that there had been a nonexistent month in his life, thirty days that oblivion had eradicated the way vultures gouge out the eyes of dead cattle. And so July disappeared, swallowed up by nothingness.

August had more consistency, but its consistency was made of nothing but despair. Tuquedenne was aware of his solitude, but he didn't realize that it was only so atrocious because he didn't even recognize his own presence.

Making the heat his excuse, he had his hair cut and smarmed

down, and his mustache shaved. Thus transformed he went to show himself off in the avenue des Champs-Elysées, in the rue de la Paix and elsewhere. There were some beautiful ladies there, wearing diaphanous frocks. Tuquedenne was waiting for one of them to fall into his arms. He waited until it was time for dinner, and then went back to have that meal with his parents who lived in the rue de la Convention. In the evening he ventured on to the Grands Boulevards. A dehydrated crowd was hanging around there, tongues dangling and feet sweaty. At the corner of the rue Richelieu a prostitute said to him:

"Coming, darling?"

Embarrassed, he about-turned and an AI bus took him back from the Opéra to the Place Saint-Michel. He started strolling again. It was around ten o'clock. Near the Odéon, he perceived an individual of the feminine sex walking with a light step. There was no one else in the street. He caught her up and murmured:

"Excuse me, mademoiselle."

Thus cornered, the girl turned round and demanded:

"What for?"

She looked terribly minor. Tuquedenne said: "Excuse me," and crossed the road. He took the métro at Saint-Germain-des-Prés, and went home to bed at his parents' house, they lived in the rue de la Convention.

In the morning he hung around in the apartment; in the afternoon he hung around in Paris; in the evening he hung around among his books. He read abundantly, having taken out a subscription at the Tronche lending library in the rue Dupuytren. He went there every day, then sat down by the Médicis fountain, then followed this or that path through the town. The women were beautiful, that year. They had shortened their skirts. It was a splendid summer. Every evening Tuquedenne went home in despair. It was at about this time that he copied out this quotation from Proust, of which he was the author:

"I was incapable of sincerity. If I sometimes tried to imagine myself as I was or at least as I believed I was, I was unable to put it in writing, either because of a lack of cynicism and because of a lingering sense of shame which seemed to me at the time to be the height of absurdity, considering it to be an artificial quality and, in order to criticize it more easily, confusing it with the exasperating prudishness that made me detest the majority of moralists, or because it would have been somewhat difficult for my vanity to bear were I to set down in writing the defects that it suffered to know that I possessed. Hence I felt myself incapable of clarifying my thoughts and deeds with regard to women, not consenting to avow to myself in writing what course of action I had taken in this or that circumstance and which, upon examination, I had considered either to be stupid or to show signs of an excessive timidity which I was trying to convert into indifference with regard to what I most desired, as if the mere fact of putting into writing the fact that I had been stupid, timid or ridiculous might have increased the humiliation I felt in telling myself that I had been such, or might have solidified these defects that diminished me, by thus preventing me from one day ridding myself of them."

But because he didn't have it, he continued to despise what he most desired. In the evenings, after the family dinner, alone again, he watched himself suffer until his suffering became so acute that it disappeared of its own accord, unable to transcend this supreme point. Then he went to bed extremely weary, and the next day started all over again in the same way. Whereupon he began to lament the monotony of these days which elapsed so indistinguishably and which afforded him no hope. An ascetic through weakness, he exalted the activity of the senses. He read Gide's *Paludes* and *Les Nourritures terrestres;* he greatly approved of these two works and titillated himself with phrases such as: "There are some things that one does every day because one has nothing better to do; there is neither progress nor sustenance in such a course," or: "Angèle, *chère amie,* are you not beginning to think that our life lacks true adventure?" or again: "A life full of pathos, Nathanaël, is preferable to tranquillity." He also read other books, many other books.

Then September came.

He no longer thought about anything. He no longer suffered. He was calm. He began to visit Paris. He tried the museums, but he preferred the streets. He prepared long itineraries carefully and followed them scrupulously. He went up, and down, and around, and in zigzags. On one day he traversed the town from north to south, on another he transpierced it from east to west. He made his way around the successive circles of the boulevards. One by one he covered each arrondissement, but he didn't dare venture into the alleyways, into the culs-de-sac, under the arches. He avoided the prostitutes' streets, and was always conscious of the effect his presence might produce on the inhabitants of the districts he was exploring. Each new street he went down was always an object of great excitement. Then he began to worry about the changing aspect of towns and the future of their layout. He even composed a short poem on the subject, which says more about this than a long speech:

> The Paris you loved then
> is not the one we love today
> and we are slowly making our way
> towards the one we'll forget again
>
> Topographies! Itineraries!
> Towns through which we've strolled!
> Memories of timetables of old!
> The difficulty of memories!
>
> And without a map under your eye
> you will never understand our aim
> for all this is only a game
> and obliviousness of times gone by.

Charlie Chaplin came to Paris. The new *Printemps* department store burned down. A train was derailed in the Batignolles
tunnel. October brought with it a beautiful, brand-new sun.
Vincent Tuquedenne continued to waste his time. He continued not to think about anything. He allowed all his admirations
to dissolve and with a cold eye appraised the skulls of great
men, dead or alive. Lying in their tombs or in their beds, the
great men didn't blench. Vincent Tuquedenne didn't forgive
them the slightest transgression. Geniuses also have their
weaknesses, so it is said: he wasn't prepared to accept this.
Heroes no longer existed for him. Every day he went home to
dinner with his parents, who lived in the rue de la Convention.

Once again he was alone, face to face with himself. Bits of
debris lay scattered around him. His life continued to be calm
and bitter. He was beginning to resemble the debris. He was no
longer interested in anything at all. One day he realized that he
was disintegrating. He took a bit of paper and wrote: "*I'm disintegrating,*" underneath which he made a note of the time,
23:13. A few days later he discovered this saying: "*You are
becoming littler all the time, you little people! You are disintegrating, you who like your comforts, in the end you will
perish,*" but he didn't want to perish.

October continued to be a month the like of which had never
been known, in the way of good weather. Vincent Tuquedenne
suddenly began to formulate ambitious projects, to set himself
timetables, to make plans for study. He would attend classes at
the Collège de France, the Ecole des hautes études, the Faculté
des lettres and the Faculté des sciences; he would learn three
or four living languages and four or five dead languages the
knowledge of which he considered necessary; in short, every
day he went home to dinner with his parents who lived in the
rue de la Convention.

Towards the end of the month Hublin wrote to tell him that
he was coming back from Le Havre. Before going to meet him
at the Café de la Sorbonne, Vincent Tuquedenne went to a

barber to get his hair cut. He rarely went twice to the same hairdresser, as he never managed to get himself tricked out to his satisfaction. He detested that talkative, tyrannical race. That day his choice was particularly unfortunate. He fell into the hands of a pervert and was unable to refuse him a wave. When the thing had been done and the artist had relinquished his hold, he discovered himself in front of a mirror and was aghast at the waves rippling through his locks. He disgusted himself enormously. For a moment he thought he wouldn't keep his date. He hesitated, but finally made up his mind. Jean Hublin was waiting for him. He still wore his hair very long.

"Hallo, old man," said Tuquedenne, sitting down.

He put his hat down on the banquette. Hublin examined him.

"What a mess you look," he observed.

Tuquedenne blushed.

"Well, how are you? Did you have a good holiday in Le Havre?"

"Pah!" Hublin snorted, absentmindedly regarding the waves.

"Did you see Rohel?"

"I caught a glimpse of him several times but I didn't really see him to speak to. He created a bit of a disturbance two or three times, at the casino and elsewhere. Drunken scenes. Muraut told me about them in detail. He was one of the gang too, wasn't he just proud of it!"

"What did they do?"

"How should *I* know? They leave me cold, their stupid goings-on."

Tuquedenne was amazed at his nasty expression.

"Didn't you want to go around with them?"

"Go around with those idiots? Are you asking *me* such a question?"

"Oh, I didn't really mean anything. Didn't you see anyone there, then? Weren't you bored?"

"No. And you—what did you do?"

"Me? I read, I went for walks. Oh, I did quite a lot of things."
Hublin didn't ask him what things. Then Vincent said:

"And you—what's your position now? Are you still interested
in the hereafter?"

"Yes, I am. More passionately than ever. You know, I've discovered something. I *think* I've discovered something. I can
tell you, because you're my friend. Those imbeciles in Le Havre
—you can just imagine how it would make them laugh. I can
tell you, because you're my friend. You don't think the way I
do, but you're a friend. The others—you can just imagine how
it would make them laugh. The chaps from Le Havre, for example. Or even the professors at the Sorbonne. If it would
make them laugh."

"But what? What would make them laugh?"

"Ah yes! I'm a medium."

Hublin was becoming confidential. Tuquedenne sipped his
demi, and grunted from time to time.

"What makes you think so?"

"This summer, I tried a few experiments. Actually, it's very
scientific, spiritism is. Yes, this summer I tried a few experiments. I had a feeling that I could be a medium. A good medium.
I had a feeling that I was made to communicate with the dead.
I'd already had several messages, you know. I can tell you
because you're a friend. You can just imagine, the others, those
idiots, how they'd laugh, if they knew."

"Yes. Of course."

"I've already had several messages. But that isn't conclusive.
Victor Hugo and Tolstoy spoke to me. But that isn't conclusive."

"Victor Hugo and Tolstoy?"

"Yes. That isn't conclusive. Actually, do you know what I
want? Do you know who I'd like to get into communication
with?"

"Who? Joan of Arc?"

"Idiot. My father."

"Ah, your father."

Tuquedenne felt so ill at ease that for a moment he thought
he was going to vomit. And this was his best friend! How he
must have changed; how *they* must have changed! All this stuff
made him feel quite sick.

"I'd like to get in touch with my father," Hublin went on.
"My father's dead, but I need to talk to him. We need to talk to
each other. You remember that day when we went on to the
cliffs with Muraut and Ponsec? That was another of Muraut's
ideas. My father was ill, you remember. I'd told you. But I didn't
know that he was so ill. When we got back it was very late. You
remember? We knew perfectly well that our parents would
give us hell. You weren't too happy. You didn't quite know
what your father was going to say to you. But when *I* got home,
my father, he was dead."

Tuquedenne went "hmhm," and sucked up the froth lique-
fying in the bottom of his glass. "What a bloody bore he is," he
thought, to get over his embarrassment, and once again he
went "hmhm."

"You don't realize," said Hublin.

"I do, I do."

"You don't."

"Did you call?" the waiter asked.

"No," said Hublin.

"Personally, I could do with another *bock,*" said Tuquedenne. "What about you, aren't you going to have anything
else?"

"No thanks."

The waiter withdrew.

"Tuquedenne, do you understand me?"

"Yes, old man, of course I do."

"Do you understand this? I'd like to talk to my father. It's very
simple. There's no reason why I shouldn't be able to. Really,
you know, I believe I'm a medium. That I could be a medium."

The waiter brought the *bock.* At this moment Rohel and
Wullmar came in. They had just met, barely a quarter of an

hour before, and Rohel had just overcome Wullmar's reservations about him.

Wullmar sat down at the two philosophers' table with marked disgust. This was a feeling Rohel reserved for Hublin alone.

"Well then, so we're going to start a new year," he said, laughing. "The results weren't so good, were they? Personally I don't give a damn for results. One more, one less..."

What he was saying didn't mean much, but he was showing off in front of Wullmar.

"Are you studying medicine?" Tuquedenne asked Wullmar.

"I've chucked it. One doctor in the family is already too many."

He was alluding to his father, a distinguished professor.

"I make out that I'm studying law," he went on, "I think that's enough. And you, still philo(sophie)? Still got your nose permanently stuck in a book? Books, personally, I can do without them. I'm no keener on being a bookworm than I am on being a hospital worm."

Rohel thought Wullmar splendid. He picked up a book Tuquedenne had put down on the table. It was Jacques Maritain's *Théonas*.

"Are you interested in Thomism?"

"Among other things."

"You certainly seem to live for ideas!"

"I'm passionately interested in ideas," said Tuquedenne.

"Personally, I've never taken an idea seriously," said Rohel.

Tuquedenne looked at him, deeply shocked. Rohel drank his *demi* in one go, very proud of himself. Even so, Vincent asked him for his address.

"81, rue Monge."

"What an idea, living there," Wullmar exclaimed scornfully. "*I* live in la Villette."

"La Villette?"

"It's a terrific district. Full of people just spoiling for a scrap.

Go and see for yourself!"

"No kidding—do you really live in la Villette?" Rohel asked.

"It's a terrific district," Wullmar repeated. "There's brawls every evening. Only yesterday I saw a couple of guys having a go at each other. It was really something. In the end, one of them stuck a couple of fingers in the other one's eyes. Magnificent. He couldn't see, then. The first one brought him down with a kick in the stomach. The cops arrived, so he did a bunk. That's what I call a terrific district."

"To be sure," said Rohel, amazed.

Hublin stood up.

"I'm off," he said.

The others made no effort to stop him. Tuquedenne shook his hand absentmindedly.

"If your pal turned up on the quai de Valmy with his long hair," said Wullmar, "some jokers would be sure to chuck him in the canal."

"He's perfectly free."

"He's perfectly free. Like you to get your hair waved."

"Naturally," said Tuquedenne.

"I've had enough of this bistrot," said Wullmar. "And in any case I have to go. I've got a date at the Chatham bar."

He stood up, threw a five-franc note folded in sixteen on to the table, and made tracks.

"He's quite someone," said Rohel.

Tuquedenne didn't agree.

12

MADAME DUTILLEUL was telling her fortune with the cards. There was a tap on the door.

She said:

"Come in!"

It was he.

"Then you didn't like the kid?"

"It's not that I didn't like her. To start with it wasn't too bad, but afterwards it wasn't right at all. She always seemed to be bored with me. What I need is a kid who isn't stupid, and who has some imaginative qualities. Whereas your laundress, she never thought anything up of her own accord. Ah well . . ."

He sighed.

"And now it's winter again," he added. "It's going to be a bad winter, a very bad winter."

"Who told you that?"

"A waiter I know in a café."

"And what does he know about it?"

"He predicts the future."

"With the cards?"

"No, he gets his information from the planets. And with incredibly complicated calculations!"

"I'd certainly like to meet him, your waiter."

"Shh! That's not possible. It's a secret between him and me."

"All right, all right. Like a game of piquet?"

"No, my dear, I haven't got time. A very important business appointment."

"May one know what it is?"

"A profiteer who's going to entrust me with a certain sum of money to find him an apartment."

"Will you find him something?"

"No. He's a filthy swine. He made a pile while other people were getting themselves bumped off at the front. He's only got one eye, he wasn't in the war. A stinking nouveau riche."

"You only ever swindle people you find antipathic."

"In general. And then they can't be called swindles."

"What I wonder is why you don't try to pull off something really big."

"I'm a modest man."

"It's a mistake," said Madame Dutilleul. "But ambition may drive you to it yet."

"Oho!" said Monsieur Dutilleul. "In any case, it's all over with the laundress, eh. And now I shan't bother until next year."

He rested his lips on an impure forehead, and left. He walked down the rue Saint-Roch as far as the rue de Rivoli and took the métro to the Hôtel-de-Ville. The filthy swine was waiting for him in a café on the corner of the rue de la Verrerie. But Monsieur Dutilleul had only just turned into the rue des Archives when he perceived a huge, muttering crowd. At first he attributed it to some accident or some minor brawl, but then he observed with dismay that the café he was making for was at the very heart of this ant heap.

"What's going on?" he asked a fellow.

"A chap's been murdered," this person replied.

Monsieur Dutilleul approached anxiously, pushing his way through the crowd with his white waistcoat. He could hear the rumors multiplying around him.

"A chap's been murdered."

"By a woman."

"A woman put his eyes out."

"She chucked vitriol at him."

"A man split his skull."

"That's not true. He bit his ear off."

"It's an atrocious crime."

Policemen were calming the populace. Then they heard the bell of an ambulance; it braked outside the café. Police reinforcements came and maneuvered over the people's feet. The café door was wide open. Necks were craned. Monsieur Dutilleul insinuated himself into the front row. Borne by two volunteers, a big lump went by, its head covered in bandages, and groaning. It was shoved into the ambulance which disappeared, ringing its bell. Monsieur Dutilleul had recognized his nouveau riche.

"I'm out of luck at the moment," he murmured.

He listened without pleasure to the excited comments of the people around him. In the meantime the police had completed their investigations and were roughly dispersing the crowd that had gathered to see a bit of crime. The owner of the bistrot, to avoid snoopers, was shutting up shop. Monsieur Dutilleul went up to him.

"Ah, Monsieur Blaisolle," said the café owner. "Do you know what has just happened?"

"Tell me."

"Well! come on in, Monsieur Blaisolle. But I'm going to shut the door behind you. If I let all that lot in, they'd pinch all my billiard cues. Oh, it's terrible, it's horrible."

There were only a few regular customers left in the café. Monsieur Blaisolle knew them all. They greeted him with exclamations in which pride was mixed with horror.

"Tell me," said Monsieur Blaisolle.

"Well! What happened—Monsieur Tormoigne, you know him very well, don't you, Monsieur Tormoigne, the man who had only one eye? Well! He was here, having a drink with us. My goodness, I have to say that he was a bit fuddled, he must have been at least on his third Pernod. In short, we were playing manille and kidding each other when here comes a queer customer wanting to buy a stamp. He was a queer customer because his hair came halfway down his back, worse than an artist. So Monsieur Tormoigne, who just happened to be in a joking mood, said just like that: 'Huh, there's Absalom!' Naturally that made us all laugh, even the ones who didn't go to catechism classes and don't know any Bible history. The fellow pretended he hadn't heard. He was waiting for his change. Then Monsieur Tormoigne said even louder: 'I tell you, that's Absalom!' And we started to laugh too, and my wife, it was all she could do not to go into convulsions under the freak's very nose. 'The barbers can't be making a fortune with fellows like that,' Monsieur Tormoigne went on. That made us chuckle. The chap takes his stamp, licks it and sticks it on his envelope. Then Monsieur Tormoigne adds: 'Hair like that is very pretty, but it must pick up the dust.' Me and my wife were laughing so hard she almost pissed her knickers it was so funny. But the freak simply opens the door and goes out, he was all red and pretending to smile but he must have been fuming, just imagine. 'Good-bye, Absalom,' Monsieur Tormoigne shouts after him, 'if your mother's too poor I'll buy her some shears.' Really, everyone was laughing. The fellow goes out and shuts the door behind him, nice and gently, and we go back to our card game when what do you know, barely five minutes later the long-haired chap comes back; he shuts the door, goes and stands at the counter and orders a *bock*. And then Monsieur Tormoigne, not in the least impressed, says, just like that, not looking up from his cards: 'Huh, here's Absalom come back.' You can just imagine how that set us all off again! We even made the bottles rattle. But the chap, he wasn't laughing. He even looked mighty serious. 'Oh,' Monsieur Tormoigne says to him, 'so we're looking for trouble, are we? We aren't content to have such pretty curly hair?' At that point no one had the slightest idea what was going to happen, we were only thinking about having fun, and with good reason, well then, Monsieur Blaisolle, do you know what happened? The freak goes up to Monsieur Tormoigne and then wham! he sticks his penknife in his eye. Just like I'm telling you. I even saw it glinting, his little penknife. Goodness! didn't he just yell, Monsieur Tormoigne. My wife fainted and the chap scarpered so fast that he hasn't been found yet. He's completely disappeared, it's as if he never existed. And Monsieur Tormoigne was still there bellowing, and mucking up his ace of spades with the stuff oozing out of his eye. A little penknife, that's what he did it with, the artist. And poor Monsieur Tormoigne, now he's blind."

"It's horrible," said Monsieur Blaisolle.

"You can say that again. It's horrible."

"I hope they'll guillotine him, the wretch who did that," said the café owner's wife.

"They ought to burn him at the stake," said someone.

"Criminals aren't punished severely enough," someone else added.

"Poor Monsieur Tormoigne," the boss repeated. "Now he's blind."

"Did he lose his other eye in the war?" an inquisitive fellow asked.

"Not likely!" a nasty customer replied. "During the war he made a pile, while other people were getting themselves killed. It was worth his while being one-eyed, believe me!"

"They could at least have taken him on as a noncombatant," said somebody unnamed.

"There have been and there always will be injustices," said somebody else.

"All of which goes to show that criminals never pay the penalty for their crimes," an individual added. "They're protected by the law. Look at Landru . . ."

Monsieur Blaisolle left them holding forth and went out, murmuring:

"It's horrible."

In the street, Monsieur Dutilleul grumbled:

"A couple of thousand francs slipping through my fingers."

At the Soufflet, Monsieur Brabbant asked the waiter:

"Tell me, Alfred, was it a good day today?"

"It all depends what for, monsieur."

"That's true. Ah!—and then, if we were obliged to think about all those things . . . Does it never happen to you to make a mistake, Alfred?"

"Oh, personally, monsieur . . ."

"Well then, Alfred," said Brabbant, satisfied with this answer, "bring me a Pernod and *l'Intransigeant.*"

13

"WELL, HAVE YOU seen that, Madame Whatsit, Landru has been condemned to death."

"What do I care, it's none of my business, and anyway, if you think I have time to read the paper."

"Me neither, I haven't got time, I heard it from a pal."

"What a carry-on, eh, just for ten women who've disappeared."

"You aren't much of a champion of your own sex, Madame Whatsit."

"Oh la la, huh, aren't you just gallant."

"Hang on, someone downstairs wants you."

"What is it?" she yelled.

"Isn't Monsieur Hublin here?"

"No! He left with his suitcase, he's gone back to Le Havre. Is that all you wanted to know?"

"Thank you, madame," whoever-it-was answered from downstairs.

"The student made tracks yesterday," she explained. "Family business, he said. Just as well, because he frightened the life out of my little girl with his hair."

A time. A space.

"Ah, Wullmar, how are you? It seems you're chucking medicine?"

"And how. Here, did you see that Landru's been condemned to death? You who made out he didn't exist."

"Of course he doesn't exist. It's all a fabrication. They invented him to get the Treaty of Versailles through. Everyone's concentrating on Landru and not on the future of France."

"My dear Muraut, you have the soul of Joan of Arc."

A time. A space.

"Well then," said Rohel, "have you seen that 'they' have condemned him to death?"

"Yes. The swine."

"Peasants, shopkeepers, daring to judge that marvelous man! Do you know this story? He dressed up as a marquis and went the rounds of all his fiancées. He said to each one: 'Will you forgive me if I only stay five minutes? You understand . . . a masked ball.' "

"And Fernande Segret's memoirs in *le Journal,* have you read them? When she heard that the war was over, you know what she said? 'It's over too soon.' "

A time, a space.

"Well then, monsieur, 'he' has been condemned to death."

"The poor man," sighed Monsieur Martin-Martin.

"What, monsieur, you're sorry for him?"

"I'm convinced he's innocent."

"You're certainly the only person who thinks that."

"Yes, I'm convinced he's innocent."

"I wanted to ask you also whether you've thought any more about what you told me yesterday?"

"What did I tell you yesterday?"

"You promised to pay me for the two months you're in arrears."

"How unfortunate. The deal slipped through my fingers. My customer met with an accident. You can surely wait until next week?"

"The thing is, I've got my old mother to feed, Monsieur

Martin-Martin, and two little brothers who're still very young."

"Did your mother have children very late?"

"At eleven months, monsieur."

"What a witty girl! A real Paris sparrow."

A time, a space.

"Didn't you see it in the paper this morning?" asked Monsieur Tolut, trembling with emotion.

"What? Landru's death sentence?"

"No no, oh no. That horrible news item. Didn't you see it?"

"My goodness, no," replied Monsieur Brennuire.

"An artist put out the eye of a passerby who made fun of his painting."

"Really? But that's abominable."

"It happened near the Hôtel de Ville, that terrible thing. No doubt the artist was painting one of the picturesque sites which are so numerous in that district. Although it isn't very clear, because the journalist said that this abominable crime took place in a café."

"You know, Tolut, journalists always embroider the facts a bit."

"But I haven't told you the most atrocious thing of all. Which is that this passerby had already lost one eye."

"The other one?"

"The other one."

A time, a space.

"Then your mother's better?" Muraut asked.

"Yes," Ponsec replied. "Here, do you know who I met in Le Havre?"

"No. Did you see that Landru has been condemned to death? Lot of humbugs!"

"You'll never guess who I saw in Le Havre."

"Hm, I met Wullmar just now. It's quite true that he's chucked medicine."

"I bet you anything you can't guess who I met in Le Havre this morning."

"Hublin?"

"How did you know?"

"I just said it haphazard."

"I see. Believe it or not, he's had his hair cut."

"No?"

"And he's going to Brazil. It seems his uncle has got him a job with a coffee company."

"You're having me on."

A time, a space.

"Hallo, gentlemen. Alfred, a Pernod!"

"Hallo, my dear fellow. What do you think of that death sentence, then?"

"Actually, there wasn't the slightest proof," said Brabbant.

"Even so, even so," said Monsieur Brennuire.

"I've already demonstrated to you many times that there wasn't the slightest proof."

"You may not be wrong," said Tolut. "And anyway, burning dead women in a stove is no more terrible than blinding a one-eyed man in his good eye."

"What's that you're saying?"

"Here, read this news item."

A time, a space.

"Did *you* know that Hublin was going to Brazil?"

"Who told you that?"

"Ponsec. He saw him in Le Havre this morning."

"Brazil . . ." said Tuquedenne.

A time, a space.

"Don't you think it must have been a cubist painter?"

A time, a space.

"He's gone to Brazil. Just like that, from one day to the next. He's chucked everything to go there."

"I can't believe it."

"And *we* are still here, stuck in our old rut, the Sorbonne, the Latin Quarter, Sainte-Geneviève, the cafés."

"And the street . . ."

". . . la rue de la Convention."

A time, a space.

"That swine has made me lose two thousand francs. Wait till I catch him! And that profiteer Tormoigne, who's blind now. Just my luck. Getting to my age only to come a cropper over things like that. It's true that I'm too modest."

A time, a space.

"Don't you think that death sentence is unjust, mademoiselle?"

"What gives you the right to speak to me, monsieur?"

"I saw you reading the paper. I am most interested in women's opinions on the Landru affair."

"If you only knew how it bores me to read the papers. But anyway, I'm not talking to you."

"If you're bored, we could go and see *The Kid* at the Max-Linder."

"What's that?"

"A Charlie Chaplin film."

"I was that *bored*," said she.

A time, a space.

The time, night; the space, a bedroom in Paris. Vincent Tuquedenne is seeing Jean Hublin leaving for Brazil. It's the sea breeze that torments us. Adventure was very fashionable that year. A little review called *Aventure* was founded. Vincent Tuquedenne read Mac Orlan's *Le Chant de l'équipage* a dozen times and stayed in Paris.

A time, a space.

The time, night; the space, a liner. Hublin, classically leaning over the railings, is watching the lights of the town disappear in the distance. He's in coffee, now.

Alfred

WELL! THIS TIME it's all over, they've condemned him to death.
I had foreseen that, as indeed I foresee that he will be guillotined. It's all written in the planets and in my calculations, I
only had to glance at them to see what was going to happen.
Monsieur Landru will be guillotined. Monsieur Brabbant
seems to be much affected by this sentence; *he* doesn't believe
in his guilt. He discusses it very knowledgeably: he must have
read everything the papers have written about it. It's an inexplicable business, that's certain, and it would be terrible to cut
his head off if he was innocent. He didn't say a word, he isn't
going to say a word. Monsieur Brabbant hopes he will be par-
doned. But I know very well that there's no hope: his head will
fall into the basket. When I say that, I'm talking about Monsieur
Landru's head, not Monsieur Brabbant's. The more I see of him,
the more curious I find this customer. He's inexplicable, he's
like Monsieur Landru, but in his own way, and personally that
doesn't surprise me because, owing to the planets, people of
the same type happen to be circulating in the world at the
same time; but each one in his own way. Because of the planets
and my calculations I can see very clearly that there happen to
be families constituted of people who have never met, and for
me Monsieur Brabbant is like a brother of Monsieur Landru. I
don't mean to say that he burns chopped-up women in a tiny

little stove, always supposing that that really was what happened in Gambais. Nor do I mean to say that there's a mystery in his life that's anything like the one in Monsieur Landru's life. No—but they are still as alike as two brothers. Actually, I do know who he is, that Monsieur Brabbant. I do know. I am neither a naïf nor a simpleton. I have a certain experience of life which enables me to recognize people, to see at a glance what planets govern them, in which statistical column to arrange them, in which statistical range to collate them. For Monsieur Brabbant it's very simple; he's a crook. I'll even add: a petty crook, a small-time crook, a very small-scale crook. It has to be said: that was also a little bit Monsieur Landru's style. Monsieur Landru too was a petty crook, a small-time crook, a very small-scale crook. True, he did do away with ten women and a young man, that's what sets him apart, but I'd seen quite clearly what sort of person he was. Monsieur Brabbant is much the same, but he too must have something special about him, otherwise he wouldn't be Monsieur Brabbant. He has a name, and a name—that counts. What I'd need to find out is what kind of swindles he goes in for. Every so often he asks my advice. "Do you think I'm going to pull off this coup?" But he never tells me what kind of a coup it is. He's a terrible gambler, too. If they opened the Enghien casino he'd be there tomorrow; and he's always prepared to bet on anything and everything. That's not at all Monsieur Brennuire's or Monsieur Tolut's style. *They* only play billiards and piquet. That's the difference.

I can see very well what's special about the entrepreneur—it's the two gentlemen he has an aperitif with almost every day. With Monsieur Tolut he often goes and has a game of billiards in the neighborhood. They've known each other for almost a year now. I remember it very well. Monsieur Brabbant wasn't letting on but he was trying to get to know those gentlemen. He managed it, but nothing has changed. I thought vaguely: "He isn't hoping to get anything out of Monsieur Tolut, he doesn't look rich enough, it's more likely Monsieur Brennuire who interests him. He must have quite a bit stashed away and Monsieur Brabbant is going to advise him to invest it in a reliable business, mines in the Congo for example, or a firm selling rabbit skins in New Zealand." Such things have been known. But nothing of this order seems to have taken place between them up till now, and therefore there's still nothing to show what it is that makes Monsieur Brabbant Monsieur Brabbant and not somebody else.

At all events, it's been going on for a year now. It began with the winter, with the year. Another winter has begun now, and the trio is still there; there are new people, young men who're beginning to acquire habits and to catch venereal diseases from the cocottes who come here to smoke a cigarette. Some little reviews have been started this year too, but those things don't take place here anymore. Well, it's none of my business, I only mention it in order to take account of time, as indeed to take account of the appearance of overcoats, of braziers and chestnut sellers, and of people treading the dead leaves on the asphalt underfoot while they're waiting for the tram in the rain. There's no arguing about the seasons.

I, who am a philosopher in my own way, I watch them go by and I say to myself: "Ah, we're going to see this again, we're going to see that again," and it never fails to occur. Unless there's a catastrophe—the war or the Spanish influenza, but even they don't surprise me. All that, that's the business of the planets. The planets go round in circles just like people do. *I* remain fixed in the middle of saucers and bottles of aperitif and the people revolve around me; they go round with the seasons and the months. *I* don't budge, but *they* revolve and repeat themselves. They're more or less content with that. I look at them, but they don't look at me. I'm quite content to complete my calculations and then finally go to the races to fulfill my destiny; for such is my fate. I myself have read my destiny in the stars. It's extremely convenient to be able to do that on your own and not to have to ask anybody for anything or let anybody stick his nose into it. I win all along the line, that's my destiny, such as the numbers have written it in the sky with little lights.

Talking of destinies, there are some odd ones. I was just saying that to myself the day Monsieur Landru was condemned to death, or rather the next day, when it was in the papers. And I wasn't saying that to myself apropos of Monsieur Landru (although I might have), but apropos of a one-eyed man who had his other eye put out by a chap. Monsieur Tolut even got far more worked up about this than he did about Monsieur Landru's death sentence. It was very badly reported, that incident. It's hard to know what happened. It remains mysterious. In any case, the one-eyed man is blind now. There's a destiny for you! Ah, it's a strange thing, destiny. I suppose that one-eyed man used to go to the same café every day, maybe for the last twenty years—just a supposition. He used to go there every day, then, and return like the sun every morning and the stars every evening, and he went through the yearly cycle with the seasons. When the first leaves appeared, he must have said: "And now it's winter." And the same waiter would have served him the same aperitif every day, and no doubt he had been expecting things to go on in the same way for a long time, perhaps he even imagined: forever. But now it's all over. His expectations have been thwarted. Even so, that must have been in the planets, but who thought to look at them?

And when I see my little world revolving around me, I think that one day a destiny gets fulfilled—and then someone departs. Sometimes it takes years and years for that to happen. They've become old men, every year completing the cycle of the seasons, mounted on their date of birth as if it were a horse in a merry-go-round. When you observe their regularity, you might think that they'll never stop and that the axle is so well greased that they'll go on revolving forever. But one day their destiny gets fulfilled. Which is to say that one day they die. The younger ones don't revolve for so long, and when they disappear it's to go and revolve elsewhere. As for me, I'm not caught up in the cycle of the seasons and I remain indifferent to their evolution. It's the planets that make the seasons, and as I know the motion of the planets it's as if I were responsible for the course of the seasons. The habitués don't know it, but sometimes this makes me feel like laughing.

15

THE SORBONNE LIBRARY was much better heated than the
Sainte-Geneviève library; therefore Rohel couldn't find a seat.
He detested libraries, but having decided a few hours earlier
that he was going to study seriously for his exams, he felt
obliged to go to one to read the fundamental works, notably
those written by his esteemed professors, in order to get some
slight idea of the correct thing to think about language, about
involution as opposed to evolution, about the primitive men-
tality, Indian castes, judgmental methods and the last period
of Platonic philosophy. This zeal for work coincided with the
fact that he was now living with a girl he had met one day when
she was sitting bored stiff over a coffee; craftily he'd taken her
to the cinema; they were now a couple, and had been for a
week.

Rohel perceived, then, that there were no unoccupied seats.
And anyway, he had chosen a somewhat awkward way to start
his new life of study; it was already half past four. He had only
an hour and a half left for work; he got to Sainte-Geneviève at
around twenty to five. There it wasn't so warm, but it was full of
customers because you didn't need a student's card to get in.
The atmosphere was more severe than at the Sorbonne, but
also more insipid and slightly corrupt. Rohel walked around
the tables looking at the girls, and sat down opposite a student

of the great-big-eyes-and-flowing-tresses type, who was reading a Foignet. He pulled some papers out of his pocket, rustled
them noisily, and by various antics endeavored to attract the
young person's attention. She was studious, though, and didn't
look up more than twice.

And now he had to choose which work he would try to
extract from the malevolence of the assistants galloping up
and down behind the grilles. In their wake trotted an assort-
ment of customers prepared to suffer any kind of persecution
to get their hands on the coveted octavo. Every time Rohel
ventured into this place he had an argument with these itiner-
ant officials. He began to consult the card indexes, looking for
a shelf-mark. That was another thing he had a horror of. Those
little bits of greasy cardboard disgusted him. Finally he filled in
his application form, handed it to an assistant and in his turn
began to follow him around. And after all that, the work was "in
use." Discouraged, Rohel went back to his seat; then he caught
sight of Tuquedenne, his nose buried in a calfskin-bound book.

"How're you doing then?" Rohel asked him.

Tuquedenne stammered something; he didn't like to be thus
taken unawares.

"What's that you're reading?"

"Oh, it's an old book," Vincent replied, closing it.

Rohel didn't insist.

"Are you leaving now?"

"And you?"

Rohel led him out. They walked down the rue Cujas.

"Do you work a lot?"

"A bit. But in general, what I do is fairly irrelevant to the
syllabus."

"What were you reading just now?"

"Cardan's *De vita propria.*"

"What gave you the idea of reading that?"

"Bayle. Haven't you ever read his *Dictionnaire?* It's amazing."

"To hell with all that! Erudition will be your downfall, old man. What the devil do you care about Bayle's *Dictionnaire!* I can only put up with all that ancient stuff if it's on the syllabus."

"Hm, so you agree with Brennuire now."

"No, but joking apart, do you take it seriously, the philo(sophie) degree?"

"No, of course not."

"Well then? What's the use of wasting your time on those ancient books? The best thing would be to make a bonfire of them. A fire at Sainte-Geneviève, what a liberation! All those spiders' webs should be incinerated."

"The Louvre too, eh?"

"The Louvre too!"

"I've already read that in the Dada reviews," said Tuquedenne. "Only the thing is, they didn't burn anything at all. As for Cardan's book, it's an extraordinary work, and I can't see any reason why you'd like to stop me reading it."

"I don't want to stop you. But really, *is* it of any interest?"

"Yes. It's very modern."

"I'll have to read it."

"Here—what you ought to read is *Le Cornet à dés.* It's superb. All modern poetry stems from Max Jacob and Apollinaire."

"Didn't Max Jacob convert to Catholicism?"

"Yes. That doesn't change the poetic value of his work."

"Of course not."

"Personally, I'm an atheist," Tuquedenne said abruptly.

"Shall we go in here?"

They informed Alfred of their desire to drink some beer.

"Ah—and what about Hublin!" Rohel exclaimed. "Have you any news of him?"

"None. I really don't think we'll ever hear from him. He's gone."

"It's unbelievable, that business. What on earth can have got into him?"

"Nothing. He's just quite simply gone."

Rohel considered this an elegant answer.

"What are you doing tonight? How about having dinner with me?"

"My parents are expecting me."

"Your parents? You can surely ditch them for one evening. You're not a child anymore."

"They're good to me, you know. I wouldn't want them to worry."

"Phone them."

"They don't have a phone."

"Send them a *pneu.*"

"Where shall we have dinner?"

"We'll see."

"Right, I'll send them a *pneu.* Let's go to the post office in the rue Danton."

For some time Rohel had been examining an old gentleman sitting at a nearby table; two other old gentlemen came in and went up to him. Rohel was able to hear his name. It was indeed old man Brennuire.

"Hm, there's The Lozenge," said Tuquedenne, who had just recognized Tolut.

"Let's make ourselves scarce," Rohel suggested, calling the waiter.

They went out before the old professor spotted them, but Rohel had had time to recognize the third old man as well: he was that Martin-Martin whom he'd been to see about a job as secretary. But was it really he? Old Brennuire had just called him by a different name. That old idiot Brennuire, who had it in for him because of a miserable bottle of brandy . . .

Outside Crès's bookshop, he stopped.

"I'll have a look at the latest books while you go to the post office."

Tuquedenne told himself that he too would have a look at them, but when he had sent his *pneu* he met Rohel at the door of the post office. Rohel led him off to the rue Monsieur-le-Prince, and there pulled a bundle of books out from under his overcoat. He showed one to Tuquedenne: it was *Le Cornet à dés.*

"This *is* what you advised me to read?"

"Yes, that's it. What else did you buy?"

"*Buy?* For goodness' sake, who do you take me for?"

"Did you steal them?"

"That's right, shout it from the housetops."

Tuquedenne shut up.

"It's dead easy there," Rohel went on. "Picart's, though, have put mirrors up, it's become very difficult. I can pinch anything I like from Crès's, but obviously it's more amusing at Picart's. Haven't you ever tried?"

"I don't think I'd have the knack."

"The main thing, you know, is to do it quickly. I'll go home now and get rid of these books."

Rohel turned the corner into the rue Racine.

"Shouldn't we go straight on?"

"No. That's true, I forgot to tell you. I live in the rue du Cardinal-Lemoine now."

"Usen't you to be in the rue Gay-Lussac?"

"I like a change, you know, and anyway I'm fed up with hotels. I'm renting a furnished room with a kitchen now."

"Do you use the kitchen?"

"Of course. I wouldn't be able to get by without it. What's more, I'm fed up with cheap restaurants, too."

They continued on their way thus, chatting absentmindedly, each harboring various sentiments towards the other. They climbed the high steps of a dark old staircase, then Rohel kicked open a door that was already ajar. Sitting on a bed, a woman was mending a run in a stocking.

"Suze" (that was what this person liked to be called), "this is a pal."

Rohel put his books down on a table. Tuquedenne stayed in the doorway; he was rather amazed. Suze stood up, kissed Rohel, and then, looking at Tuquedenne:

"Anyone would think you take me for an exotic animal!"
She laughed very loudly and they shook hands.

"As Tuquedenne is free tonight..." Rohel began.

"Ah, you're called Tuquedenne," Suze interrupted. "That's a funny name."

She always said that; she found it very tiring to remember names.

"As Tuquedenne is free tonight," Rohel began again.

"Are you usually engaged in the evenings, monsieur?" Suze asked, very much the society hostess, and remembering the "monsieur" at the last moment.

"Yes, and he's free this evening. So..."

"Are you a student too, monsieur?"

"Oh, shit! are you going to let me speak?"

"All right, all right, I've got it, we're going out to dinner tonight. I'll just put my hat on and I'll be with you. I hope we're going to have an aperitif."

"That's right," said Rohel.

Tuquedenne turned over the pages of *Le Cornet à dés,* looking for the poem entitled "Fantômas." When he had found it, he showed it to Rohel who read it and then started looking through the volume, uttering enthusiastic little exclamations.

"Okay, I'm ready," said Suze.

"Just a minute," Tuquedenne said to Rohel, "read this one too."

And he found another poem and showed it to Rohel, who read it out loud.

"Oh, really! can't you tear yourselves away from your book?" demanded Suze, who was becoming impatient.

"We're coming," said Rohel, abandoning the book.

He put out the gas and double-locked the door. Suze and Tuquedenne waited for him outside, not saying a word.

"Well, where are we going?" Rohel asked.

Suze suggested a café in the Latin Quarter; Rohel protested. He was bored to death with the bistrots in the Quarter. *He* voted for the Café de Versailles. Since Tuquedenne had nothing against it and Suze only made vague objections, they all jumped into a Z bus which happened to be passing. The journey was rather gloomy. In the café, they ordered aperitifs. The men filled their pipes and Suze lit a cigarette. The people around them were talking in loud voices, it was a provincial clientele, spiced with a tart or two. Outside, people were shivering; inside, it was nice and warm. The New Year's Eve menu was written up on notice boards. The waiters circulated like ghosts in the midst of a fog of triple origin: human, alcoholic, nicotinic. Fixed in space like a target, the manager was bowing his head first to one side, then to the other.

After half a glass, Rohel and Tuquedenne felt better.

"Do you write poetry?" asked the former.

Tuquedenne hesitated.

"Yes."

"Have you ever published any?"

"No."

"Haven't you ever tried?"

"No."

"You ought to show them to me."

"No kidding," said Suze, "are you a poet? Well, I never!"

"What d'you think a poet *is?*" Rohel asked her.

"Oh, I can see you coming. You'd like me to say it's a chap with a big black hat and a floppy bow tie, so's you could make fun of me afterwards. No, my sweet. I know that it's only photographers that dress up like that these days. I knew one once, a poet, at the Rotonde. He only traveled in wagons-lits, he injected himself with morphine and he was kept by women, yes, my sweet."

Rohel and Tuquedenne collapsed onto the table, laughing.

"It's true, he was kept by women and he was a poet, a modern poet even."

"Your modern poet, you didn't by any chance meet him in the pages of *Mon Film?*"

"At the Rotonde, I tell you."

"In any case, I don't suppose I look much like a poet," said Tuquedenne.

"Oh, no!" exclaimed Suze, carried away by sincerity.

"What does he look like?" asked Rohel.

"Like a student, of course."

Tuquedenne made a face. Rohel rubbed his hands.

"You see, you mustn't have any illusions."

"Where are we going to eat?" Suze demanded.

Rohel suggested the Duguesclin, nearby. It wasn't too expensive and he liked the food there. As for Tuquedenne, who never dined anywhere other than the rue de la Convention, he felt he was having a great adventure.

Suze was very hungry; she never had anything but a cup of coffee and a croissant for lunch.

At the restaurant they treated themselves to two carafes of rosé d'Anjou, a little wine that goes to your head, as everyone knows. Suze wanted to go dancing afterwards; Rohel wasn't in the mood that evening. It was true that he couldn't dance, which he didn't dare admit to her. Tuquedenne, who was in the same position, declared himself satisfied with another of Suze's suggestions. They'd go and have a drink at the Rotonde. They might even see the famous poet there.

Tuquedenne and Rohel, who were setting foot in this café for the first time, affected the casual air of regular customers and took good care not to gawk like provincials at the Negress or the chap in the turban.

"Hey, there's Kiki," said Suze. "She's a model."

Suze had been there three or four times with a chap who had vaguely pointed out to her the personalities who frequented the place; she was proudly repeating what she had learned. But Rohel didn't allow himself to be impressed. Tuquedenne made severe judgments on the paintings hanging on the wall. The two of them began to talk painting; neither knew much about it, but they could mention names. Their preference was for the cubists.

"Have you ever seen any cubist paintings?" Rohel asked his girlfriend.

" 'Course I have," replied Suze. "You think I'm just up from the provinces? *I* can tell a Braque from a Picasso. That surprise you? I've known some chaps who keep up with the times, you understand."

"It isn't difficult to tell a Braque from a Picasso," said Tuquedenne.

"Oh, *you*. You have to know everything better than everyone else."

"He knows everything," said Rohel. "He's read everything, even the works of Gerolamo Cardan. Do you know Gerolamo Cardan?"

"Oh, the hell with your boring old books."

"That's what I told him earlier on. You read too much, erudition will be your downfall and you'll end up a librarian."

"That's not so sure," said Tuquedenne.

Suze yawned.

"No kidding, don't you really want to go to Bullier's?"

"Not tonight," said Rohel. "And anyway, Bullier's isn't very amusing. It's lousy with students."

"And aren't *you* a student?"

"All the same, when there are ten students together, that makes ten imbeciles."

"Good thing there's only two of you."

"How very logical you can be, my little Suze."

It was Tuquedenne's turn to be bored. Suze called the waiter and ordered another coffee. The others asked for beer. More saucers were piled up.

"Basically," said Tuquedenne, going on to more general considerations, "logic has just taken a terrific punch on the nose."

Rohel didn't answer. Suze yawned.

Whereupon Wullmar came in, looking like someone who's looking for someone. He noticed the trio and at first wanted to pretend he hadn't noticed them, but having noticed that the trio had noticed him, he went up to it. They greeted each other. Rohel introduced Wullmar to his girlfriend and his girlfriend to Wullmar.

"I can only stay five minutes," the new arrival announced, sitting down.

He ordered a whiskey, which greatly impressed the two philosophers.

"Well then, what's become of you?" he asked.

He was only addressing Rohel. Tuquedenne didn't interest him.

"Nothing much has become of us," sighed Rohel. "And you?"

"I'm still studying law," Wullmar replied, with irony.

The irony certainly consisted in the fact that he, Wullmar, might actually be studying (anything).

"And what else are you doing?" asked Rohel, who had understood.

Wullmar smiled.

"I was looking for someone, he isn't here, I'll go and look in the Dôme now. If he isn't there either I could take you for a spin in my Amilcar, but it only has two seats. See you one of these days!"

He knocked back his whiskey and stood up.

"We could make a date," said Rohel.

"I shan't be free before January."

"What day?"

"How about the third? At about seven, at the Criterion?"

"Right."

Wullmar paid for his drink and left a big tip. They shook hands. He left.

"He's splendid," exclaimed Rohel. "No, don't you think so?"

"And then, Amilcars, they go fast," said Suze.

16

WULLMAR WAITED FOR a few minutes and then the typist showed him in. Monsieur Martin-Martin, slumped behind his desk, motioned him to a chair.

"My friend Rohel sent me," Wullmar began. "He advised me to apply for the job of secretary that you offered him. He can't accept it because he has a splendid situation at the moment which he can't leave."

Monsieur Martin-Martin seemed surprised.

"I didn't know that. What is it?"

"Private tutor."

"With some very rich people, no doubt?"

"Probably."

Monsieur Martin-Martin smiled.

"I thought you were a friend of Monsieur Rohel's?"

"Certainly. We see each other very often."

"But you're playing a dirty trick on him."

"I may well be doing him a favor."

Silence.

"Does he remember the visit he paid me about a year ago?"

"Very well."

"I'm trying to call him to mind. Isn't he a blond young man, very thin, who makes gestures as he speaks?"

"That sounds like him."

"In that case, I saw him at the Soufflet the other day."

"He recognized you."

"That's what I was wondering."

"And that no doubt is why you wrote to him."

Silence.

"I won't ask you any questions. I already know you a little."

"Oh, you know, Monsieur Brabbant, what Brennuire might say about me . . ."

"You took your time making up your mind. But get it into your head that that name is not known here."

"Very well, monsieur."

"I must have considerably intrigued your friend."

"Oh, no, not especially so. He won't inform on you to the police."

"I can't think why he would do that. Ah, these young people, always so romantic! Plenty of people use another name than their own, there's no law against it. You ought to know that, since you're studying law now. Martin-Martin is the name of my former partner, if you're interested. But there's something else I wanted to say to you; you lied to me just now, your friend hasn't got a splendid situation."

"Let's not be afraid to call a spade a spade: I lied."

"I hope it's for the last time. I demand the highest moral standards from my employees."

"Then I may now consider myself your secretary?"

"You start work immediately. You can also act as my chauffeur, for, if my information is correct, you own a little Amilcar which might be of some use to me."

"How much a month are you going to pay me?"

"We'll talk about that later."

There was a knock on the door. The typist announced that there was a Monsieur Rohel to see him.

"Tell him I asked him to come at three o'clock precisely; it's seven minutes past three. I have found someone to take his place."

On the other side of the door Rohel could be heard protesting; then a door slammed.

"What sort of work are you going to give me to do?" Wullmar asked.

"That's what I'm wondering," Brabbant answered.

He stood up.

"For Christ's sake, I just wonder what there will be for you to do! I'll make no secret of it, I haven't got the slightest idea, for Christ's sake!"

One after the other he moved the objects littering his desk. He couldn't manage to come out with what he wanted to confess. He remained silent, although there were movements in his throat. Finally, he vomited out his secret.

"Believe it or not, young man, one day I suddenly became ambitious. It came upon me like the colic, it fell on me like a flowerpot. Do you realize the enormity of it, young man? At my age, to have had enough of mediocrity? Isn't that phenomenal and flabbergasting? Yes, now I have ambition, at sixty-eight come next summer! You simply can't imagine what it's like! A fig for your piddling little business deals and petty swindles, I want to accomplish great things! It isn't too late; look at Clemenceau, that glorious example. I still have at least fifteen years ahead of me and I'll make no secret of it, young man, that a year from now I expect to have amassed a fortune, an immense fortune. You see how interesting it is, the situation I'm offering you. I need someone young to help me. Yes, I need someone young who has drive, guts, spirit, and above all who is of impeccable morals. I believe you fulfill all these conditions, Monsieur Wullmar. But before we come to any definite arrangement you must pledge yourself in the first place to the most absolute discretion, that's only natural; and in the second place to stop seeing your Latin Quarter friends and to frequent as little as possible the cafés in the boulevard Saint-Michel and its environs, which you may well find difficult; and in the third place not to sleep with my typist. Is that understood?"

"That is understood, monsieur."

"I can't wait to accomplish great things," Brabbant sighed.

"Where shall we begin?"

"For Christ's sake! I've already told you that I've no idea. Absolutely none."

Brabbant thought it over.

"Perhaps I could teach you the basics, or at least what I used to do in the old days. In the old days: by that I mean not very long ago. I'll show you a few little dodges; they'll help you get your hand in and they'll also explain my method. Why don't we begin with the deaf man trick. It's simple and amusing. You sit down in a café next to some worthy woman, you ask her to make a telephone call for you because you're hard of hearing, and you make off with her coat or her handbag or her suitcase. There's the trick of the suit and the telephone, the trick of the provincial and the taxi, the trick of the suitcase full of foreign currency, the business of the spittle on the shoulder, and lots of others that I know although I don't practice them. You'll get your hand in and learn to keep your head, but naturally all that is mere child's play. You mustn't spend too much time on such bagatelles, Monsieur Wullmar. We have to think big, very big, and not waste our time on such trifles. It's a simple apprenticeship, not a vocation. You may not know it, Monsieur Wullmar, but there's something terrible, and that is the line of least resistance. I know people who've tried a little trick that worked once, and then gone on doing it indefinitely, all their lives."

Silence.

"That's what I used to do. It's terrible. You end up ossified. I need someone young to overcome this ossification. See you tomorrow at three, Monsieur Wullmar."

"At three?"

"Yes. To start with we shall work only in the afternoons. And there's something I was forgetting: don't try to suggest ideas to me. The only ideas I want to put into practice are my own. You understand?"

Wullmar left. Brabbant sank into a deep depression. Things were not happening as he would have wished; this secretary who was imposing himself on him seemed to bode no good and, all things considered, he found this Wullmar antipathetic. He remained inert until twilight; as night fell, he took off. What had become of the blind man? Monsieur Blaisolle took a taxi to the rue des Archives, and then made his way peacefully through the enchanted crowds streaming out of the Bazar de l'Hôtel-de-Ville. He hesitated for a moment at the door of the café. He recognized the voices of some of the habitués. He went in.

The blind man was there. Still just as fat, he was leaning his two hands and his chin on a big stick, his eyes hidden behind dark glasses. he was sitting with a team of four manille players, three of whom were his former partners; they had found a replacement for him. He was paying great attention to the remarks, interjections, jokes, oaths, gibes. He added his own. He got them to explain every move, and shook his nut sadly, because in his opinion they all played very badly now.

Monsieur Blaisolle went up to them. The manille players recognized him.

"We never see you anymore," said they.

"I've had quite a bit of business to do in the provinces," Brabbant replied.

"Huh! Monsieur Blaisolle!" the blind man exclaimed. "We never see you anymore!"

"Business in the provinces," Brabbant repeated.

"Sit down, sit down," said Tormoigne. "Did you hear what happened to me?"

But without giving the other time to reply, he began to recount "the terrible attack of which he had been the victim." One of the manille players sympathized with Blaisolle and, passing the back of his hand over the sides of his face, gave him discreetly to understand the immense boredom that Monsieur Tormoigne was in the habit of generating. What most outraged the latter was the fact that the papers hadn't spoken at greater length of his dreadful misfortune.

"It seems they only put it in the news-in-brief. Such a horror, and they stuck it in the news-in-brief! and you know why? You'll never guess why. Well! This is why: because that day the papers had no room for anything but Landru. That was the day he was condemned to death. If it hadn't been for that I'd have been on the front page and it would have made a real splash. Well! Didn't you know? Personally I find it a consolation. I tell myself that I am still very much alive, whereas Landru, whoosh! They're going to cut his head off and shove him under six foot of earth with his head between his arms. That's what he'll have got, and that's what I tell myself."

He waited for approval. Brabbant cleared his throat, and Tormoigne seemed satisfied with that.

"And what about my flat? Have you been thinking about my flat?"

They embarked on a fierce discussion. But Brabbant got the better of it. Not only did he obtain three thousand francs instead of two thousand, but he also left with Tormoigne's wallet in his pocket.

It was his first theft.

17

TUQUEDENNE STOPPED meeting Rohel; he didn't particularly want to see him again. On the other hand he struck up a friendship with Brennuire, who taught him to play billiards. And every day they spent an hour or two or three at the Ludo. Sometimes they caught sight of Tolut and Brabbant who were also having their game. They greeted each other from a distance. The young ones sometimes preferred to go to any other café rather than having to be subjected the one to a former teacher and the other to an uncle. As for the second old man, he didn't interest them.

"I met Rohel," Brennuire said one day. "He asked me a whole lot of questions about old Brabbant. I wonder what he finds interesting in him."

"It's a long time since I've seen Rohel," said Tuquedenne.

Every evening, when the dining room table had been cleared of its polluted plates and bread crumbs and was serving as his desk, he bemoaned the day he had just lived through. He was there, alone. His parents retired early and read serial stories in bed. In a room a little farther away his grandmother was aging. He was there, alone. From time to time a tram passed, or a lorry. He was distressed at having lived through this day in this way. At moments he thought about love, and couldn't see how it could ever happen to him: to meet a woman he loved—and who loved him. And at other moments he thought about the past, about all those days that were always the same, about the hideously monotonous life he led, the family meals, the Sorbonne platitudes, the customary caroms. And at still other moments he thought about the future. What would he become? He could see himself threatened by gnawing mediocrity, by the rats' teeth of mediocrity. Or perhaps adventure? Maybe one day he would go away like Jean Hublin? But some ordinary, everyday affliction always rendered him helpless; he perceived that he didn't know how to telephone, or that he gave way to despair because he had just broken one of his shoelaces. How to get out of it then?

Every evening he was alone in the little dining room in the family flat. He worked. When he was too bored he would get up and drink a glass of wine; or he would look out of the window, but then the deserted street seemed to be a nightmare, and in particular the shutters on the hardware shop. He masturbated. This too was quite a business. He would very much have liked to cure himself of this habit, but how could he do so except by sleeping with women, and how can you sleep with women if you never meet any? Occasionally he followed one in the street but at a considerable distance, and after a short time he let her go. And if a tart accosted him, he fled.

He thought of suicide, but never for very long at a time. He managed to put it all out of his mind and set himself to getting his confidence back. Two things took him out of it: reading (not work) and Paris. He loved Paris, or more precisely the streets of Paris. When, disgusted with the monotony of his life, he decided to spend a day without meeting Brennuire and having a game of billiards, he walked across the town in zigzags. He interested himself in the alterations to the bus routes and in the new lines that were brought into service; he didn't despise the lowly trams and he even had a lively affection for the métro. He didn't like the town itself, its topography. He only knew its skeleton, not its flesh. And yet the twilight always seemed to him to be a moving hour, when the newspaper sellers cry their wares, when the café terraces emerge glittering from a fog heavy with mechanical roars, when the sun like a big red balloon goes and gets deflated behind the Arc de Triomphe, over by Saint-Germain-en-Laye.

He also escaped his despair through reading. Certain books became an event for him, as for example Chesterton's *The Man Who Was Thursday,* and Johan Bojer's *Le Caméléon.* He read Goethe in order to find some sort of equilibrium, even though he couldn't stand Goethe, and as a concession to a certain intellectual fashion he began a passionate study of Thomism— he, the atheist.

In the meantime his grandmother, who was decaying in the end room, had aged so much that she was beginning to give up the ghost. Her death throes lasted two days because she was hard to kill, as Tuquedenne senior said. From time to time Vincent went to see how things were going: the old girl was still giving the death rattle and tugging at her sheets. He watched her for a few minutes; then they told him there was no point in his staying there; so he went. It didn't make much difference to his life. He was reading *Le Sens commun,* the work of a reverend father, which he found of extreme interest; and he had made so much progress at billiards that that day he beat Brennuire. When he got home it was more or less all over. They had paid a woman to keep a close watch on the march of Death while knitting woolen socks for her husband who was a gas man and had delicate feet.

The family sat down to dinner.

"The poor old woman, she isn't conscious anymore," said Tuquedenne senior.

Madame Tuquedenne sighed. She was only her mother-in-law, but she'd never done her any harm. If it hadn't been for her, how would they have got this flat? They would have been obliged to leave Vincent in Paris on his own, and God knows what would have happened to him.

After dinner, the table was cleared. Vincent began to work, his father to look through the paper and his mother to read a novel. On the stroke of ten Monsieur Tuquedenne stood up and said:

"I'll go and have a look."

The gas man's wife told him matter-of-factly that it could still last some time.

He went to bed; his wife joined him. Vincent, left alone, worked until one o'clock. Then he felt thirsty. He drank a glass of wine. Some cesspit emptiers went by in the street; there must have been at least a dozen; he recognized them by their ponderous, peaceful progress. He thought he ought to go and see what was happening in the end room. He opened the door slowly. The gas man's wife was asleep. So was Grandmother. She was all yellow and her eyes were open. She was clutching the sheets with her short, fat fingers with their long, dirty nails. Vincent closed the door gently and went off to bed thinking vaguely: "that's all," "it's simple," "it isn't much." He fell asleep at once.

In the morning, his grandmother was nicely laid out with a chin strap round her head. The formalities had to be seen to. Vincent went with his father. It wasn't a very amusing day and in the evening Monsieur Tuquedenne felt pretty tired. As they were sitting down to dinner he even suddenly shed a tear in a totally inexplicable way, but his wife put him to shame. That evening Vincent finished reading *Le Sens commun,* the work of a reverend father.

Then they put Grandmother in a coffin and buried her. Without a religious ceremony, because the Tuquedenne family was not a family of bigots. The old girl had a vault in the Montparnasse Cemetery; her husband had been waiting for her there for decades. Everything went off normally. A few vague relations came, and then went. Vincent tried to think about death.

He couldn't manage it.

Monsieur Tuquedenne exchanged his four-roomed flat for a three-roomed flat, likewise in the rue de la Convention, but nearer the métro. This made him a small profit. Vincent would have liked to move to another district (adventure), but the old folk had acquired their habits in the present one. The only advantage he could see in the change was that he had a small desk in his room; his capacity for isolation was thereby increased. But none of this changed his life very much. He continued his games of billiards and his reading. And was periodically overwhelmed by abominable fits of despair from which he was abruptly extricated by a ridiculous but stubborn optimism, an absurd love of life.

In the meantime, they had guillotined Landru.

One day, Tuquedenne discovered the Place d'Alleray, and sat down on a bench. It was ten in the morning. It was a lovely day. A vehicle passed, occasionally. Occasionally, a pedestrian. Children were playing. Sitting on the terrace of his café, the *patron* was reading the paper and smoking. From time to time, in a house, a woman began to sing. It was a lovely day. It was ten o'clock. Tuquedenne sat down on a bench.

It was true that none of these things contained its raison d'être in itself, and all of them, submerged in Aristotle's "becoming," were destined to perish. What was their reality? Did it not depend on something other than themselves? Where was their reality, then? What made their reality? Was it Being, was it the One? If Being constituted the reality of things, why then did these things not exist? For to be destined to-be-no-longer is not to exist. If it was the One, why then were things several? Why then did they exist, why then must they perish?

One of the children began to cry. An old man came out of one of the houses and dragged himself over to a bench, smoking an old pipe. The *patron* of the café had finished both his reading and his cigarette and was yawning in the sunlight. Two housewives were shouting at each other from opposite sides of the square. An old-clothes man began to sing. A cat ran from one street to another, obliquely. The trees were becoming green, for it was that time of year. Against one of them a dog pissed, after having sniffed it, and then paid a visit to another. The woman was now singing "Le Temps des cerises." Tuquedenne felt he could weep, and was moved to pity over the inexistence of things.

How can they be saved? Yes, how can things be saved? How can things be rescued from nothingness, how can they be delivered from Being? How can the instant be given both becoming and eternity?

He remembered a saying of Goethe's that he had copied out. He took a notebook out of his pocket and looked for it. On the first page there were some addresses; on the following ones, dates and a series of figures, showing the progress he had made at billiards. After that came the Goethe quotations, the first of which, in capital letters, said: *Niemand demoralisieren.* Goethe continued:

"If you want to penetrate into the infinite, advance on all sides into the finite. Do you want to extract a new life from the Whole? Then know how to see the Whole in the smallest object."

"Yes, I do," said Tuquedenne. "But when the smallest object has disappeared, where shall I see the Whole?"

"Let reason be always present when life enjoys life," said Goethe. "Thus the past continues, the future lives in advance, the instant is an eternity!"

"That's what I was looking for! The past continues, the future lives in advance, that's certainly 'becoming' as it is lived according to the laws of reason. The instant is an eternity: how is that, then?"

"I have never been anybody's master," Goethe replied, "but I do dare call myself a liberator. My example has allowed people to see that it is from the inside to the outside that man must live and the artist must work."

Whereupon Goethe departed; a bibliography replaced him.
R. P. Pègues, *Commentaire français littéral à la Somme de Saint Thomas,* Toulouse, 8 vol.
Farges, *Cours complet de philosophie scolastique,* 9 vol.
Hugon, *Cursus philosophiae thomisticae,* 6 vol.
Jean de Saint-Thomas, *Cursus philosophiae thomisticae,* 3 vol.
There were several pages of this sort. Even so, though, Tuquedenne hadn't read it all.

There followed some scholastics' aphorisms about actuality and potentiality, about form and matter, about movement, about causality, about purpose. At the top of each page Tuquedenne had written the fundamental principle: *est, est; non, non.*

"Every being," says the school, "by the very fact that he is, is what he is and not what he is not."

"That was certainly the question. But why is he what he is, this being? Why must he perish, if Being is immutable? Why is there a becoming? If it was necessary for there to be a becoming, did Being therefore depend on it? If this being is, why does he become? And if he becomes, why is he not?"

The theologians remained silent. A curé wanted to ascend the pulpit. Tuquedenne smiled and turned the page. On it there were a few personal notes such as: "Logic, 6 March, forms of classification." (He had passed the exam for this certificate; it was the first.) Or: "Stop going to la Source, or to any other café in the boulevard Saint-Michel; stop looking in the window of the bookshop next to the Ecole des mines; stop imagining that I'm changing for the better because when I'm going home I walk on the right-hand pavement instead of on the left-hand pavement; stop believing that I've become someone else because I don't go to la Source anymore or look in the window of the bookshop at the above address; stop my knees trembling when I pass a woman in the street because I think she's looking at me (very difficult); stop arguing with my father when he says I ought to become a teacher in a school in the provinces (let him talk but do nothing about it); stop wearing braces." Next, this quotation: *Et quid amabo nisi quod rerum metaphysica est?*

The aspect of the little square had changed. It was now eleven o'clock. More cars were passing. On the café terrace, some builders were having a snack, with some beautiful liter bottles of red wine in front of them. The old man was smoking his third pipe. The woman had stopped singing. The children were still playing; laughter and quarrels alternated. The sun was heating the paving stones but a light breeze was ruffling the young leaves on the trees and the people filled their lungs with this fresh air saying: isn't it lovely today, and isn't it fine.

"Isn't it lovely today," said the people, "and isn't it fine."

"*Est, est, non, non,*" declared the philosopher.

"I don't know anything about anything," sighed Tuquedenne.

"Ονδεις ημων ονδεν οιδεν, ονδ' αντο τοντο ποτέϱον οιδα-μεν η ονκ οιδαμεν," said Metrodorus who happened to be passing, on the next page.

"Another bloody foreigner," exclaimed the people. "What's he on about? He wouldn't be insulting us, would he?"

"We don't know anything," Tuquedenne translated, "not even whether we know anything or nothing."

"But he's a skeptic, that chap," murmured the scandalized crowd.

"How to deny it?"

He shut his notebook and returned it to his pocket. He stood up. He went home to have lunch with his parents, who lived in the rue de la Convention.

18

ROHEL WAS GOING through a period of bad luck. Slates fell on his head with every step he took. He had a solid skull. He looked at the debris and laughed. That was his way of fighting.

The draft board had presented no problem. He had gone to Le Havre in Wullmar's car. Declared fit for combatant service (after all he wasn't a runt), he had asked for and obtained a deferment of a year. So he wouldn't have to think about it again for the next eleven months. Binges and conviviality in the lower part of the town decorated this little excursion.

Then there was Monsieur Martin-Martin's letter and Wullmar's disappearance. For a time, Wullmar had never left Rohel and Rohel had never left Wullmar. One fine day, Wullmar disappeared. Rohel waited; then searched, and discovered that Wullmar had played a fine trick on him. He decided to forget about it, but without the Amilcar life became boring. Suze wanted to force him to learn to dance. He sent her packing. She disappeared, she and her nickname. He found himself alone in the midst of cans of food and a few dirty dishes. He washed the dishes, opened the cans, and began to work frenziedly, for the exams were approaching.

He failed.

He considered that there was no point in getting upset. He took the métro and, changing at every connecting station, began to zigzag underneath Paris. Even more than Tuquedenne, he loved this means of transport, and in particular the Nord-Sud line because, he claimed, that was where you met the most beautiful women. When he emerged from his subterranean journey he had forgotten his failures and setbacks and was talking in a way that was beginning to become quite intimate to a charming person who didn't want to confess her nationality. She agreed to meet him the next day. He went home full of joy.

But there, he found Suze. Suze had made herself up to look tragic. He took her upstairs; and there she informed him that he'd done it now. What had he done? She explained it to him, quite crudely, and expressly invited him to sort it out as soon as possible for she had no wish to keep it, o-ho no! Rohel attempted to make a few jokes about the advantageous situation of a mother of a family in our present-day society and about the names to give the child. But Suze considered that there was nothing to laugh about and insulted him. He, preserving his dignity intact, assured her that he would arrange things. He asked her to come back the next day. She had been vaguely hoping that he would let her stay; he didn't even invite her to dinner. She left, hinting at threats.

This new business didn't seem to him any more serious than the others. It ought to be easily arranged. He only had to go and see Muraut or Ponsec. Muraut seemed preferable. He would find him in the rue Monsieur-le-Prince in a little restaurant where he dined every evening with other medical students. It was only five o'clock. He lay down on his bed, but after ten minutes he had had enough of his teeming thoughts. He went out.

He walked down the rue des Ecoles. He stared with interest at every woman he passed. Sometimes she gave him an answering smile. But he walked on. He didn't even look back. He went on playing this game until he reached the boulevard Saint-Michel, which was overrun by the great after-work crowds. He thought that an aperitif would buck him up a little. It was a mild, insipid day. Rohel sat down on a café terrace and read the evening papers. Then he looked at the passing women. He saw more than one pretty one and several beautiful ones. He thought that Suze was a good deal better-looking than most of them. But when it came to learning to dance, nothing doing. So it was just too bad. He left without paying to see what happened. The waiter didn't notice. Rohel thought that this was a good sign. He laughed aloud and alone, when he suddenly remembered the day when he had left some dive without paying and had heard the manager come galloping up behind him, yelling; but he was chasing someone else, who was less crafty than he. Whereupon he went into Picart's bookshop and appropriated a copy of *Introductory Lectures on Psycho-Analysis,* a work that was being much talked about.

In the little restaurant in the rue Monsieur-le-Prince, Muraut was beginning to come out with the series of jokes that had earned him a certain renown among first-year students. He was finishing his portion of sausage-and-butter when Rohel tapped him on the shoulder. He immediately suspected something and teased him about the venereal diseases that he imagined were the reason for this visit. Rohel sat down at his table, which was already adorned with four other first-year students. In the presence of the literary man, the representatives of medicine immediately began to come out with their small stock of corporate witticisms and then, invading their opponent's territory, to lavish high praise on *the stupid nineteenth century.* Rohel listened to them indulgently; he recited some Victor Hugo to give them some idea of what it was. The others argued vehemently, with great shruggings of the shoulders.

When Muraut had finished wiping his mush and when he had carefully folded his napkin and threaded it through a red wooden ring, Rohel led him out into the street and told him his little story.

"Pff, pff," said Muraut. "Nothing easier."

He knew of a radical drug, the genuine article, a most effica-
cious whatsit. He would bring him some the next day and he
could guarantee the result. Rohel made a few jokes at his own
expense and Muraut patted him on the shoulder, he thought
he was such a good fellow, and so amusing. They decided to go
and have a drink together. Rohel felt a vague desire to tread on
his toes. They joined the four first-yearers who were playing
billiards in the back room of la Source. The evening ended in
the rue Bernard-Palissy. Rohel refused to go upstairs because
brothel women disgusted him. The whole gang finally got
themselves thrown out and, finding themselves on the sinister
paving stones of the long rue de Rennes, dispersed. Rohel
walked home taking great strides and gesticulating, because
his head was full of alcohol. Near the Place Maubert he was
accosted by a tart; he insulted her. A pimp suddenly emerged
from the shadows, swinging his hips so as to play his part
properly. Rohel was getting ready to hear a pretty speech
regarding the respect due to ladies and to get a few kicks on
the nose. But some bicycops came past. The pimp faded into
the shadows and Rohel continued on his way with increased
speed. When he got to his block he was overcome by giddiness,
and measured his length. He got up, swearing, then climbed
the stairs as far as his room, opened the door without hesitation, didn't shut it behind him, curled up, and fell asleep at
once.

The next day Muraut didn't show up. Rohel looked for him
everywhere but didn't find him. He started to prowl around
the Ecole de Médecine, stopping at the displays of the medical
booksellers Maloine and Le Soudier. He helped himself to
another copy of *Introductory Lectures on Psycho-Analysis,*
because the day before, he had lost it. As Muraut didn't appear,
he dragged himself off to the little restaurant. Muraut arrived at
about one, with the drug.

In the rue du Cardinal-Lemoine, Suze was becoming impatient. Rohel gave her the medicine and explained how to use it.

She listened very carefully. When she finally understood she put the bottle in her bag and stood up. She said: "Right," and held out her hand. She went out slowly. He heard her going down the stairs, and then made out her footsteps growing fainter.

He expected to get a letter from her, but never did.

Alfred

THEY HAD JUST started to dismantle the Big Wheel and then
the spring arrived and Monsieur Einstein arrived too, which
excited quite a lot of people. Serious gentlemen filled the café
and talked rapturously about relativity, the curvature of space
and the shots you fire into infinity which come back to you six
hundred years later with some contemporaries who have no
more than a two weeks' beard to shave off. I listen to their
stories and I don't even laugh to myself because I respect
science, even though that sort of science isn't up my alley. I
don't base *my* science on hypotheses and calculations that
simply consist of letters, I base it on real, solid facts and on
calculations that consist solely of figures. And I mean it when I
say that my facts are solid and real, for what is more solid than a
planet, and what is more real than a horse? So I don't laugh
when I listen to them but they don't impress me, these gentlemen who talk about Manchurian clocks, about semicircular
light rays, and tensors with little Greek letters top and bottom.
I don't allow myself to be influenced by fashion. When Monsieur Einstein has gone back to his own country the readers of
le Matin won't talk about him anymore. For my part I have a
goal, and I don't let current events divert me from it, whether
it's the trial of Mécislas Charrier or the cubist film being shown
on the boulevards, or even, as I was saying just now, Monsieur

Einstein's stay in Paris. If I were obliged to take all that into account I should never get to the end of it. Naturally, if someone came and asked me: "Are the planets propitious today?" I would answer yes or no. That comes under current events, if you like, but I would only do it as a favor to a colleague or a customer. I should rather say to *the* customer, because Monsieur Brabbant is the only one who asks such questions, sometimes, from time to time, once in a while, not every day.

At the moment he isn't asking me anything because he's away. Monsieur Brennuire has had a postcard of the Leaning Tower of Pisa, and Monsieur Tolut has had a postcard also of the Leaning Tower of Pisa. They were signed Brabbant. I might have hoped to get one also of the Leaning Tower of Pisa, but Monsieur Brabbant didn't remember me. Recently Monsieur Brennuire has stopped coming regularly but Monsieur Tolut still comes. So I make conversation with him, to cheer him up. He talks travels to me and I talk planets to him, he talks adventures to me and I talk statistics to him, he talks exoticism to me and I talk figures to him, he talks lumbar regions to me and I talk racecourses to him. He's a worrier, that old gentleman. He's longing to go somewhere very far away, so I give him something else to think about because at his age they'd lead him straight to the grave, adventures would. Sometimes I might feel like laughing, but as with the people who spend their time thinking about Monsieur Einstein's clocks without understanding the first thing about them, I don't do anything of the sort because I respect other people's opinions. If Monsieur Tolut wants to travel, it's nothing to laugh about. The other day he was talking to me about China. What did I think about China? Naturally I didn't think anything about it, but *he* thought quite a lot of things. Next he wanted to go to the Andes. That's in South America, that idea. The Andes? I let him talk as much as he likes. When I go and serve another customer and then come back, I notice that he's been talking to himself all the time I wasn't there, which means that I don't always follow the thread of his argument very well, but that's of no particular importance. Recently he asked me: "Your calculations—can they tell me whether I'm going on a long journey?" My goodness, nothing easier. He gives me the basics and I work the thing out for him on a corner of the table. In the end I found there were more than 991 chances out of a thousand that he'll still go on a journey abroad. He couldn't get over it. He had two drinks and left me a big tip, from his point of view at least. On another subject, he can't wait for Monsieur Brabbant to come back and play billiards with him again. When Monsieur Brabbant isn't here he does try to get a game with people he doesn't know, but as they're better than he is, his defeat spoils his whole evening. Monsieur Brabbant, that's who he needs, in no way an opponent to be despised, but one with whom he's always sure of dining in a good mood and going to bed likewise.

That's the way we talk, the two of us, while we're waiting for the others to come back. The others *will* come back, until one day everything gets set in motion, until one day their destiny is fulfilled. I think Monsieur Brabbant will certainly have something to do with it, because it can't be for nothing that he tried, and managed to make the acquaintance of those two gentlemen. It will all be explained in the end. For my part, I shall wait quietly for the machine to stop working. I shall wait, without waiting, since it's none of my business. Sometimes I might say to myself: "Monsieur Tolut won't come back, he's gone on a long journey, he's taken ship for the West Indies, or even for the East Indies." All day long I try to imagine it. But at around five o'clock I do a few sums and I see that there are 991 chances out of a thousand that Monsieur Tolut will come again that evening. It's true that there are nine chances that he won't come. Only, towards six o'clock, I see him coming; then I smile and say to myself: "Decidedly, my calculations always turn out to be correct, I shall soon be able to go right ahead," and this is how I shall go about it:

I go and see the manager and tell him: "A thousand apologies, but I'm leaving." He'll ask me why. And I shall reply: "I have things to do." He'll immediately think that it's the races that are the cause of it and he and my colleagues will say: "Alfred, we'll soon see him back, when he's left all his dough in the pari-mutuel booths." I shan't leave anything at all there. Between the pari-mutuel and me it's a man-to-man affair. I shall turn up on the course with a rotten little ten-franc note, and in one single stroke I shall restore the balance thanks to a so well-calculated double that no horse will be able to lose, and no combination will be able to fail, a double that will give me back the 201,643 francs that are owing to me. After this wonderful coup I shall buy a house in the country where I shall be able to grow old in peace.

Or else I shall come back here. I'll give the boss a tip, a little thousand-franc note, and I'll resume my duties. I'll get my habitués back, all my habitués. I shall have been gone such a short time. "What happened to you then, Alfred?" they'll ask. I shall answer: "I had a whitlow, you can't imagine how painful they are," and there's sure to be an habitué who'll tell me: "Oh, whitlows, I know what they're like, I had one, they're horribly painful." And I shall see Monsieur Brabbant and Monsieur Brennuire and Monsieur Tolut again, because nothing will have happened yet. And I shall go back to serving endless drinks nonstop, hot ones in winter and cold ones in summer, and spirits in all seasons. And I shall see the habitués come back every day, and the passing customers change every day, as the seasons return every year and as people's ages change every year. And I shall be immutable and perfectly balanced because I shall have recovered my lost fortune, thus fulfilling my destiny. I shall watch all their agitated movements, the young and the old, the males and the females, the men and the dogs, the cats and the mice, the leaves on the branches, the clouds on the rooftops, the old newspapers on the pavements, the ideas in the craniums, the passions in the hearts, the penises in the trousers. Immobile and immutable, I shall watch all that just as the water in a lake reflects the flight of migrating birds without allowing its surface to be rippled by the beating of their wings.

20

BRABBANT LEANED OVER towards the man sitting next to him who was consulting a railway timetable with obvious inexperience. Slightly raising his hat, he entered into conversation with him.

"Forgive me if I am being indiscreet, monsieur, but I see you are puzzled. I would simply like to tell you that there is a good train for Dieppe at 14:15."

"Thank you."

The man had replied without turning his head.

"It's a very good train," Brabbant went on. "You get to Dieppe at . . ."

"Thank you, thank you."

The man wasn't prepared to listen any longer. He closed his timetable.

"It's a lovely day today," said Brabbant.

The man called the waiter, paid, and left. Brabbant began to wait again. Soon afterwards a new customer came and sat next to him. He didn't ask for any sort of timetable. Brabbant sized him up out of the corner of his eye. The customer, turning towards him, said with the air of a connoisseur:

"It's a lovely day today."

"Magnificent," said Brabbant, going one better. "What a superb summer we are going to have!"

"One can't commit the future like that," the other retorted. "Often, after a fine May, we have a terrible summer."

"That's very true, what you say there, monsieur."

"Where I come from, we have a saying: A fine month of May, the summer'll be grey."

"Ah? Really? And what part of the world are you from then, monsieur, if I am not being too indiscreet?"

"Not at all, not at all. I am a native of Touraine. Near Chinon."

"Very beautiful region," said Brabbant. "Very beautiful region."

"Touraine, monsieur, is the garden of France."

And so on and so forth and so on and so forth, until finally the native of Touraine got around to saying:

"You might not think it to look at me, monsieur, but I am in a most embarrassing situation."

"What's happened to you, then?"

"Oh! I don't want to bore you with my little difficulties."

"Oh, but do, do."

"Believe it or not, I'm in quite a predicament. A predicament —that's even putting it mildly. I find myself without a sou in Paris. I don't know how I can have allowed it to happen. I haven't a sou. Well of course, I have a ten-franc note or two, but to last me over Sunday that isn't much, you'll agree."

"Yes indeed," said Brabbant.

"Only the thing is, I have a little suitcase containing quite a large sum in dollars which I've deposited in a hotel. I would be happy to give them to you as a guarantee."

Brabbant smiled.

"I was about to suggest the same thing to you," he said.

The man examined him very closely, called the waiter, paid for his drink and disappeared. Brabbant pulled out his watch and looked at its dial with a gloomy eye: three wasted hours. Anxious, he stood up and went to join Wullmar at the Ville-de-Rouen.

"Well? On your own?" Wullmar asked.

Brabbant sighed.

"Nothing this morning."

Wullmar shrugged his shoulders. His nerves were on edge. He'd drunk three glasses of port while he was waiting for the boss.

"I've had enough," he said. "I've had much more than enough."

"Do you expect it to work every time, young man?"

"It's not that! But I've had enough of your rotten little dodges. I know them all like the back of my hand; the this-trick and the that-trick. I'd be quite capable of doing them on my own now. But they leave me cold!"

"So?"

"Where's your ambition, Monsieur Brabbant, what have you done with your ambition?"

Brabbant scratched his head.

"I haven't had an idea yet."

"Would you like me to suggest one or two?"

"Don't do that!" exclaimed Brabbant. "Whatever you do, don't do that! The ideas have to come from me."

Wullmar shrugged his shoulders.

"We could open a subscription for the pope," he said.

"For the pope?"

"Yes. We'd say that he's been incarcerated in the Vatican cellars."

Brabbant gave him a severe look.

"What *are* you talking about? I told you to keep your ideas to yourself."

"I'm fed up," said Wullmar.

"Let me invite you to lunch," said Brabbant, and he offered a bottle of Burgundy and liqueurs.

Wullmar ended up somewhat tipsy.

"*I* want to do great things," he said.

"You're quite right. We shall do great things. I shall do great things. But we must be patient. We must wait until I get some ideas."

"No, I don't want to wait! I want to do great things *now!*"

Brabbant was discomfited.

"Have you still got the two suitcases?"

"Yes, but I can't be bothered with things like that anymore. Nothing doing. They're just stupid. We'll end up in jug if we go in for third-rate tricks of that sort."

"Shh, shh."

Wullmar shut up, and thought things over.

"Tell me, what do you want from old Brennuire?"

"What do I want from him? Why, nothing at all. We're friends, that's all there is to it."

"Ha ha! I don't believe you."

"Be so good as to speak to me more politely, Monsieur Wullmar. Don't forget that I'm your employer."

"Tell me honestly: what d'you want to get out of old Brennuire?"

"Why, nothing at all."

"You'll never get me to believe that."

They remained silent for a few moments.

"It intrigues me no end," Wullmar finally said.

"I've no idea what you're getting at, or even what you could be getting at."

"Ah well! I won't insist. And what are we going to do now?"

"We could try the trick of the suitcase full of dollars," said Brabbant.

"I've already told you that I can't be bothered with that sort of thing anymore."

"You're my secretary; your job is to obey me."

"Don't make me laugh," said Wullmar.

Brabbant scratched his head.

"Would you like me to give you the afternoon off?"

"It isn't a question of that. I simply want to do something interesting, something really big."

"We'll have to wait until I've had an idea."

"I can wait for a long time."

Brabbant stood up, furious, and banged his fist on the table. Everyone looked at him. Waiters came hurrying up. He sat down again, clearing his throat and fiddling with the knot of his tie.

"A glass of water and the bill," he demanded.

Wullmar looked at him with interest. They left without exchanging a word. The Amilcar was waiting outside the hotel. Brabbant squeezed into the little bus and put the two suitcases full of dollars on his knees, the one with the counterfeit dollars and the one with the old newspapers. Wullmar got in behind the wheel.

"Where are we going?"

"Let's drop in at the office. I'll leave these, as we shan't be using them today."

Brabbant looked tenderly at the two suitcases. He had got away with that trick so often that he had a very particular affection for it.

"Have you never done anything in your life but swindle people?" Wullmar asked, as they drove down the rue Tronchet.

"Shh! You mustn't use words like that," said Brabbant. "I've told you a hundred times."

"Incidentally, you got very angry just now."

"Ah yes, that's true. I was forgetting. You're becoming presumptuous. We are not partners, and don't forget it. You are only my secretary."

"Yes, monsieur."

"You mustn't be impatient. Have confidence in my star. I'm sure that in a very short time a magnificent idea will germinate in my brain."

"Yes, monsieur."

"It seems to me, moreover, that so far you have nothing to complain about. I've paid you well."

"I have expenses. Petrol costs a lot. Don't you think we could buy a proper car? It would be very useful to you. It's easy for people to spot us with a sports car like this."

"That's an idea," said Brabbant. "I shall buy a proper car. A sedan, I suppose?"

"I know of one that's going quite cheaply," said Wullmar.

He stopped at a corner. Brabbant got out with his two suitcases. Wullmar waited for him.

"And what are we going to do now?" he asked, when Brabbant came back.

"Nothing. I'm going to think things over. I shall go for a walk. I have a feeling that I shall get an idea today."

"The one about the pope shut up in the Vatican cellars, don't you think that's good?"

"Spare me your jokes. I'm going to work. We'll see about the car tomorrow. For the moment, you're free."

Wullmar waved, and immediately disappeared to the accompaniment of gigantic farting noises.

"It's unfortunate, though," Brabbant mused. "He has qualities, that boy, but he's ruined by the cinema. The pope shut up in the Vatican cellars! Where did he dream that one up! I wouldn't be surprised if he didn't write poems in which he makes *hallebarde* rhyme with *miséricorde*."

And he began to follow . . . "a little bit of fluff," to use his own expression.

21

"COME OFF IT, Grandpa, you haven't looked at yourself in the mirror," said the little bit of fluff.

"Oh, mademoiselle! How could you imagine that my offer was dishonorable? It is pure, absolutely pure."

"I'm not so green as I'm painted, old cock. I know your sort. Aren't you ashamed, at your age?"

"But, mademoiselle, I assure you . . ."

"I know it by heart, what you're going to come out with."

"I am very fond of the company of young people, mademoiselle. That is why I invited you to spend a little time with me. Although naturally I would not want your parents to become worried, if it would make you late."

"And what were you thinking of offering me?"

"A glass of port? At the Café de la Paix?"

The chick whistled admiringly.

"Let's go," she said. "What do you do, monsieur? Senator?"

"Do I look like a senator?"

"No. That was a joke. Hasn't anyone ever made a joke with you?"

"Yes, yes."

"Well then, tell me, what do you do?"

"I'm in business."

"Are you married?"

"Oh no!"

"That's interesting."

"Why so?"

"Tell me, is it a serious business?"

"It's a very serious business. Buying, selling, and managing property."

"That's a shark's trade. It's tip-top, their port."

"I'm glad you like it."

"You've got a funny sort of look. No kidding, *is* your business serious?"

Since he had pinched Tormoigne's wallet, which event had made enough of a stir to justify a quarter of a column in the newspapers, Brabbant had been subject to sudden fits of anxiety which he described as stabbing pains.

It was the first time such a thing had happened to him.

"Property is extremely safe. And t'isn't subject to the fluctuations of the foreign exchange."

"Why jou say *t'isn't,* stead of *it isn't?* It doesn't sound nice."

"Very true, very true what you say, mademoiselle."

"And what's your name?"

"Martin-Martin. Monsieur Martin-Martin."

"That's a bit of a mouthful. But I'm not going to call you Tintin, even so!"

"I'm sorry that I am unable to change my name."

"Mustn't take offense. They're chic, names with a hyphen."

"Are you very much interested in grammar, mademoiselle?"

"Not half. We might go and have dinner."

Brabbant suggested the Brasserie Universelle.

"That's a terrific idea," said the chick. "I can't wait to tuck in to all their hors d'oeuvres."

Brabbant called the waiter and paid like a noble lord.

"You're a bit of a dope to leave him a tip like that. Thirty sous would've been heaps."

"I wanted to manifest my joy at having met you."

"You certainly do have strange ways."

She began to sing under her breath:

> *Evohé, these goddesses*
> *Have such strange ways.*

"It's divine, isn't it, *La Belle Hélène?* Don't you like it?"

"I adore Offenbach," said Brabbant.

It was true. They went into the brasserie. The hors d'oeuvres were brought.

"Oh my!" said the chick, "I'm not sorry I came. It's just like they told me. I thought it was a lot of baloney. Here, you might at least ask me my name, don't you think? The saveloy was gorgeous."

"I didn't dare ask you."

"Don't give me your bashful act. My name's Fabie, that's shorter than Fabienne. My father's a compositor, he's no fool, my father isn't, what with all he reads. He's a decent bloke, but my mother's a bitch. Let's forget it. And then, I've got two sisters. You'll never guess what they're called?"

"I can't guess."

"I didn't think you could. The oldest one's called Suze and the other one's called Nivie. Suze, that's for Suzanne, and Nivie, that's for Caroline."

"Ah! Really?"

"Yes. I'm not having you on. My my, I can't believe what I'm putting away. Don't give me too much wine, it'll go to my head. After, I don't know what I'm doing."

"A little more of these delicious mushrooms?"

"No, pass me the brawn instead. It's first-rate, their brawn. Suze, my sister, she's a funny one. She knows heaps of artists, painters, students. No kidding. Not so long ago she was always driving around in a car, a natty little Amilcar."

"Ah! Really?"

"Couldn't you change a bit? You never stop saying: 'Ah! Really?' It gets on my nerves. Still, let's forget it. What was I saying? Ah yes! My sister, she had some pals who had an Amil-car, she was always going here, there and everywhere. They were a couple of students, real clowns."

"Law students?"

"How should I know? Are you interested? One of them was called Rohel and the other one was called Wullmar. What is it? Something the matter?"

"I'm perfectly all right, thank you."

Fabie looked at him; a pitiable sight.

"I scared you, didn't I?"

"You scared me?"

"Don't give me your ignorant act. You know it very well, the little Amilcar, you were in it earlier on. I recognized it all right, and the chap too, that Wullmar! What a laugh I had, when I saw you were following me! I said to myself: 'If that old boy accosts me, I'll tell him a tale that won't half surprise him.' No, but— you aren't his father, by any chance?"

"No, no, not his father, not his father."

"Oof. I thought I might have put my foot in it. Maybe you're his uncle?"

"No, no, not at all, he's my secretary."

"Your secretary? Don't give me that! He's rolling in money, he's not going to amuse himself working. Suze told me all sorts of things about him, he's not the type that goes to work."

"What did she tell you about him?"

"You don't really think I'm going to squeal on her, do you? I'll have a pêche melba, I adore them."

Brabbant didn't look very cheerful, no doubt on account of his stabbing pains.

"It's true that sports cars are very conspicuous," he said dreamily.

"They're very conspicuous," Fabie repeated.

She ate her pêche melba in silence. Brabbant was staring straight ahead of him. She shook his arm.

"Come on, mustn't take on like that. We'll go to the movies

to give us something else to think about. No kidding, is he really your secretary?"

"Certainly."

"That's a lot of bunk. I'm not so green. Still, it's none of my business."

"And your sister, does she still see the Rohel fellow?"

"He finally gave her the push, the bastard. And that made her want to travel, so she's gone to the Argentine. That's really traveling, don't you think? But that's enough of my sister. Are we going to the movies?"

"Excellent idea."

"Get a move on then, Tintin, or we'll be late."

They went to see *L'Atlantide*. Fabie was engrossed, but Brabbant was thinking of something very different. It was the first time in his life that this had happened to him: he was afraid of being arrested! That's where it gets you, trying to depart from your speciality! And yet, what the hell, he certainly had to depart from it if he wanted to do great things. And he still had no ideas.

After the movies he took the chick to have a *demi,* because sand dries your throat. He found her cute, smart, and most amusing; but he was afraid she might put the evil eye on him. It was stupid to have such ideas. He'd have to ask Alfred's advice; but really, a sports car was too conspicuous. Wullmar was right. He'd have to get another.

"Midnight!" Fabie exclaimed. "I'll never dare go home."

Brabbant was now in a quandary. "I only hope she doesn't bring me bad luck," he thought.

"Now I'm really in trouble," she said. "What'm I going to do? What'm I going to do?"

Suddenly, all his fears, all his anxieties left him. How absurd to have thought that anyone could find Monsieur Blaisolle. Monsieur Blaisolle didn't exist. How could anyone find him? And as from tomorrow, the car would be changed. Fabie appeared to Brabbant as the harbinger of a new existence placed under the sign of ambition.

He took her home with him.

Passing the concierge's lodge, he called out:

"Monsieur Brabbant."

"I was pretty sure Tintin wasn't your real name," Fabie whispered.

22

BRABBANT DICTATED A few letters; then, all the while tapping his left-hand thumbnail with a mother-of-pearl paper knife, spent the whole morning daydreaming while waiting for Wuilmar, who didn't turn up. He left his office at midday, went and had a vermouth chez Crucifix and lunched on his own chez Armand, near the Opéra. He was missing Fabie, who had gone to fetch her belongings from her parents' place, but he didn't for a moment doubt that she would come back. While drinking his coffee he read through the small ads very carefully. He still hadn't had an idea. At around half past two he was back in his office, waiting for Wullmar. He dictated a few more letters.

"Business isn't doing too badly," the typist remarked.

"Yes, it's going quite well," he replied absentmindedly. "It's going quite well."

"In that case, you might perhaps think about my arrears. And about a little raise. All my girlfriends earn more than me now, and the cost of living goes up every day."

"How much of a raise do you want?"

"A hundred francs a month, Monsieur Martin-Martin."

"Well well! You certainly don't go in for half measures, mademoiselle. Still, as business is going well at the moment, I'll let you have it."

"Thank you, monsieur. And my arrears?"

"I'll think about them, I'll think about them. Leave me to work on my own now."

Wullmar entered.

"I've been wondering where you'd got to," said Brabbant. The typist went out of the room.

"I've fixed it," said Wullmar. "On Monday we shall have a sedan, a brand-new eleven horsepower Georges-Irat."

"Eleven horsepower isn't much," said Brabbant.

"With a forty horsepower you'll be just as conspicuous as with a sports Amilcar. You aren't reasonable," Wullmar added, laughing in his face.

Brabbant studied the door handle in front of him.

"I'm beset by ambition."

"I understand," said Wullmar. "And that great idea?"

"I already have the rudiments of one."

He was lying. Wullmar knew it and, naïvely, looked him straight in the eye, hoping to make him blush.

"May one know?" he asked.

"Not yet, not yet. It's still only in the preliminary stages. That's it, the preliminary stages."

"I understand."

They fell silent.

"Do you need me today?" Wullmar continued.

"Well, not really. Unless you'd like us to try..."

"No, no, I'm not playing. I've already told you that..."

"All right, all right," cried Brabbant.

"Incidentally," said Wullmar, "I've got to sit for some exams in the next few days. And in three weeks I'm going on holiday. I hope you'll give me a holiday too, and a bit of time off to study."

"Naturally. I'll be putting the finishing touches to my plan during that time."

Wullmar stood up.

"On Monday I'll show you the car."

Brabbant smiled, pleased.

"I'll go on holiday with it," Wullmar added.

He went out. Brabbant did nothing for a good hour, vaguely musing on various incidents in his past. Suddenly, at around four o'clock, he decided to go and see Madame Dutilleul.

"Well! I haven't seen much of you this year," said that person, giving him an affectionate look. "Is anything wrong?"

"No," he replied gloomily.

He was putting on a bit of an act; he wasn't as gloomy as his eyebrows wanted to make out.

"What's wrong, my poor Louis?"

"Ambition."

"Ambition?"

"Yes, do you remember what you told me? I was too modest. Now that you've put that in my head, nothing goes right."

"Louis, I'm really sorry. I didn't want to do you any harm."

"The harm's done now! Nothing goes right for me anymore. I despise all that small-time stuff. But in the meantime, I haven't got a bean."

"Are you broke, my poor Louis? Maybe you'd like me to lend you some money?"

"That wouldn't hurt."

"An old client like you, nobody could refuse him. How much do you want?"

"Five thousand francs, for example."

Madame Dutilleul's heart gave a hiccup. That was a lot of money. She opened a little chest and handed Brabbant five wads of banknotes. He stuffed them in his pockets, which seemed to be capacious.

"Thank you," he said simply.

"And what are you thinking of doing now?"

"I've no idea. I mean: something big, but I don't know what it'll be."

"Aren't you afraid of . . ."

He shrugged his shoulders.

"I'm not afraid of anything. A sly dog like me."

"And you haven't the slightest idea what it'll be?"

"No."

He hesitated.

"There's been a change in my life recently."

"And what might that be?"

"I have a secretary now. He's a charming boy, energetic and resourceful. A splendid boy. I also have a car, a sports car. It goes like the wind, it's terrific."

"I don't recognize you anymore!" said Madame Dutilleul, laughing.

Brabbant stood up; he straightened his tie.

"There was one more thing I wanted to tell you . . . Don't rely too much on my custom from now on."

"No more love?" asked Madame Dutilleul, who had misunderstood.

"No more!" said Monsieur Dutilleul sardonically. "It's only just beginning!"

He departed, squeezing the wads of banknotes in the bottom of his pockets. He still had about four hours before he met Fabie. He took a taxi and had himself driven to the Ludo. While he was waiting for him, Tolut was watching some champions playing a complicated version of the game.

"Shall we go?" Brabbant suggested.

But there were no free tables.

"I'm the first on the waiting list," said Tolut.

A waiter pointed out the table that would no doubt fall to their lot. The two old men went over to it. It was occupied by Tuquedenne and Brennuire.

"Ah, I've caught you at it!" Tolut exclaimed, as a joke.

The others heard his sour voice without enthusiasm.

"We shan't be long," said Brennuire. "Eighty-six to eighty-one."

"Who's winning?"

"Tuquedenne."

The others sat down on the banquette while they were waiting. Tuquedenne missed a carom.

"You didn't give it enough spin," said Tolut.

Brennuire in his turn failed to score.

"You ought to have aimed at the red," Brabbant remarked.

"And head on," Tolut added.

Tuquedenne miscued.

"That's what comes of not chalking your cue before each shot," said Brabbant, pointing the moral of the business.

Brennuire failed to bring off a screw-back stroke.

"That was risky," said his uncle. "You ought to have tried to play off the four cushions."

The young people thus reached the highest pitch of nervous irritation under the critical eye of the older generation.

"Are these your books?" Brabbant asked, indicating two lying about on the banquette.

Tuquedenne nodded.

Brabbant glanced at them. *Lord Jim,* he read on the first. It was in English, it meant nothing to him. The other was entitled *Les Caves du Vatican.*

"What sort of a story is this?" he asked casually.

Tuquedenne gave him a scornful look.

"It's the story of a young man who kills an old one," he answered insolently.

Ever since he had been wearing a belt instead of braces and ever since he had been smoking English tobacco and ever since he had been reading Conrad in the original, he had been feeling a certain self-assurance.

"Isn't there anything about the pope in it?" Brabbant insisted.

"Oh, you know, the pope! . . ."

Tuquedenne scored his hundredth point. The table was free. The two young men fled in disgust. The others played their little game. But Brabbant, who wasn't going out of his way to humor Tolut that day, made a break of twenty-five and won by forty points. The Lozenge couldn't get over it.

"Well, my dear fellow! you *were* on form today. What got into you?"

Brabbant put on a modest act. He still had half an hour to go before meeting Fabie at the Taverne du Palais. He went with Tolut to the Soufflet and had a quick Pernod. Monsieur Brennuire wasn't there. The Lozenge excused himself for a moment, seized with a sudden need to piss. Brabbant took advantage of this to call Alfred.

"Tell me, Alfred, was yesterday a good day?"

"For affairs of the heart or affairs of the head?"

"The heart, Alfred, the heart. But don't tell anyone."

"Monsieur knows how discreet I am."

He consulted a brand-new notebook.

"I was thinking about you," he said. "I prepared your calculations in advance."

Brabbant came across with twenty francs.

"Yesterday was an excellent day for you," said Alfred. "Especially for what you were telling me about."

Brabbant looked pleased. But a moment later he became anxious.

"Listen, Alfred, you never tell me about anything but successes. Are there no black-letter days for me, then? Or is it that you don't tell me the whole truth, to please me?"

Alfred showed his notebook.

"The calculations are there, Monsieur Brabbant. It's a science. I don't add anything."

"I believe you, Alfred, I believe you."

Tolut came back.

"Are you off already?" he asked, seeing Brabbant putting on his hat.

"I'm so sorry, some urgent business. Give my regards to Brennuire."

"On Monday I'll get my revenge," said Tolut.

Brabbant nodded "yes, yes," and went out in a great hurry.

With a rapid step he walked down the boulevard Saint-Michel to the Taverne du Palais. He went in, trembling with emotion. Fabie was already there.

23

VINCENT WALKED UP the boulevard Saint-Michel to the Port-Royal station. It was hot and he had just passed the history certificate for the philo(sophie) degree. A U bus went by. It was very hot. Vincent crossed the road and sat down on the terrace of the Brasserie de l'Observatoire. He drank a *demi.* He walked home to his parents' place, which was in the rue de la Convention. Brennuire had now got a degree in both arts and law; he was going on holiday that evening with his sister. He said good-bye to him. This year again, Vincent was staying in Paris. Brennuire was going off to do his military service in November. They would probably never see each other again. Brennuire said good-bye to him and their friendship evaporated. The street, heavy with heat, smelled of dust and dung. Vincent watched the people and things going by without thinking too much about these people and things. Brennuire—he didn't really like him but for the past six months he'd been seeing him more or less every day. Vincent counted on his fingers to see if it really was six months, but it was a little less. Brennuire, equipped with solid credentials, was preparing to become a reserve officer, and later he would be a civil servant. Vincent considered all this very sad and very contemptible. Brennuire shook his hand and said good-bye to him and went on holiday. For his part, Vincent never went on holiday and never traveled, but he felt he was changing since he had been wearing a belt instead of braces, smoking English tobacco and reading Conrad in the original. And Defoe, and Stevenson, and *Barnabooth,* also in the original. He didn't travel but he did read a lot, and he despised this humdrum, banal, everyday life from which he made only puerile attempts to escape. He drank another *demi,* because it was exceedingly hot. A U bus went by. A crowd gathered because it was nearly the end of the day and the end of work. On the terrace, people sat down here and there and also there, and began to drink, because of the heat which caused sweat to form on the foreheads of the obese, on the hands of the lymphatic and on the feet of most of them. In this crowd there were some exceptional and marvelous people, but no possible relationship could be established between *them* and him. So he rapidly judged. He had no desire for the most charming of these women to come and sit near him because he was absolutely certain that he would not dare speak to her. Rohei had achieved some academic successes, according to the notices pinned up in the corridors of the establishment on the hill, but he couldn't be found. Brennuire. Rohel. Vincent added a third name, and the person who bore it was no doubt in a position to see the austral constellations embed themselves in the sky every night. Vincent never traveled. *So many ships leave from Le Havre.* He was quoting himself. Brennuire, Rohel, Hublin. His friends were disappearing from his life, as if they had only been created for a short time, merely to play a part in his universe; Brennuire, he wasn't much, Rohel was a real friend, but Hublin, now, he was a mystery, the living affirmation of Adventure. In Vincent's eyes, Hublin validated such notions as the Fortuitous, the Gratuitous, the Uncertain, those cardinal notions that alone, in his view, could give meaning to any life. When Vincent calculated what separated him from all that, he who lived so inadequately and in so banal a fashion, it was enough for him to think of Hublin and to have lived in his vicinity, to conceive as immediately possible an abrupt transformation of his existence which would deliver him from the odious ropes he bound round himself and which became tighter with every effort he made to release himself. And so he lived this inadequate life, convinced that that moment would come; and when he became aware of this hope, he cursed himself for his revolting optimism, because pessimism after all seemed to him the only acceptable conception of life and the only one in conformity with reality. He made pessimism his profession of faith. He paid for his *demis* and left.

Vincent walked towards Montrouge, experiencing his solitude through his contact with the crowd swarming in front of the grub shops in the avenue d'Orléans. Three friends, three departures: it had ever been thus, ever since his childhood, from the one who had died and whose name he barely remembered to the one who was working for a wholesaler in Le Havre and with whom he exchanged rare and totally uninteresting letters. Vincent was gradually discovering his isolation; brushing aside to right and left the odd vague individuality, he saw himself as being absolutely alone on earth, and he was terrified.

The rue d'Alésia runs from the Montrouge church to the railway bridge. The rue de Vouillé runs from the bridge to the rue de Cronstadt. Then comes the rue de la Convention. Tuquedenne senior was impatiently awaiting his son's return, very much doubting that the news could be good. Madame Tuquedenne had confidence; she was sure Vincent had passed but she kept touching wood to ward off ill fortune. She was tall and thin, and rather like the rue de Vouillé, as she dressed in dark clothes and was lugubriously stiff, like a hanged man's phallus. For his part, Monsieur Tuquedenne thought highly both of sauces and of stews, said views and stews being shared by madame, and this was what constituted the basis of their understanding. On the off-chance, they had told the maid to cook a big dishful of sheep's trotters with sauce poulette for the evening meal, and this was the way in which they were preparing to celebrate the success of their heir. If he'd failed, the sheep's trotters with sauce poulette would be made to do for two meals instead of one.

Vincent came in. It was good news. So they polished off the sheep's trotters with sauce poulette. This ingestion was washed down with Burgundy. Vincent chattered, perorated and glibtalked, his forehead covered with sweat, for it was extremely hot. Tuquedenne senior envisaged the future with confidence; Vincent would have finished his studies next year, he would be a reserve officer, and then a civil servant. Vincent spoke of Brennuire. The family admired him very much. Vincent considered himself a coward; he attributed this to the Burgundy. With the dessert, Tuquedenne senior opened a bottle of sparkling wine and he too announced some good news. They were going to spend a month with their cousin Borchard who kept a bistrot-cum-diner somewhere in the backwoods south of Nantes. Their departure was fixed for the first of July.

Their departure took place on the first of July. It was a journey of great banality punctuated by vulgar incidents and modest hitches. They spent the night in the train. Vincent couldn't sleep.

They arrived in Nantes in the morning and visited the town and the port, making comparisons with Le Havre. They took a little local train in the afternoon and at around five o'clock the Tuquedenne family got itself out at the appointed place. Cousin Borchard had come to meet them in his carriole; he drove them to his lair, a weatherboarded house overrun by the sands. The cousin's wife produced food for two unfortunate residents who seemed to be enchanted by the dreadful stuff. A semi-imbecilic maid served the rare customers. There were very few tourists, because it was impossible to bathe, the beach was muddy at low tide and at high tide dangerous. Opposite, the Isle of Noirmoutier lay flat in the sun. Vincent liked this place, but Madame Tuquedenne was disappointed. On the first day there was a little argument between the father and the cousin apropos of the cost of their board and lodging. But everything got sorted out. The days began to glide by, the days before the nights.

Among Cousin Borchard's customers was a future law student, aware of his elegance and concerned about his beauty. They wondered what mystery had caused him to run aground on this beach. There were also two Russians who lived in an isolated villa guarded by dogs. When they came, they put the gramophone on and danced. The future student had exchanged a few words with Vincent, but they hadn't hit it off. The former asked nothing better than to be dazzled by stories about the Latin Quarter, but Vincent didn't come out with any, and furthermore he didn't understand the vestimentary and cosmetic anxieties of the young man from Nantes. They came quite often, then, wound up the gramophone and danced. Cousin Borchard finally discovered that the young man was the lover of "the superb Russian woman," as he called her. At night, they could hear the dogs at the villa howling in the distance.

When they came, the Russians, it made Vincent suffer, and especially the presence of the woman. He couldn't watch her dancing with the young man without a feeling of unease which was almost anguish. The man, the Russian, drank brandies and water all day long. While the others were dancing he got another record ready and wound up the gramophone. The Borchards and Tuquedennes commented on all this and laughed in an unpleasant way which made Vincent indignant. He went for long walks in the countryside, but always avoided the Russians' villa. Everything became painful and oppressive to him. It was with relief that he heard one day that the young man had drowned.

"That's not going to attract customers to the district either," said Cousin Borchard.

The Russians left the district, without paying for the brandies and water. The weather changed and it rained nonstop. The dead summer contaminated all the horizons and livid clouds dragged themselves through the sky like decaying carcasses. The hut-hotel became swollen with humidity, it was feared that it might die of dropsy. The maid took a header into the soup tureen while suffering an epileptic fit. The Borchards lamented their fate. The Tuquedennes wanted to go home. Alone in his room, Vincent read.

24

IT WAS A SATURDAY. Cindol was having a day off. He took the tram to the casino. He went down the steps opposite the baths and, slipping on the pebbles, came to a beach hut painted light grey. Muraut, lying in a deck chair, was reading a rakish magazine. Ponsec was mending a football.

"Good old Cindol," said Muraut.

He looked at him from bottom to top and from top to bottom.

"Well, how're you doing?"

"Want a glass of whiskey?" said Ponsec. "Rohel swiped a bottle from the casino yesterday."

"Good idea, we'll have a whiskey," said Muraut, standing up. "Only, there isn't any ice."

He exhumed the whiskey and a syphon from a dark corner.

"It was Rohel who pinched it?" Cindol asked.

"Yesterday. We had a good laugh," said Ponsec.

All three sat down, glass in hand.

"Well, how're you doing?" Cindol asked.

"Still doing medicine," Muraut replied. "We don't talk shop during the vacation."

"And Rohel, he's got his degree now?"

"What a hope. He has precisely a quarter of his degree. Incidentally, a rotten thing happened to him last winter. He got a chick pregnant, he was in a fine mess. Luckily I fixed it for him."

"How did you do that?"

"Curious, aren't we! If ever you need my services, just let me know."

"That's right, just let him know," said Ponsec. "It'll only cost you a hundred francs."

"What a filthy liar! I didn't charge Rohel anything. He'll tell you so himself, you bastard!"

"Isn't he writing for some of the reviews?" Cindol asked.

"Who? Rohel?"

Muraut had never envisaged this possibility. He shrugged his shoulders.

"And Tuquedenne?" Cindol asked.

"Oh, him! We don't often see him these days. We only meet him by chance. And then he looks down on us from the heights of his grandeur. No kidding. *We* are only poor unfortunate medical students, whereas *he* reads Saint Thomas in Latin and knows which way up to look at a cubist painting. It's obvious; you can see why he despises us."

"And who's he, Saint Thomas?"

"Pah! A fashionable gimmick. Propaganda invented by the curés."

Cindol preferred not to talk about the curés.

"Did you know that Hublin's coming back at the end of the year?"

"*There's* someone who impresses them."

"Who impresses who?"

"Rohel and Tuquedenne, of course. My dear chap, when his name crops up they can talk of nothing else. Don't you remember all the things Rohel used to say about Hublin in the old days, and how he used to sneer at him? Now they see him as an adventurer, someone there's never been the like of. Just because he had his hair cut and went off to buy coffee in Brazil for his uncle. It seems that that's transcendent. No kidding. It's very simple though. No mystery to be found there."

"Even so I did get a shock," said Ponsec, "when I met him here the day before he left. There was no way anyone could have foreseen it, all the same. I found it rather bizarre."

"Oh, life's quite simple," said Muraut. "There's no point in looking for things that aren't there."

"People talked about it quite a lot here too," said Cindol. "Everyone thought it was strange."

"Provincial gossip," Muraut retorted.

"But how do *you* explain his departure?"

"It's simple. He'd had enough of lousy student life and he went into business. *You*'ve gone into business."

"Of course, but he did it from one day to the next."

"Doesn't it ever happen to anybody to make a sudden decision? And how d'you know that it hadn't been arranged for a long time but he just didn't talk about it?"

The others fell silent. Muraut went on:

"They irritate me, people who look for a mystery everywhere. Life is simple and clear, you only have to look around you to realize that."

"Me, I'm not so sure," said Ponsec.

"Me neither," said Cindol.

"And anyway, shit," concluded Muraut.

Rohel entered.

"Well, you might have waited for me before you drank my whiskey. Aren't you going to bathe?"

He undressed.

"How's Tuquedenne?" Cindol asked.

"I haven't seen much of him recently. I never go to the Quarter."

"What a snob."

"Shut up, you."

Rohel was in his shirt. A girl going by gave a little scream. He began to prance around. She fled.

"You'll get us into trouble with her daddy and mummy,"

said Muraut.

"If they don't like it, we'll screw her for them, their daughter," said Rohel.

"We were talking about Hublin just now," said Ponsec.

"Much good may it do you," said Rohel.

"He's coming back at the end of the year," said Cindol. "He wrote to me."

"Is that all he said?" asked Rohel, interested.

"Oh, that's all. It seems that he's done very well there. A chap in his firm told me so."

"Does he still impress you?" Muraut asked Rohel.

"More than you do," Rohel replied.

He made his way towards the Channel, which happened to be a few meters away. Ponsec and Cindol began a game of chess. Muraut filled his pipe and pretended to be thinking, lying in a deck chair. Rohel came back, curling up his toes.

"Was it warm?" Muraut asked him absentmindedly.

Rohel nodded "yes, yes," and rubbed himself down, puffing and blowing. He dressed, and drank a glass of whiskey.

"That's a game I can't stand," he said, looking at the chessboard. "Didn't my brother come?"

"No," Muraut replied. "But tell me, don't *you* think that basically life is simple?"

"What d'you mean?"

"I was thinking of Hublin. You've been imagining all sorts of things about him. But what actually happened? He'd had enough of being broke in Paris so he went into business."

"And he went to Brazil. That's already quite something."

"Ah yes, there's Brazil. But you know, there's heaps of people who've been to Brazil. Millions."

"And anyway, it's not a question of Brazil," said Rohel, "but of transforming your life from one day to the next, suddenly. You'll never understand that."

"Of course not," said Ponsec without looking up.

Rohel lit a cigarette.

"Here—do you remember The Lozenge?"

"That old swine," said Ponsec.

"I met him the other day near the Luxembourg. He recognized me right away, he grabbed me by the sleeve, I couldn't shake him off. I didn't regret it afterwards, though, because I found him terribly interesting."

"Another one," said Muraut.

"Can you guess the idea he's got into his head? No, you'll never guess. He's full of remorse. And why is he full of remorse? Because he's afraid he taught us geography badly. And why is he afraid of that? Because he's never traveled."

"He's completely gaga," said Muraut.

"And so he'd like to travel. Naturally that wouldn't change the fact that he'd anyway have taught geography without having traveled. But in any case, he's chock-full of remorse, he's oozing it. He asked me seriously whether they'd been any use to me, his geography lessons."

"He's completely gaga," said Muraut.

"I bet you told him they hadn't been the slightest use to you," said Ponsec.

"No, not at all, but I strongly encouraged him to go round the world."

"You want to make him kick the bucket," said Ponsec.

"So it's old Tolut who interests you now," said Muraut.

"Yes. Don't you think it's amazing, what he told me?"

"Pah! He's become gaga, that's all there is to it. Life is very simple, my dear chap."

"Ah well, I'm off," said Rohel. "I'll leave you to talk crap in peace. If my father comes you can tell him I've gone home. See you tonight at the casino?"

Agreed. They'd get good and drunk once again.

25

TOLUT WALKED UP the boulevard Saint-Michel to the Port-
Royal station. It was hot, and he had just played a game of
billiards with Brabbant, the last game of the season. A 91 bus
went by. It was really hot. Tolut crossed the road and sat down
on the terrace of the Brasserie de l'Observatoire. He drank a
demi. He strolled home. He lived in a nice quiet guest house
near the Observatory. Brabbant was going away and wouldn't be
back until October, Brennuire was going on holiday to Dinard
with his children. Tolut alone was staying in Paris. The street,
heavy with heat, smelled of dust and dung. Tolut watched the
things and people going by without thinking too much about
these things and people. He tried to remember how long he
had known Brabbant, and did some sums on his fingers. He was
looking for landmarks to help him fix the date. He searched the
past like a weevil, but the past had hardened behind him and
he couldn't manage to bore his way into it. All he could ex-
hume were facts such as: he had met Brabbant in Paris and not
in Le Havre, and consequently he couldn't have known him for
more than three or four years. Moreover, he could no longer
remember whether it was four or five years, or more, since he
had left the provinces. The war didn't in any way help him to
establish his chronology. At all events he had certainly known
Brabbant for several years. A fine billiard player, he considered,

but not as good as himself. Tolut couldn't understand how he hadn't managed to win a single game recently. He had got into a habit, that of beating Brabbant, but now he had to change it and get used to being beaten. Nothing was more disagreeable to him. He was beginning to find his opponent less likable, and drank another *demi,* because it was exceedingly hot. A 91 bus went by, full. It was the end of the day and the end of work. Tolut mused that he had certainly earned his retirement and that he had behind him a life of honor, work and professional conscience whose merits his superiors had not properly appreciated but of which he could be proud. Certainly a little decoration had come his way to recompense his locally erudite research, but he sometimes thought that he had acquired enough merit to aspire to the Legion of Honor. And yet, did he really deserve that decoration? Since he had no longer been a teacher he had been subject to remorse, which was at first vague but which became more explicit every day. He who for years and years had taught geography, he had never traveled. At first this had been only a rather interesting observation, but it had finally become a terrible fact. In the beginning, he merely thought about traveling for his own benefit, to make up for the years of immobility. But he had come to the conclusion that to have taught geography without ever having traveled was an abuse of trust and a swindle, of which thousands of children and parents had been the victims. He had not led a life of honor, work and professional conscience, but a life of lies and deception. He did try to reason with himself; he told himself that geography had nothing to do with travels and that what he taught to children did not necessitate an actual knowledge of the places he talked about; he also told himself that the earth was very vast and that it was impossible to visit the whole of it and that if that were a necessity, no geography would be able to exist; he told himself a lot of things, but nothing could prevail against the terrible fact that he had taught what he didn't know. Ah! if only he had traveled like Brabbant! Brabbant seemed to know every country, every town; at every turn of the conversation his recollections of some far-distant country cropped up. What place in the world had he not been to! Tolut envied him and, now that Brabbant beat him at billiards, he was jealous of him. He was not far from hating him, for he thought that Brabbant must have a clear conscience and that he was a truly honorable man, whereas he, Tolut, though outwardly respectable, was nothing but a crook. A moral crook, of course; he immediately allowed himself this reservation to appease his guilty conscience. Brabbant, Brennuire, what did they have to reproach themselves for? *They* knew their job. He didn't know his. He paid for his *demis* and left.

While trotting off towards his domicile, he let his mind drift on to his solitude on earth. Never had he been so aware of it. Perhaps he was getting really old. He ran through the list of the people he knew or had known or had met. True enough—he really was alone in the world. To whom could he have confided his misgivings? To his brother-in-law, to his nephew, to Thérèse? To Brabbant, perhaps. Perhaps to Brabbant. But Tolut didn't like losing at billiards.

In the guest house he lived in, mealtimes were extremely regular. Dinner was at half past seven. At 7:25 he sat down at his place. Some of the guests were already unfolding their napkins. The others came in, one at a time or by the dozen. The mistress of the house supervised the seating arrangements. At half past seven, operations commenced. Tolut ate slowly, being very careful to taste what he put between his jaws. It wasn't that he was a gourmand, but simply that he didn't waste his time at table. After each course he wiped his mouth carefully. When the cheese arrived, the mistress of the house uttered a little interior scream; she had forgotten to give Monsieur Tolut his mail. As he never received any letters, it was excusable that when for once there was one she shouldn't think to give it to him.

Tolut wiped his knife on his bread and slit open the envelope, at the same time swallowing his mouthful. He unfolded the sheet of paper and looked at the signature. It was true; he had a brother, a younger brother. They hadn't been on speaking terms for thirty years. He hated him almost as much as he hated box tricycles. His brother had written him a long letter telling him that he was going to die and that before this painful event he would like to see him. To justify this request, he appealed to the highest and most noble sentiments such as brotherly love and the honor of the family. Tolut guffawed. He remembered his brother very clearly now, and how they hated one another. And now he's offering peace, because he's going to die. Tolut guffawed. As a postscript, his brother added that naturally he would pay for his trip. Tolut guffawed. What a way to go on! Still as much of an oaf as ever. He looked at the address. The letter came from London. He picked up the envelope and admired the effigy of George V. He finished his dinner, thinking in a very confused fashion. He wasn't aware of what he was thinking about. He felt very ill at ease, his mind was ill at ease.

He went up to his room. Through his open window he could see the trees in the grounds of the Observatory. He sat down, waiting for it to get really dark. He tried to remember why they hated each other so much. Actually, no, *he* didn't hate him, it was his brother who hated *him*. And why? because he had stopped him making a fool of himself. There were no other reasons; and his brother, instead of being grateful to him, had wanted to kill him. Tolut had gone about it very skillfully, not despising any stratagem. The woman disappeared. His brother, instead of being grateful to him, had wanted to kill him. Maybe now, near death, gratitude was germinating in his ungrateful heart. Tolut guffawed, and then suddenly faced up to himself and became serious. It was his duty to accept this reconciliation. He had some small savings; a trip to London couldn't be so very expensive. And anyway, hadn't Théodore offered to pay for his ticket? That was very thoughtful of him. The night was becoming coal-black. Tolut shut the window and turned on the electric light. He looked at the envelope and deciphered the date stamp: London S.E.26. And so he, Tolut, was going to travel. He fell asleep admiring the nobility of his sentiments and telling himself once again how his life had been a life of honor, work and professional conscience.

The next day he began to comply with the requisite formalities for the issue of a passport, which he did with puerile enthusiasm. Then he waited impatiently. He went to the Gare Saint-Lazare to inquire about prices and departure times. He wondered whether he would be seasick. He was. At Newhaven, he observed that English was a foreign language. He got off at Croydon and caught another train for Penge. At the station, an obliging individual drew him a map on a piece of paper showing him how to get to the place indicated. After a twenty-minute walk Tolut came to a long road uniquely composed of identical villas. The left side was the reflection of the right side and the right side the mirror image of the left side. At number 145, Tolut rang. A housewife came and opened the door. She said something that he naturally didn't understand. He made little signs with his head. The inside of the house was rather squalid. The woman showed him the way. They went up to the first floor. She pushed a door. Tolut insinuated himself into the room and saw Théodore in bed, certainly dying. "It's quite true, he's going to die," Tolut said to himself. He didn't know whether to hold out his hand. His brother smiled, but Tolut immediately realized that this smile boded no good. And then his brother began to speak. He told him of his hate in no uncertain terms, and added that he wasn't the man to change his mind at the last moment. That was what he wanted to say to him. Tolut was shaken. Before his very eyes, his brother died laughing—the dreadful death.

Tolut departed, very much distressed by this obstinate ingratitude. At Penge station he made inquiries about how to go back to France. He didn't understand a word of the explanations he was given. In the end he spent a very bad night in a little suburban hotel. The next day he returned to Paris, worn out by this excursion. Only then did he realize that he might have taken advantage of it to visit London. But traveling was the last thing he was thinking of now! He had just lost his taste for adventures and far-off countries. Now, what he was thinking of was death. His own.

26

"HERE I AM," said Fabie.

"Huh!" said Nivie, "I thought we were never going to see you again."

"I'm glad you're in, I've got things to tell you, and incredible ones, my dear, incredible."

"Is your old man all right?"

"Him, what a guy, a guy like I've never met before. But you know, everything I'm going to tell you, keep it to yourself."

"My lips are sealed."

"He's really old, you know. He's seventy."

"Wow!" said Nivie.

"He doesn't look it. And you know what he does?"

"I don't know."

"He manages apartment blocks. Foreign apartment blocks that belong to French people, and French apartment blocks that belong to foreigners."

"That's a funny sort of business."

"Funnier than you think, because the apartment blocks don't exist."

"No kidding?"

"No. It's all window dressing. In actual fact he's a comic, my old man, an old crook."

"You're having me on."

"No, no. You'll never guess where he's been."

"Don't keep me in suspense."

"In a penal colony."

"Is he a murderer?"

"No, an ex-lawyer."

"Now you're in the soup."

"How come?"

"You'll end up in prison one of these days, with a guy like that."

"Nonsense! He's smart. He's never set foot in prison."

"What about the penal colony?"

"Oh! that doesn't count."

"Is he rolling in it, your banker?"

"Fair to middling. But there's going to be something better. He's working on a terrific stunt that's going to make a packet."

"What is it?"

"Ah, that! That I can't tell you, you understand. And for the rest, keep your mouth shut, eh."

"I should think so."

"Ah! and then, you remember the guy that used to take Suze out in a car?"

"The one who had an Amilcar?"

"The same. Well, he's Brabbant's secretary!"

"Brabbant?"

"My old man's called Brabbant. Antoine Brabbant. It's a ter-rific name, eh? Well, he has dozens of names, each one more terrific than the others."

"Just like Landru."

Fabie took on the appearance of someone struck by lightning.

"What did you say?"

"Does that frighten you?"

"Me? No, not in the least."

"Well, you look as if it does. It's true, you know, he may be a chap like Landru. You ought to watch out."

"My dear girl, I didn't come here to listen to your drivel,

did I? I tell you he's a crook, and nothing else."

"I believe you. You know him better than I do."

"Guess where he took me the other day? To see the Car-pentier-Siki match."

"That must have been top-notch."

"You can't imagine. It was magnificent. Siki, he's splendid. He que-nocked the other one out, you should've seen how. You can't imagine how it fascinated me. All the more so because we had a bet on it. I was scared shitless that the old boy would lose, but he seemed to know what he was doing."

"Did he bet on Siki?"

"A thousand francs at ten to one."

"*He* wasn't scared."

"He knew what he was doing. A waiter had given him the tip."

"What did he know about it, his waiter?"

"Ah, that! that's another long story. Seems he's a fellow who can see the future. He looks at the stars, he does some sums, and that's it. He's never wrong. When the old boy wants to bet on something he goes and sees him to find out what's going to happen. Or when he's cooking something up, then he goes and sees him, and according to what he says he carries on or he doesn't carry on."

"That's a real carry-on!"

"You can say that again, and you know, with the old boy, there's things like that nonstop. In any case, Siki's win brought us in ten thousand. And while you're waiting to strike it rich, that's not bad."

"Hope you won't forget me."

"I remembered you."

She took a five-hundred-franc note out of her bag.

"You can buy yourself something with this, and you can pay Papa's debts at the bistrot."

"You're a real sister, you are."

"And you'll never guess where we went, after that."

"I can't guess."

"We took a little trip down to the Côte d'Azur. You can't imagine how beautiful it is. There's palm trees, you know, like in *L'Atlantide,* and then the sea's really blue. It isn't a bit like in Dieppe, there aren't any tides. That's a laugh, isn't it? The old boy told me that. He knows heaps of things. Even more than Papa does. He's a wizard."

"Did you go to Nice?"

"Of course. Nice is splendid, my dear. There's a big boulevard all along the sea, I've never seen anything like it. And the elegant people—masses of them!—and whacking great motorcars!"

"Has he got a car, your old boy?"

"No. But he's going to have one. When he strikes it rich. And *then* you'll see."

"You won't forget me?"

"No, Nivie my pet. I've had an idea. You know what I'll do with you? I'll marry you off into the nobility."

"Oh!"

"The old boy told me that one, too. Seems that there's counts and marquises that are stone broke, and so people marry them. It costs a certain amount. And then you become a countess or a marchioness. Or else, you know what I'll do for you as well? I'll make you a movie actress. It was the old boy again who told me how it works. All you have to do is pay. Then you become famous, and you get your picture in *Ciné-Magazine.*"

"You're addling my brain with all your stories."

"Ah! And then, I was forgetting the best part. We went to Monte Carlo. We played roulette. It's thrilling. We stayed there all night. Me, I lost all I had, but the old boy pocketed quite a few notes of a thou."

"He's got a lucky streak, then?"

Fabie hesitated.

"I think actually he swiped some chips from a guy who was winning all the time."

"He seems to have a hell of a nerve, your old boy."

"Whatever happens, not a word to anyone, eh? You can see what a mess I'd be in if all this got out."

"You can trust me, I'm as silent as the grave."

"Don't talk like an undertaker, it gives me the willies. To come back to Wullmar, he's the one the old man wants to pull off his masterstroke with. He told me that he's trained him and taught him a whole lot of things and that the boy's good and ready. Me though, I advised him not to involve him. You know, these young people, need to be on your guard. They're liable to talk when they're sozzled. What I think, we'd do better to get rid of him and then it's also a question of conscience, you understand, my old man runs the risk of ruining the young man's life. What if he gets himself nabbed, eh? He could be sorry later on. However, we haven't decided yet."

"I don't think you're wrong."

"I'm quite sure I'm right. To my mind, the best thing would be for the old boy to do it on his own. There'd be less risk and more dough."

"You're no fool, Fabie."

"Don't worry, I know how to paddle my own canoe. It's full of grey matter in here."

She tapped her skull with a freshly varnished index fingernail. Suddenly, though, she seemed less satisfied with herself.

"You're an idiot to have said that just now."

"Said what?"

"That he was a chap like Landru. You've scared the shit out of me."

"I was only joking."

" 'T's'not very funny, your joke. 'T's'even stupid, when you come to think about it. Brabbant like Landru! You make me laugh."

"Because it'd be a pity to hear that you'd been chopped up into little pieces and roasted in a stove."

"It'd be Papa who wouldn't be pleased! That'll do. Incidentally, give him my love. Don't forget to do what I've told you. And when I strike it rich I won't forget you, my little Nivie."

They kissed.

"By the way, Fabie, there's something I'd like to ask you."

"What is it?"

"You won't be angry?"

"Say it anyway."

"Well: have you got a lover?"

"Do you take me for a tart?"

" 'Bye then, Fabie."

" 'Bye then, Nivie."

27

EVER SINCE HE'D squandered the last of the few thousand-franc notes he'd appropriated from a light-headed gambler, Brabbant had been up against it. Fabie asked him every day how the masterstroke was doing; he replied: "It's coming along, it's coming along," but she'd almost got to the point of not believing him anymore. He didn't want to go back to the stations circuit and the provincials' track because he was out of practice and the idea of getting pinched for a trifle upset him no end. He importuned Madame Dutilleul once again but she only lent him a few louis. One day he thought he'd got it, a really ingenious solution. He rushed off to the Soufflet and sat down at an Alfredian table.

"I've got a proposal to put to you."

"I'm listening, monsieur," said Alfred, very guardedly.

"What would you think if I were to subsidize you to exploit your knowledge of the planets and magnetism?"

"I don't understand, monsieur."

"Well, yes, you'd dress up as a fakir or a maharaja, to make an impression, and you'd predict the future. I'd bring you some clients. As you never make a mistake, you'd acquire a formidable reputation and we'd make a fortune."

"The thing is, I don't like disguising myself," Alfred replied; "and then I don't like trade, either. Shopkeeping—that really wouldn't interest me, and selling people their fortunes, even less. Monsieur knows very well that I have only one goal: to win back on the racecourse what my father lost there. Apart from that, I'm only a waiter, not a fortune-teller. And monsieur will understand that if I tell him this or that from time to time it's just as you might say out of good nature."

"I understand you, Alfred, I understand you."

Brabbant didn't insist, and about-turned.

Alone in his office, he was now babbling, and without hope. And his little Fabie who believed him to be a great man—a great crook. It was enough to make you smash your skull against the wall. He could no longer manage to put two ideas together, two words, two rudiments of thought. Alone in his office, Brabbant, demoralized, was breaking up.

The typist knocked, and showed a few curls through the half-open door.

"It's your secretary," she said.

"Aha!" said Brabbant.

Wullmar came in and sat down, crossing his legs.

"Well?" he asked calmly.

"Well what?"

"The great idea."

"Ah, it's true," said Brabbant, "you're my secretary."

"You'd forgotten that. I hadn't. I'm still interested in your great projects."

Brabbant didn't answer.

"Aren't you pleased to see me?" Wullmar asked.

"Go to the devil," Brabbant murmured.

Wullmar whistled in amazement.

"Things aren't going so well, I see."

"Things aren't going at all. If you've come for my ideas, you can go back where you came from. I haven't any to give you."

"You're yellowbellying, then?"

"Watch your language, young man. Don't forget that you're talking to an old man."

"To a crook."

Brabbant shrugged his shoulders.

"You're a child."

"If I understand aright," said Wullmar, "there's no more for me to do here."

"My goodness, no."

"You're sacking me."

"Let's not exaggerate. I know that you don't depend on me for your livelihood. Your respected father . . ."

"Leave him out of it. In any case, you've no need to worry, I shan't inform on you to the police."

"You're too kind, my friend."

"I always did think you were nothing but a humbug."

"Don't you think you might perhaps go?"

Wullmar stood up.

"And to think that I risked going to prison because of you."

"It wasn't I who made the first move."

"Hm, that's true. Good old Rohel, I've probably saved him a lot of problems."

"You see, you won't regret everything."

"I don't regret anything, dear monsieur. If I'm not being too indiscreet, may I ask you what is going to become of you?"

Brabbant turned pale.

"Don't worry about me. Be good enough not to worry about me."

"I won't worry, just to please you. As for me, if you want to know what's going to become of *me*, I'm going to join up."

"In the Colonial Army, at least?"

"Naturally."

"My hearty congratulations."

Brabbant extended his mitt, to sheikhands. Which they did. And Wullmar departed.

"A good-for-nothing, that boy," said Brabbant, when he was alone once more.

He began to walk round and round his office, thinking about

the ambition and the love that were throwing his aged life into turmoil. They were linked together, and they would sink together because he had no imagination. Ah, if he'd only put his mind to it earlier, maybe his younger brain would have begotten great things; now, though, he was as dry as goat's cheese. Brabbant was much moved by this comparison. He sat down in despair, and suddenly made a discovery: he could commit suicide. But he immediately found this idea repugnant. Whereupon his typist made a semi-appearance and announced Monsieur Brennuire. Amazed, Brabbant majestically gave the order to show the visitor in.

Monsieur Brennuire entered, looking very gay, and discreetly examining his surroundings.

"It's very nice, this office," he said.

"A bit small," said Brabbant. "Given the continuing growth of my business, I shall have to expand."

"Have you many employees?"

"Just a typist and a secretary. They are enough for me, as I do an enormous amount of work myself."

Monsieur Brennuire looked surprised.

"I have other offices in the rue Notre-Dame-de-Lorette," Brabbant hastened to add, "for my legal and accounts departments. There, I have about fifteen employees."

"It's a big firm," said Monsieur Brennuire.

"Well, yes," said Brabbant, "but not so big as it could be."

"That's just what I thought," Monsieur Brennuire murmured.

He remained hesitant for a moment, like a tomcat on three legs. Then he put down the fourth.

"Listen, my dear Brabbant, I'm going to make you a proposition which you will not be obliged to accept, of course. I would very much like my son to come and work with you when he's finished his military service. And as a guarantee, I should be very willing to invest some capital in the business."

"I should be only too delighted to have your son as a collaborator."

"It isn't only as a collaborator that I would want you to have him, but as a partner. I will add right away, my dear Brabbant, that I am prepared to put fifty thousand francs into the business as a guarantee. And here is the third part of my proposition: it would give me great pleasure to entrust to you the management of a few apartment blocks I possess in Paris."

Brabbant bowed.

"Does this offer suit you?"

"My dear Brennuire, I never bargain with a friend. It's a deal. I approve of your investing your money in this manner, because it will bring you a return of a minimum of 40 percent."

"I remember you one day mentioned 25 percent."

"And Germany, my dear Brennuire? And Germany? Thanks to the collapse of the mark we're going to buy blocks upon blocks, we're going to buy as you might say the whole of Germany, and when the mark has recovered its normal value, the return on the capital with which we have been entrusted will no longer be 40 percent but 60 percent, 80 percent, and possibly even more. But for that we need vast financial possibilities, and the former firm of Martin-Martin is forthwith going to be transformed into an international society for the management of property, the Société Internationale de Gérance Immobilière, with a capital of ten million. Ten million to start with, of course. The main object of the SIGI will be the one I have just succinctly described to you. The shares will cost a hundred francs. Naturally your son will have the same situation that he would have had with Martin-Martin. Not at all, my dear Brennuire, there's no need to thank me. I'm glad to be of service to you in this way. Moreover, if you have any friends who would like to invest in this business I shall do my best to satisfy their wishes. I say 'I shall do my best,' for the ten million will soon be subscribed and the increase in the capital, which won't happen immediately, will favor the first shareholders. You can imagine the incredible profits we are going to make when you consider that even so the mark can't go on falling forever. No, not at all, my dear Brennuire, don't mention it, there's no need to thank me. I am really only too glad to be of service to you. And now, if you like, we will talk of something else. Let me think, what time is it? What would you say to going for a drink on the boulevards?"

"With pleasure," said Monsieur Brennuire. "And . . ."

"And not another word about the SIGI. Ah yes, though, just one. I would like to ask you when you will be able to have your capital available."

"But whenever you like. Sometime this week."

"Excellent," said Brabbant. "Well, let's go and have something at Pousset's. Ah, the boulevards! I adore the boulevards!"

"I shall be really pleased to have a chat with you, we don't often see you in our old Latin Quarter these days."

"Alas, you can't imagine how I regret it. And my old friend Tolut, how is he doing?"

"Badly."

"No? Ill?"

"He's as fit as a fiddle, but he has lugubrious ideas all the time. After a while it becomes very disagreeable."

"I can understand that," said Brabbant.

"It's since he went to London for the death of one of his brothers. Would you believe it, I was completely unaware of the existence of that brother. My wife had never even mentioned him. He must have been, I fear, a very bad lot. And my goodness, even though after all he was my brother-in-law, I didn't go into mourning for him."

"One shouldn't be too punctilious," said Brabbant.

"At all events, our poor Tolut hasn't got over that journey, I'm afraid. It was a terrible blow to him. I fear he will never recover from it. And then you know, my dear fellow, he's beginning, let's not be afraid of the expression, to talk through his hat."

"Aren't you exaggerating a little?"

"Not at all, not at all; feeling remorseful about geography even!"

"Hm—what are they all looking at like that?"

They raised their heads. A plane was writing "Citroën" in the sky in letters of smoke.

"What don't they invent nowadays!" Brennuire exclaimed.

"That's progress," said Brabbant.

28

TUQUEDENNE APPROACHED this third year with the firm determination "to put an end to it," which for him meant to destroy a whole series of behavior patterns ranging from laziness to cowardice. He went about it in a peculiar fashion: by becoming a hypochondriac. He noticed that he was afflicted with half a dozen illnesses and infirmities which it was incumbent upon him to get rid of as soon as possible. From September on, he began to go the rounds of the doctors.

These individuals informed him that his urine settled in sedimentary layers at the bottom of test tubes and indicated phosphaturia. He watched himself functioning, swallowed pills and began to simulate bulimia; for he had no doubt that he was anemic as well. Four or five times an afternoon he downed some hard-boiled eggs and a tumblerful of white wine. He licked the platters clean. He hoped thus to piss clearly and distinctly and get the better of his lymphatism.

This did not only concern his digestive system and his bone structure. His attention was also turned to the extremely excessive activity of the glands that obstructed the inside of his nose. For years, Tuquedenne had had a cold from the autumn until the summer; at that moment he got hay fever; he got it even without leaving Paris, which was evidence of the profound malfunctioning of his respiratory system. A specialist in a cheap clinic informed him that he was suffering from hypertrophic rhinitis, at least that was how Tuquedenne understood it. Whereupon the doctor did not hesitate to burn the back of his nostrils and to make him pay fifty francs. For several days, Tuquedenne breathed in the Universe as if it were gradually becoming worn out, like a dishcloth. This was not the only unpleasant occurrence he had to suffer: in the middle of consuming a ham sandwich nicely smothered in mustard his nose began to bleed and he fled to the washroom. The torrent only decided to stop flowing after half an hour. Tuquedenne then finished his sandwich, which was getting stale. A week later he went back to see the operator. Who cut his turbinate bones with a pair of nail clippers and once again roasted his sternutatory glands. He asked him to come back on the following Wednesday. But Tuquedenne didn't go back, determined as he was not to pay for the second butchering. He congratulated himself heartily on this small swindle; and he had really had enough of having cotton wool in his nose, of sniffing the world as if it were garbage being incinerated and of making bloodstains all over the hard-boiled eggs he consumed in various bistrots in order to be finally able to urinate in Cartesian fashion. He also solved an optical problem which had constituted a source of humiliation for him since his childhood. He decided to wear glasses. From the aesthetic point of view, he admired their tortoiseshell. From the practical point of view, this gave him an excuse for many satisfactions. He became so proud of his sharp eyes and his specs that he began to read the newspapers as if he were longsighted and to decipher the names of actors on the Morris columns on the other side of the boulevard.

He also envisaged divers other pathological possibilities such as tuberculosis, hereditary syphilis and broken blood vessels. Gradually, these fears retreated. By the beginning of the winter, Vincent Tuquedenne was able to consider himself more or less healthy, providing he regularly took various medicines—the ones syrupy, the others powdery.

But his transforming attention did not focus only on his flesh, but also on the manufactured products with which it had to clothe itself in order to appear in public. His father was in the habit of buying him waisted jackets and high boots. Tuquedenne took to feeling ashamed of them, and he finally came to see them as the very symbol of his cowardice; after numerous discussions, during which Tuquedenne senior was in despair at seeing his son becoming perverted in this way, Vincent managed to dress in a straight jacket and to wear lace-up shoes. He felt he was becoming a different man, all the more so in that the antiphosphaturic tablets were nearly finished, as was the syrup that was good for the respiratory tracts. He turned his victory into a triumph by the acquisition of a British cap and a sturdy walking stick. These two objects gave originality and assurance to their owner. Yes, truly, Tuquedenne felt a different man, a different young man, since he wasn't yet twenty.

The winter looked as if it was going to be very hard. Thanks to the cauterizations of the unpaid specialist, Tuquedenne's nose bore its rigors bravely. Cap on head and stick in fist, Vincent went out in the cold in pursuit of something he didn't know and which he didn't even know he was in pursuit of. Once again, he was very much alone. Brennuire was looking for promotion in some overseas barracks. Rohel remained invisible; on the other hand his brother had put in an appearance. He was studying for the entrance exam to the science department of the Ecole normale and spoke disrespectfully of his elder who, he said, was living in the suburbs with a bird while waiting for his inheritance. Tuquedenne could only exchange polite, but distant, words with him. The only other relations he had with the society of men were with a few students whose names and the palm of whose hands he vaguely knew. He sometimes went so far as to chat with some of the girls studying psychology, but without pursuing this advantage.

Ever since he had seen *The Cabinet of Doctor Caligari,* Tuquedenne had treated himself to the cinema several times a week. He assiduously frequented the Ciné-Opéra, which had a reputation for showing art and avant-garde films, and also Parisiana, which screened up to three or four comic American films; out of this number there was always one, and it was this one that Tuquedenne came to see, that was located on a beach and enlivened by bathing beauty girls with a grace that no one in those days could have suspected of one day becoming a little obsolete. Solitary, melancholy and ingenuous, he watched these incarnations of luxury and voluptuousness disporting themselves on the shores of the Pacific Ocean. And without being chaste, he was still a virgin. He liked images and respected shadows.

After having been preoccupied to the point of obsession by his physiological evolution, Tuquedenne lived for his dreams. In the mornings, he cast the net of memory and fished up some dreams that he watched all day choking and perishing of light; in the evenings he let himself be borne away on the nocturnal sea and he repeated, like the poet, because in a sense there is only ever one:

> *oh may my sleep*
> *. . . as it is lasting, so be deep!*

And, taking pride in quoting illustrious authors, he prolonged the night into the day, but didn't encourage the day to penetrate the night.

At this same period he started to read—more dreams—the entire thirty-two volumes of *Fantômas.* He scoured the *quais* to buy prewar copies whose covers were on glossy paper. Rohel junior caught him carrying out this research and mocked him for his old-fashioned tastes; *he* was learning Russian and taking part in demonstrations. Thus passed the first months of this winter which was rendered illustrious by the exploits of the *piqueurs,* who went around stabbing people in the métro, some incomprehensible and multiple explosions in stoves, and Mussolini's accession to power.

29

A CITRON STOPPED outside number 80 *bis* rue des Petits-Champs. A puffy old man finally managed to wriggle out of it.

"Wait for me," Brabbant said to his chauffeur, thinking he was still living in the days when he used taxis.

He went upstairs, whistling gaily; at the fifth floor, panting hard, he tapped on a door with a curved and decided index finger. Madame Dutilleul received him in the little room that served as her boudoir and which was pervaded by her taste for fragile, highly colored objects of reduced dimensions.

"Well! Aren't you just decked out!" she exclaimed. "I've never seen you so elegant."

"You think so?"

He asked this question, which was both timid and anxious, while looking at himself in a mirror. He kissed her hand and sat down.

"To what do I owe this pleasure?" Madame Dutilleul asked.

"Er . . . I came to wish you a Happy New Year."

"That's very nice."

"And then, I've brought you a present."

He took a Louis-Philippe ruby ring out of a waistcoat pocket and, while Madame Dutilleul was going into ecstasies, pulled a wad of thousand-franc notes out of his wallet and put it down in front of her.

"Here's the money you lent me. Thank you very much, it did me a great service."

"But what's got into you? Have you become a millionaire then?"

"Not yet, but I'm not far off."

"Then you've pulled off your masterstroke?"

"I'm halfway there."

"May one know what it is?"

"It isn't a swindle."

"*What* did you say?"

Brabbant smiled modestly.

"I've become an honest man. I'm going to buy Germany."

"My poor Louis! You're cracked!"

"I'll explain. It's extremely simple: the firm of Martin-Martin, which only dealt in fictitious business, is becoming the Société Internationale de Gérance Immobilière, which is going to deal in real business. The aim of this society is to take advantage of the fall in the mark and to buy property in Germany. When the mark rises again, as it inevitably will after the occupation of the Ruhr, we shall make what you might call an insane profit. The capital to be subscribed is ten million. The shares cost a hundred francs. If you like, I'll reserve some for you."

"It sounds very interesting, your business."

"More than five hundred thousand francs have already been subscribed, three hundred thousand of them by Doctor Wullmar, Professor at the Faculty of Medicine in Paris."

"Some clients might be interested."

"I'll send you some prospectuses; some circulars, I mean. And if you would like to subscribe, I'm at your disposal."

"I'll think it over."

"It's a gold mine, and it'll enable me to enjoy a peaceful old age."

"How old are you now?"

"I just can't remember."

"You're getting vain. Is it since you took your custom away from me?"

"Oh, not at all, not at all. I simply meant that I didn't think about it anymore. About my age."

He remained silent, looking at the notes which Madame Dutilleul had not touched.

"Well, that's that," he said.

And he stood up.

"I'll send you some prospectuses. A doctor of law drafted them for me. He charged enough for it, the swine."

"I might perhaps subscribe twenty thousand or so."

"Don't leave it too long. Just think, it'll bring you in at least 120 percent."

"I'll think it over."

"You do that."

He went, and Madame Dutilleul remained pensive with admiration and perplexed with astonishment. He, climbing into his car, had himself driven to his tailor's, and then to his office, where he engaged in a great deal of activity in the middle of the files Brennuire had entrusted to him. He took the management of these properties seriously but, knowing nothing about it, got nowhere. Finally he decided that he needed a secretary, a real one, who knew bookkeeping and all the rest of it, not a silly young man who was only good enough to be an accomplice. He didn't want anything to do with the crooked fellow who had drafted his prospectus; he tried to recollect all the individuals who had come when he had put advertisements in the papers "just to see," but so far as he could recall, none would be suitable, especially not that Rohel whom he had nearly involved in various crimes and punishments. All he could do was advertise again.

Having reached this decision, he looked at his watch. It was six o'clock. He wasn't meeting Fabie until eight. Poor little thing, she hadn't a moment to herself any longer, her entire time was taken up in shopping. He thought tenderly of her, trotting round the department stores, high-hatting the skirt-chasers. Not knowing what to do he went out, tested the wind, and then drifted. At the Châtelet he bought an evening paper and read with satisfaction the account of the advance of the Franco-Belgian armies into the Ruhr. No doubt about it, the mark would fall even further, but there was equally no doubt that it would rise again one fine day. It couldn't go on falling indefinitely. The important thing was to choose the right moment. At all events, he could always wait, and content himself with imaginary transactions while he was awaiting the real ones. For Brabbant did believe that one day he really would possess some properties in Germany and that he would thereby become immensely rich and honest. He dreamed that he was buying whole villages and that the SIGI would end up acquiring entire provinces. Continuing this meditation, he came to the conclusion that it would be a good thing for the SIGI to specialize in the methodical conquest of the Rhenish provinces and thus serve the interests of France on the left bank of the Rhine. In that case it became preferable to buy land, even if it was unproductive, rather than buildings at infinitely greater cost in relation to surface area; and the moment you brought annexationist aims into it, territory—that was what counted.

Thus dreaming, Brabbant found himself in the rue des Ecoles; suddenly becoming aware of this, he decided to carry on as far as the Ludo, being sure he would find Tolut there. Walking along the wall of the Sorbonne, he remembered with amusement that he had made Tolut's acquaintance by mistake, having taken him for a meridional barber who had come to Paris to collect an inheritance of five million and in connection with whom he had thought up an ingenious scheme to swindle him out of a few hundred francs. He was modest in those days, and ridiculous. At all events, he had shown flair in continuing to frequent the old teacher. He had always had a feeling that fortune would come to him from that direction, that some sort of a deal was hiding in the corner. He hadn't been mistaken. Now he was an honest man, useful to his country, and soon to be rolling in wealth.

He went into the Ludo. It was the usual winter crowd. On the right, Poldevians and Moldo-Russians were earning their livings playing chess at twenty sous a game against carefully chosen rabbits from Normandy or Brie; on the left people had taken up a square formation around a champion of the green-baize table. Brabbant went the rounds of the billiard games without seeing Tolut. He even ventured into the back rooms where the bridge players and the enthusiasts of English billiards hold sway. But Tolut wasn't there.

Brabbant went out, speculating vaguely to himself about the possible fate of the old teacher, and walked down to the Souf-flet, where he found Brennuire with the poet Sybarys Tulle, the essayist Minturne and an individual who was introduced to him as a journalist on *le Matin*. These gentlemen were discussing politics; some were in favor of the occupation of the Ruhr, others not. Brabbant listened to them respectfully; he too had his little idea on the subject but he kept it to himself. Then the talk turned to the imminent collapse of bolshevism and the insurmountable difficulties being encountered by fascism. Finally they considered various hypotheses in connection with the epidemic of explosions in stoves. After half an hour, these three individuals left.

Brabbant, now alone with Brennuire, inquired after his children. Georges was in Algeria, and Thérèse was studying for her philosophy degree. "The whole family, then," Brabbant joked. And Tolut? Tolut was still very depressed. Brennuire inquired after the progress of the SIGI. Brabbant informed him that negotiations had been entered into for the purchase of vast plots of land not far from Mainz and of a large block of apartments they would let out in Aix-la-Chapelle. But Brennuire was worried. He wondered whether later on the German government would allow a French firm to have full liberty of action. Brabbant smiled; he explained that the SIGI wouldn't own anything in its own name, but only through the intermediary of a company they would float in Germany and which, being German, would not worry the authorities. Reassured by this fable, Brennuire took a sip of Pernod, thinking of the future with satisfaction.

30

IT DIDN'T AMUSE him all that much, Hector Lanterne, to go to this funeral. But well, you have obligations in life; after all he was an old customer, and what was more he owed him some money. All that, it counted. Naturally he would have preferred to go to the cinema or to the Châtelet theater, but well, you have obligations in life. And for Hector Lanterne, that was what it was, to go to this funeral. He did so sufficiently grudgingly to arrive just at the moment when the procession was leaving the deceased's domicile, making its way slowly toward the Pantin-Parisien cemetery. Hector Lanterne followed it, in the very last row. It had a long way to go. Lanterne was bored. He tried to enter into conversation with the man walking next to him, a chap with an arm missing, but the one-armed man conveyed to him by means of the appropriate sign language the fact that he was also deaf. Reduced to mutism, Hector Lanterne began to think; he wondered whether his wife wouldn't take advantage of his absence to be unfaithful to him on the billiard table in the first-floor room with the new waiter. To amuse himself, he tried to imagine how it would take place, and was thus just getting to the point of envisaging several bawdy possibilities when he became aware that a dry-as-dust little old man walking by his side seemed desirous of exchanging a few remarks with him.

"Is it Pantin we're going to?" the old codger asked.

"Yes. It's a mighty long way."

"That's the disadvantage of living in a big town. The cemeteries are at the other end of the world."

"Why do they have to go and put them so far away?"

"Well, they can't put them in the Place de l'Opéra."

"Of course not."

"And just think—there isn't any more room in any of the Paris cemeteries. Père-Lachaise, Montmartre, Montparnasse, Vaugirard, Passy, Picpus, Belleville, Grenelle, Saint-Vincent, Saint-Pierre, Bercy, La Villette, Charonne, Auteuil, they're all full. Paris is full of corpses, monsieur, full to bursting. And so we're reduced to going to the suburbs, unless we have a family vault. You haven't got a family vault, have you?"

"No, monsieur, I'm not rich enough."

"My family has a vault, I'm not saying that to put you down. No. You know very well that it was customary in the old days for every family to possess its vault. It was a sign of prosperity, of modest prosperity. My family has a vault in the cemetery in Le Mans. Do you know Le Mans?"

"No, monsieur. Is it a nice town?"

"I haven't been there for nearly twenty years. What was I saying, then?"

"You were talking about your family vault."

"Ah yes. Believe it or not, there were two places left. One for me, the other for my brother. But he won't occupy it."

"Dear, dear."

"No, he won't occupy it. He died abroad. You can quite understand that I wasn't going to have him brought back. The transport would have cost me a fortune. When I go back to Le Mans, my heirs will have to pay through the nose."

"Me, actually, I don't much fancy being put in a vault."

"That is the question!" the little old man exclaimed in tones that made some of the procession look round, shocked. "That is the question: I wonder what I shall choose in the end, the vault or loose soil. And you know, there's one thing that worries me, and that is, the place that will remain unoccupied. They might finally put a stranger in it, an I-don't-know-who; in that case there's no longer any point in having a family vault."

"Of course not."

The old man made an irritated little snapping noise with his lips.

"I really don't know where to go."

"What about cremation? What do you think of cremation?"

"Obviously, obviously, there's cremation. And there you avoid the danger of being buried prematurely."

"That's a nasty business."

"It's a question that preoccupies me enormously, and to which the authorities have never paid enough attention. And yet it is a real danger. There would be a way to avert that danger, though, and that would be to equip graves with little bells."

"That's not a bad idea. The stiff would ring and, when the caretaker came, he'd ask him for his coffee and a croissant."

"There is nothing to jest about, monsieur."

"A bit of a joke never hurt anybody, especially when they're talking about things that aren't gay in themselves."

"You're quite right to say it isn't gay. Do you often think about death?"

"Huh, no thanks! Fat lot of good it'd do me to think about death!"

"But today, you've had to think about it."

"Yes, that's true, because of my customer."

"What customer?"

"The one they're carting along in the hearse. He was a customer of mine."

"And what did he do?"

"Hm! You don't know what he did? Don't you know the deceased, then?"

"My goodness, no."

"Then . . . you're going to the funeral . . . just for fun?"

"I am going to this funeral, my dear monsieur, while I'm waiting for people to come to mine."

"Well! You don't have very gay ideas."

"Do *you* think it's gay, to die?"

"Of course not, of course not. But you've got plenty of time ahead of you, even so."

"No need to flatter me. And anyway, you don't know anything about it. I know that I'm going to die soon and I don't find it at all funny, monsieur. Just think that every instant brings me nearer to the fatal moment when I shall become a corpse. Every moment brings you nearer to it too, monsieur."

"Oh, look here, don't try to scare me."

"And when we're dead, what happens?"

"I've no idea."

"What, don't you even want to know whether you'll go to hell or be reincarnated in the body of a Patagonian. . . ?"

"*That*'s a funny idea."

"Or whether you'll disappear completely."

"I can't be bothered with all that stuff."

"Don't you believe in hell?"

"That's curés' stuff!"

"And in reincarnation?"

"That's a big word."

"And in complete annihilation?"

"I've no idea."

"There's no other hypothesis, though."

"Oh yes there is though, and this is going to shake you, there *is* another."

"I can't help wondering what."

"There's heaven."

"I suppose you think you're intelligent, monsieur? I suppose you think it's intelligent to mock an old man who is just about to succumb to the embrace of death, monsieur!"

"I didn't mean to say anything to offend you. I'm positive I didn't."

"Let me tell you, monsieur, that while hell may perhaps exist, heaven certainly does not exist."

"That's very sad, what you've just said."

"Sad but true."

"I wonder how you came to think such things."

"My whole life has led me to think that. What if I was mistaken, though? What if, on the other hand, my whole life . . . You think it exists, heaven? I'm asking you as man to man, I'm asking you for an honest answer."

"It's curés' stuff! It doesn't exist."

"Ah, you see! And what about criminals, eh, criminals? Criminals who go unpunished during their lifetime? Afterwards, do you think there's a judgment afterwards?"

"It's to be hoped that there is. That way there'd be fewer unpunished criminals in circulation. Well yes, like the one that put my customer's eye out."

"What's that you're saying?"

"Oh, it's a long story. But you don't even know the name of the deceased. Tormoigne, his name was. He was a good customer, because I'm a café proprietor by trade, monsieur. Tormoigne had only one eye, so he didn't fight in the war and he earned quite a bit of money while the rest of us were getting clobbered. Ah well, no point in holding that against him now, poor chap. Because I was in the war, monsieur."

"You must have seen a lot of dead people."

"There was certainly no shortage. But it wasn't the same thing as it is here. Ah well, let's not talk about it. To come back to my Tormoigne. Believe it or not, one day last winter he was having a game of manille when a queer-looking character turns up and wants to buy some stamps. I say a queer-looking character because his hair was as long as that, halfway down his back. I thought he was an artist and I didn't have any objection when Tormoigne suddenly takes it into his head to josh him about his hair, so's to make everyone laugh. Well, monsieur! You'll never guess what he did to him, what the artist did."

"He put his eye out."

"How did you guess?"

"You told me just now. Ah! my God! I remember now, though. Wasn't it in the papers?"

"I should say it was. It was the very same day they reported Landru's death sentence. And that detracted from the crime, I must say."

"I remember that atrocity perfectly."

"Atrocity, that's the right word. Well, monsieur, he's never been seen since, that artist hasn't. He's still at large. And would you believe it, after that, Monsieur Tormoigne met with one misfortune after another. He still came to the café but he became a bore because he never stopped telling his story and he wanted to advise the manille players even though he couldn't see the cards, so people began to make fun of him, not nastily, of course. But then one fine day some bastard took advantage of the fact that he couldn't see and stole his wallet. Blaisolle he was called, that man. Well! He's never been seen since, either. Isn't it incredible? And do you know how he died, Monsieur Tormoigne? He went out early last Sunday, a car ran him over and he died of it; a fractured skull. And, monsieur, you needn't believe me if you don't want to, the car didn't stop and hasn't been seen since. And now he's being taken to the cemetery."

"That's a very strange destiny."

"You've said it, a strange destiny."

"And very terrible."

"Terrible, that's the right word. But now at least he's at peace."

"Is he or is he not, that is the question. Have you read Shakespeare?"

"Oh, you know, in my trade you don't get much time to read."

"I am a teacher."

"I rather thought so, monsieur. You talk well."

"Alas! poor Yorick! Hm—in this cemetery we are now entering, I'd like to go and see the gravediggers who take the skeletons out of the communal grave, then I'd take a skull out of the pile of bones, I'd hold it between my hands, look straight into its empty orbits and exclaim: 'Alas, poor Tolut!' "

"Well! No one could say you have very gay ideas. And who is he, this Tolut?"

"I am he, monsieur."

31

"DID YOU NOTICE," said Tolut as they left the cemetery, "the sound the earth makes when it falls on the coffin? It's a hollow sound. It's as if there isn't anyone inside. Do you think he was inside, that Monsieur . . ."

"Tormoigne. You can well imagine that I didn't go and look."

"Naturally. At all events, that's him dispatched, eh. One more. And did you see how many there are? Thousands and thousands! What a lot of graves! What a lot of graves! Just think, a big town like Paris, what a lot of dead people it must provide. And one day, soon, it'll be my turn."

"You say that, but you don't think it."

"Ah! You believe that? But I think of nothing else, my dear monsieur."

"Your life can't be very gay, with ideas like that trotting through your head all the time."

"I don't expect to have a gay life. At my age, that's the last thing I expect!"

"All the same, it wouldn't do you any harm to think of something else. I'm not trying to give you advice, but all the same it seems to me that that wouldn't do you any harm."

"It's easy for you to talk. Dying isn't so simple, don't think it is. Even if one could die in peace."

"And why wouldn't you be able to die in peace, monsieur?"

"Are you going back by tram?"

"Yes, as far as the République."

"Well! So am I. From the République I can go on to the Latin Quarter. That's where I live."

"I understand that, if you're a teacher."

"A teacher! That's precisely what's preventing me from dying in peace."

"What d'you mean by that?"

"Well, yes, just imagine, my friend, I spent years teaching something of which I was completely ignorant."

"But how can that be?"

"Ah, that's precisely it! It's just what I said, though. For years and years, children have been entrusted to me for me to teach them geography, yes, geography. Well! I didn't know a single word about it. I was totally ignorant of it. Isn't that a swindle? a theft? My whole life has been a deception, yes, monsieur, a deception. Isn't that terrible?"

"I'd never have thought it possible."

"What? To teach geography without knowing a single word about it? But you make me laugh, monsieur! It's child's play! I'm exaggerating, of course. The words, I knew *them*, only the thing is: I had never traveled. Well then, how can you expect to teach geography without ever having traveled? You teach the words, but the real things—you don't know them. You know the names, but you're totally ignorant of what they refer to. Do you understand, monsieur?"

"Very well, very well."

"My whole life I've done that, my whole life I've perpetrated that swindle. It was only when I retired that I realized it. Alas, it was too late! I felt the urge to travel, to know far-off countries. It was too late!"

"Of course. People don't become explorers at your age."

"My age has nothing to do with it, monsieur. Try and understand me, though: even if I were to travel now, that wouldn't remove the blot on my professional name. I believed I had lived an honorable, conscientious life; now that I'm reaching the end, I see that I have been radically mistaken. How do you expect me to descend into the tomb with a tranquil step, shouldering the weight of this heavy sin, yes, monsieur, how do you expect that?"

"Well, er, monsieur, well, er . . . I'm not sure I follow you."

"You don't understand me? It's quite clear, though."

"Oh yes, I understand you. But after all, monsieur, if you hadn't known anything, you wouldn't have gone on being a teacher. Somebody would have noticed."

"That's where you're wrong. Nobody noticed. They accepted it all without question: my ignorance, my swindle, everything. And how do you imagine I can make amends now? Make amends for my offense? How could I? And how could I die? Ah, if I didn't have this to reproach myself for, ah, monsieur, I would watch the approach of death with joy. That's right, with joy! I should have nothing to reproach myself for. I should close my eyes with a smile. That's right, with a smile! And afterwards? Oh, afterwards, I should have no fear! I haven't been a bad man. I should go to purgatory, perhaps to heaven, whose existence you rightly recalled earlier. Or else I should be reincarnated a few hundred centuries hence in the body of a pretty woman or a rich industrialist, if there still are industrialists in those times, because with these confounded bolsheviks, they're capable of liquidating them all. In that case I should be reincarnated on another planet. On Venus, for example."

"Do *you* believe in them, monsieur, in the spirits that appear in tables? I had a go at table-turning once with my brother-in-law and Emile, the waiter we had before the one we have now. It didn't work. It remained as dumb as a fish, just fancy."

"It's annoying, you interrupted me. What was I saying, then?"

"You were talking about the bolsheviks and the planet Venus, it certainly must be a very beautiful planet, that one."

"Had I envisaged the third hypothesis?"

"I don't remember."

"It's annoying. The moment I'm interrupted I forget what I was going to say."

"It's age, monsieur."

"Yes, it's age, increasing age. It's like an animal, age, monsieur. It's an animal that grows and grows, and goes on growing until it finally eats you alive."

"Oh, but no kidding, you give me the shivers."

"All that would be nothing if I didn't have this thing tormenting me, here, in my chest."

"I don't think it's so very serious, monsieur, what you're reproaching yourself for. Since no one noticed. I see you even have a decoration."

"That's the most terrible thing of all! I alone reproach myself. Yes, I'm alone. The others don't want to understand me, my relations, my friends. They don't want to understand me. There's no one to accuse me."

"There's lots of people would be glad to be in your shoes."

"They would be dishonest people. I am my only accuser. So how do you expect me to die? Either there will be no one left to accuse me, or I shall be accusing myself for all eternity. It's abominable!"

Monsieur Tolut began to cry. But in the 51 tram that doesn't shock anyone. People are used to it, because of all the people coming away from the Pantin cemetery.

"You must calm down, monsieur," said Hector Lanterne, "you must calm down."

Monsieur Tolut wiped his eyes with a handkerchief made of old-fashioned material. He sniffed.

"I don't know what's come over me."

"I can understand it, you're upset."

"What bothers me is that I can't remember the rest of what I was going to say when you interrupted me."

"Ah yes, when you were talking about the communists and the stars."

"Mind you, my friend, I've just thought of something. I *have* traveled since I retired. I've been abroad."

"Me too, I've been abroad, to Belgium, to Charleroi, and later to the Rhineland. But all that is more or less France."

"*I* went to London. That trip, you know, monsieur, that was the end of everything. Naturally, it isn't because I might travel now that it would make any difference to my not having traveled before; do you follow me?"

"I think so."

"All the same, I thought that if I did travel it would mitigate my self-reproach. That was my idea. Well, my friend, it was just the opposite. Whether I travel now or whether I don't travel, there's nothing to be done. I saw that very clearly, there's nothing to be done. My conscience is there, monsieur, and it doesn't forgive me."

"It's most unfortunate."

"Ah! Life isn't funny, and what's even less funny is to realize it just at the moment when you're getting ready to leave."

"Death is a journey too, monsieur."

"Yes, but that particular geography isn't taught."

"Oh, but it is, monsieur. What about the curés, isn't that what they do?"

"That's an amusing idea of yours. Where did you fish it up?"

"I don't know. I get ideas when I think."

"What would be convenient, you know, would be to go off on that journey and leave one's conscience behind. Do you understand me? Here, on earth."

"And what about ghosts, monsieur? Don't you believe that ghosts are consciences left behind in old houses who don't have their owners to torment anymore? And so they pester other people."

"Well now, my friend, you seem to be extremely intelligent. It's not stupid, your idea. Do you often have ideas like that?"

"I told you, monsieur; when I think."

"And when do you think?"

"You'll laugh, monsieur: when my wife gets herself you-know-what by a customer and they go up to the room on the first floor, the one where the billiard table is, a beautiful Brunschvicg table with Champion cushions. *Then* I think. Because I'm a great cuckold, monsieur."

"Well! You certainly look on the bright side of life."

"You have to."

"Terminus," said the lady with the money bag and the little bits of multicolored paper.

"It's very intelligent, your idea. To leave a ghost behind you, a ghost that doesn't torment you any longer. I wouldn't mind dying in those conditions. There'd be a Tolut who would go I don't care where, and then a ghost Tolut who would stay here."

He stamped his foot, to make it quite clear where here was.

"And who would finally leave me in peace."

He then perceived that the café proprietor had suddenly and totally disappeared. Monsieur Tolut was taken aback and for a moment regretted the company of that conscientious interlocutor; then, when he'd got over his astonishment, he asked himself lightheartedly whether he hadn't been a ghost.

32

TUQUEDENNE HAD carefully calculated that it must be the third door, unless there was a *bis,* a slight risk to run. He didn't raise his head in the air to look at the number before he went in; somebody might notice him. He passed in front of a butcher's where the window display was being cleaned, which made one door; then in front of the dusty display that a photographer had dared to make of saddened faces and sickly bodies, which made two doors; then in front of a bookshop that specialized in chopping up plainsong manuscripts for the use of lovers of original lampshades, which made three doors. Tuquedenne entered without hesitating; on the left of the corridor the letter boxes on the wall were encumbered by a recent delivery of the catalogues of a big store. It was on the second floor, right-hand side, according to the directions for The Smile. On the second floor, right-hand side, Tuquedenne deciphered on an enamel plate: *Massage.* He rang. The door was opened. He went in.

A guy was coming out of a room. Madame pounced on him and pushed him back in, laughing.

"I don't like my clients to meet," she said, showing Tuquedenne into a very small room furnished with a chair and a kind of banquette, on which a little blonde woman was sitting.

"This is Marguerite," said the procuress.

They talked currency.

"I'll leave you," she concluded.

Which she did. Tuquedenne had been afraid he would have to choose between Carmen and the Negress, as he had read in certain tales. He thought Marguerite was nice; but for him Marguerite was a brunette's name because it was that of one of his parents' maids who also had a mustache. Contradictorily to this memory, he remembered that Gretchen is a blonde.

"Going to sit down?"

He sat down. She took his cap in her hands.

"It's very smart, your cap."

She put it on her head.

"Ah, what d'you know, it's too big for me."

She laughed.

"Have you been here before?"

"No."

He didn't at all see the necessity of this conversation.

"Kiss me."

He kissed her.

These preliminaries out of the way, she led him into a bedroom and they made love. It cost twenty francs. In the street, Tuquedenne walked slowly away from the third door, looking the passersby straight in the face so as not to seem as if he had come from that place. He felt that the women were looking at him in a special fashion; was it true, what Rohel had told him, that when you've just made love they can guess it at once? He reached the boulevard Saint-Germain, crossed the intersection and went up the rue de l'Odéon using the right-hand pavement, because he never used the left-hand one.

It was something extremely simple and not at all unpleasant; but you couldn't say it was extremely pleasant either, because it had happened too quickly and the woman had really seemed too much to be thinking of something else. But it was something so simple that it didn't stop the trams running, and people were still coming and going in all directions in the streets as if nothing had happened. It was no doubt one of the most infinitesimal events of the day and of his own life, which after all wouldn't count for much and which wouldn't even stop him lying when he was talking women with Rohel. And once again, what astonished Tuquedenne was the simplicity of the thing. It was as simple as taking the métro or going to the cinema. It was also much more complicated: what a lot of detours, what a lot of secrets, what a lot of hypocrisies. No, decidedly, it wasn't simple at all.

Tuquedenne passed in front of Shakespeare and Company and stopped, coveting the big *Ulysses* in the blue jacket, then continued on his way towards the Odéon, glancing at the new books, and then, crossing the road, walked along by the railings of the Luxembourg in the direction of the Place Médicis. It was a long story, that of his virginity, and he would have done better to shorten it. Would he not have been really different if he'd gone whoring the moment he got to Paris; or even for that matter had not waited until he left Le Havre, a town where there's no shortage of brothels. He was afraid of diseases, though. With his usual bad luck he would certainly not have avoided them in Le Havre. He didn't find this at all funny and abominated the student jokes on the subject, as for that matter on every other subject. Stupidity nauseated him; it was glaringly present in the Quarter, and more aggressive there than anywhere else. It wasn't a question of stupidity, though, but of love; love, that was saying a lot; but Tuquedenne had no regrets.

He sat down on the terrace of the Chope-Latine and, while waiting for Rohel, began to watch the crowd go by. It became obvious to him that there were two kinds of human beings, and this obvious fact had never seemed more obvious; there were men, and then there were women. They came and went, quite casually, adopting an indifferent or offhand manner, but you only had to look carefully to perceive that without any possible doubt, on the one hand there were women, and on the other there were men. "Great and profound statement of the obvious," Tuquedenne told himself, emptying his glass of white wine. Then he began to appraise the women going by, as if they were mares; but he didn't realize this.

"Hallo, old man. What's new?"

"Nothing," said Tuquedenne.

"You look odd."

"*I* do? Are you going to have a white wine?"

"Is it dry or is it sweet, their white wine?"

"Dry. I shall have another."

"Here, would you believe it, I've just met Tolut again. You can't go anywhere around here without bumping into him. The old boy's still haunted by the idea of death."

"He's not wrong," said Tuquedenne.

"Do *you* think about death?"

"I'm not talking about me."

"He told me a most unlikely story that seems to interest him a lot; it's the story of a one-eyed man who's supposed to have had his other eye put out by an artist; Tolut specifies 'with his index finger'; after which this one-eyed man who'd become blind was supposed to have had his wallet stolen and then ended up being run over by a car."

"It's a complete fabrication!"

"It seems he went to the chap's funeral."

"Did he know him?"

"No, he went by chance. He joins passing funeral processions. That's the only thing he lives for now. He's becoming a kind of vampire."

"You could find better vampires. Poor Tolut!"

"He was by far the biggest pain in the ass of all the masters. Why do masters make what they teach such a pain?"

"To stop the pupils knowing more than they do. They discourage them."

"What a subtle psychologist you are."

"Oh, to hell with psychology. Shall we have another white wine?"

"Yes, but not in this filthy district."

They took an 8 bus at random as far as the Gare de l'Est. In the boulevard de Strasbourg, Rohel suggested having some oysters to go with the white wine; they bought two dozen that were being pushed down the street to the accompaniment of shouts, then, after a few indecisive approaches, settled down in a little bistrot in the rue de Faubourg Saint-Denis with their shellfish and a pitcher of white wine. Tuquedenne:

"Do you remember what you told me one day: that you'd never taken an idea seriously?"

"Go on! *I* said that?"

"Yes. And I think it's legitimate. But *I* take ideas seriously. Always."

"And what are you getting at?"

"I don't know. I'd like to act."

"In other words, you're an intellectual and you want to act. That's a well-known pathological case. Maybe you even want to become an adventurer?"

"An adventurer? I am one."

"It doesn't show."

"I'm an adventurer of the mind."

"Shall we order another carafe?"

"Obviously."

They gulped down the rest of the mollusks.

"Why don't we go and see Hublin?" Rohel suggested.

"Where? In Le Havre?"

"Yes, in Le Havre. There's a train at 7:45. And don't tell me your parents are expecting you for dinner! You can send them a *pneu.*"

"I'll send them a *pneu.* But I haven't any money for a ticket."

"I'll lend you some. And you can stay at my mother's."

Rohel emptied his glass.

"I'll be your professor of action," he declared.

33

ROHEL AND Tuquedenne found an empty compartment in which they made themselves comfortable with their sandwiches and their liter of white wine. They began by looking at the scenery and expressing various opinions on the qualities or imperfections of the show. At nightfall, after Mantes, they wolfed down their sandwiches and emptied the bottle which was sent to explode on the rails in spite of the company's strict prohibition. Then they filled their pipes and began to smoke.

"So you stayed in the country all last winter?" Tuquedenne asked. "That couldn't have been much fun."

"It was terrific. Sweeping the snow—that's marvelous. And the big log fires!"

"It wouldn't appeal to me. Were you living there alone?"

"You know very well I wasn't."

"Who was she?"

"What's that got to do with you?"

"Did she chuck you?"

"No. We separated. I'd had enough, both of the country and of her."

"And Suze?"

"Haven't seen her since."

"Do you remember how you disappeared last year? You really dropped me, didn't you?"

Rohel looked a little embarrassed.

"You found Wullmar more amusing, didn't you?" Tuque-denne went on. "So you dropped me."

"This is a scene of jealousy."

"Brennuire told me that he'd joined the Colonial Army."

"Wullmar? He was a right bastard."

"And why was that?"

"It's of no importance. Here, do you know an old geezer who's a pal of old man Brennuire and Tolut? We've often seen them together at the Soufflet."

"The old boy who plays billiards with Tolut?"

"The same. He's called Martin-Martin or Brabbant. I think he's an adventurer."

"That old idiot?"

"That's the vague impression I have. I should have been his secretary, but Wullmar tricked me out of the job. A right bastard. I'd told him what I thought I knew about old Brabbant (I was convinced he was a crook), and he rushed off and saw him before me. It can't have done him any good, since he's in the army now!"

"Brennuire wrote me that his father wants him to join the company Brabbant has floated and that it seems to be a job with a great future. Personally, jobs with a great future bore me. What do you mean to do in life? You probably don't think about it, do you?"

"Yes, I do think about it. In the first place, I shall start by being a capitalist."

"Congratulations."

"Odd, isn't it? Yes, I shall come into my inheritance when I'm twenty-one. In a few months. Just before I start my military service."

"Don't talk about that. And afterwards, will you work?"

"Work, it seems to me, is a kind of military service."

"We shall see."

At Rouen, some of the passengers got out; others got in.

When the train began to move again Rohel left Tuquedenne to snooze and, going from one carriage to the next, went looking for possible curiosities. There were none. Disappointed, he leaned on the copper rail in the corridor, pressed his head against the window and watched his dreams floating through the nocturnal countryside. At Bréauté-Beuzeville he sat down again and read *l'Intransigeant* in a most attentive fashion. Under the effect of the white wine, Tuquedenne had fallen asleep. He woke up between Harfleur and Graville.

"I shall disturb your mother if I arrive without notice."

"Nonsense."

"Where are we?"

"We're just coming in. Don't you recognize it?"

The little lights became more frequent.

"It's been three years since I left," said Tuquedenne. (He yawned.) "So you know, I'm a bit overcome."

The white wine had somewhat knocked him out.

"We'll soon have you in bed," said Rohel, as the train entered the station.

The next morning Rohel absented himself because he had "things to do." Tuquedenne suspected that his suggestion of this trip had not been an entirely gratuitous whim. He went for a walk in the town and was amazed at feeling so little. Time had only had a minimal effect on the town, names of streets changed, boutiques no longer there, new shops, two or three recent customs. But the sea was still pushing back the cliffs with its indefatigable waves. Tuquedenne sat down on the pebbles, reflecting on his rainwatered image. Still the same— yet hadn't he become different? He thought back to the conversation he'd just had with Rohel. In two months he was going to take the last part of his degree; no doubt he would pass; then there would be four long, hopeless months he wouldn't know what to do with, and then it would be over. One sort of slavery, then another, then yet another, and so on throughout his life. Unless. Unless what? Unless he turned it into a triumph. Unless he turned it into a triumph? Tuquedenne laughed diabolico-skeptically. As the pebbles hurt his buttocks, he suspended his reflections and stood up.

At lunch, which they had at his mother's, Rohel announced that they were going to dine at the Grosse-Tonne that evening with Hublin, Cindol, and Muraut, who happened to be in Le Havre. On account of his special knowledge, Muraut had been given the task of balancing the menu and choosing the wines. They spent the afternoon walking around the port. They went as far as the cotton warehouse, the largest in the world, say the natives of Le Havre, and came back enthusing, in spite of everything, over the cargoes that go to the end of the world. In the Place de l'Hôtel-de-Ville, they met Hublin.

They shook hands, a little embarrassed, exchanging remarks like "hallo, old man, I didn't recognize you." They resumed their walk, tongue-tied.

"What on earth are you doing here?" Hublin asked awkwardly.

"We came quite by chance," said Rohel.

"Yes, for no reason," said Tuquedenne.

Hublin looked at them in surprise.

"How's it coming on, your degree?"

"It's coming on, it's coming on," said Tuquedenne nonchalantly.

"And you, you're not going on with yours?" Rohel asked.

"Oh no. I wouldn't have time."

"Are you working for your uncle?"

"Yes. While I'm waiting to do my military service. After that, I shall go back to Brazil."

"Is it nice, Brazil?"

"Yes, magnificent. But there are times when you regret France."

"No kidding," said Rohel incredulously.

They sat down round a table at the Guillaume-Tell where Cindol was waiting for them. Tuquedenne and Rohel noticed that Hublin was getting on well with this mediocre individual. The conversation wound its way painfully through labyrinths of incomprehension. Luckily, Muraut arrived. His great lack of tact put them all at their ease.

"Good old Hublin!" he exclaimed. "Unrecognizable! How right you were to get your hair cut like Tuquedenne. No one would recognize you. And Brazil, it must be stunning, Brazil!"

"Oh yes!" said Hublin.

"What got into you when you scarpered over there?"

"You really staggered us," said Tuquedenne.

"There was no reason," said Hublin. "It was perfectly natural, my leaving. My uncle offered me a job in Brazil. So I left."

"You'd never said anything about it to me," said Tuquedenne.

"That's quite possible," said Hublin.

"I remember," said Tuquedenne, "you left the day Landru was condemned to death."

"You seem well up in French history," Hublin remarked, laughing.

Tuquedenne, offended, remained silent.

"And spiritism?" asked Muraut, slapping himself on the thigh. "Are you still a spiritist?"

"I've stopped playing the fool," said Hublin.

He seemed to be in a splendid mood. Muraut seemed no less gay. He had borrowed his stepfather's car and hidden an old bottle of excellent rum under the seat. He announced the gastronomic marvels awaiting them at the Grosse-Tonne and suggested another round of aperitifs. Cindol objected that they could have that at the restaurant. Rohel made the banal remark that the one did not preclude the other; Muraut agreed. Tuquedenne was sulking.

The dinner was a great success. They spoke of their former schoolfellows and their former schoolmasters, they recalled the fine outings they went on during the war, and they told dirty jokes, each according to his speciality. After that the party moved on to chez Pitt, for liqueurs. It was a dance hall. Rohel, slightly drunk began to raise Cain and tried to stop the couples circulating. Muraut wanted to sing medical students' songs. Cindol was clumsy enough to upset a glass over a woman's dress. The gentleman accompanying her looked menacing. Hublin, up to then very calm, took it into his head to smash his skull with an ice bucket. Finally the gang got thrown out. Muraut then suggested going down to the beach to finish off the old bottle of excellent rum.

Which they did. Sprawling on the pebbles and singing, they drank from the bottle. Finally it fell into Tuquedenne's hands. He swallowed a good few centiliters, out of ignorance. He stood up in order to make a great speech facing the sea, but almost immediately collapsed onto the pebbles. They took him back to Rohel's house, and Rohel put him to bed. The rest of them went off to finish the evening in a brothel.

Tuquedenne, very ill, vomited all over his hostess's sheets. The next morning he went back to Paris with Rohel, without seeing Hublin again.

Jules

ALFRED, NOW HE was one of a kind. I mean it: he was one of a kind.

I've certainly known some members of the corporation.

Thirty years in the trade!

I've certainly known some members of the corporation in thirty years in the trade.

I'll say it again:

Alfred, he was one of a kind.

And a decent kind.

And now he's gone.

One day he said to us: "Good-bye, I'm leaving, you won't see me tomorrow." We said to him: "Why are you leaving?" He said to us: "I have things to do." We said to him: "We know what they are. So you're going to try out your system?" He said to us: "Yes." We said to him: "We'll have you back very soon."

After that, he went to see the manager. He said to him: "A thousand apologies, but I'm leaving." The manager said to him: "Why?" He said to him: "I have things to do." The manager said to him: "I see what it is. The races, eh?" He said to him: "It's in the bag." The manager said to him: "Well, there's one person we'll soon see back, and that's Alfred."

And so he left.

He didn't look as if he was anyone special. Just a waiter like the others. You had to know him.

I knew him.

When I wanted to know something I used to ask him: "Should I do this? Should I do that?" He would take a bit of paper and do a quick sum. Then he'd tell me: "Yes." "No." "You'll bring it off." "You won't bring it off."

And he was always right. What a character!

He didn't only know how to see the future. He was also a philosopher. A real one. He used to say to me: "You see, the customers, they're like a pile of dead leaves."

I asked him why. He answered: "Leaves, when they're on the tree, if you didn't know that autumn existed you might think they'd stay there forever. That's like our customers. They come back every day as regular as clockwork: you think they'll go on doing so forever. But then one day the wind blows and carries the leaves off to the gutters and the street sweepers make little piles of them on the edge of the pavements to await the dust-cart. Me too, every year I make my little pile when the autumn arrives, my little pile of dead souls."

And he added: "You see, all that is like the drawing I saw the other day in a humorous magazine which represents a fellow falling from the sixth floor. As he passes the third-floor tenant he says to him: 'So far, things aren't going too badly.' You see the joke. Everyone has his pavement waiting for him on the ground floor."

He wasn't only a philosopher. He was also a sycologist. He knew the customers better than anyone else did and he could get them talking. He saw right through people. He pointed out old Tolut and told me: "Look at that one. He doesn't come as often as he used to. He hasn't got time anymore. It's since he went on a little trip abroad. Death passed close by him, flapping its wings. Look how he's shivering. He doesn't come so often, these days. And do you know why not?"

I asked him why not. He answered: "He's devoting his leisure to the study of deaths and funerals. He joins funeral processions, visits cemeteries and frequents undertakers' assistants. He worries about people being buried alive and goes sniffing around crematoriums. He knows what kind of wood coffins are made of and what kind of marble makes graves. He invades the kingdom of the dead with his decrepit little presence. He drools at one undertaker's, and smacks his lips at another's. He wants to become a ghost."

And then I told him: "You give me the willies, you and your blather."

But Alfred went on: "And do you know why he's like that? Because there's something that's eating his heart out, gnawing at his liver and wringing his guts. When death passes the way it passed close by him, it raises a wind, a hell of a wind, a wind strong enough to dismast the big sailing boats, a wind strong enough to demolish people's consciences. When death passes the way it passed close by him, you have to put your hat on, my dear Jules; it's the opposite of what you do at funerals. You have to put your hat on, otherwise things go badly, especially if there's something putrefying inside you which is called a professional conscience, because no one knows what else to call it."

And that was the way he knew men, Alfred. It was as if he'd turned the customers' jackets inside out and could see their linings.

"The lining, that's the most important part."

That's what he used to say. He said a whole lot of other things as well. What a character he was. And a decent one, too. He did people some wonderfully good turns, just casually. Old Brabbant, for example. I'll take old Brabbant as an example, because I've already dug up old Tolut. They're two of a kind. Well! Old Brabbant was speculating on the mark. He thought the mark would rise again. Alfred did him a bit of a sum on the corner of a table and told him: "Get rid of them, soon they won't be worth anything." Old Brabbant, he didn't want to believe it. He was sure of himself. The thing is, since he's become the manager, the administrator, and the board of directors of an important property company, he believes he's somebody. He's seen around with retired generals—and when *they*'re retired they do all right. He's seen around with people who were decorated by Napoleon in the Invalides. He's seen around with a car and a little chick who's much prettier than the ones who do the best they can in the Quarter. I say "he's seen," and not "we see him," because he hardly ever comes now, and he never tries to show off. To come back to the marks, he didn't want to believe what Alfred said.

Personally I think he'd be wrong not to listen to Alfred. Because Alfred, he was someone. I mean it: he was someone.

In thirty years, I've certainly seen some colleagues.

Well! I've never seen two like him. Not even one. I've only seen him.

He was someone.

And now he's gone.

The other day, old Brabbant comes and sits down. I hurry over. He whispers in my lug-hole: "Not here? Alfred?" I tell him: "Gone."

Then he thumped on the table:

"Ye gods!" he bleated.

I reckoned he was a bit cracked.

35

FOR THE FIRST anniversary of the SIGI, Brabbant gave a dinner in a big restaurant, a dinner to which a few intimate friends were invited, as for example: Brennuire and Dr. Wullmar, and persons of distinction, as for example: Messrs. X, X, and X. It was a great success, although some of the guests thought that Monsieur Brabbant looked a little tired. After much hesitation, Brabbant had decided to invite Tolut; but Tolut refused, because he always heard the name of the company as *ci-gît,* and this seemed to him to be of ill omen. Fabie dined at home with her sister, who kept her company until about one o'clock. Brabbant didn't come back until two in the morning.

"Here I am," he said in a somewhat fuzzy voice.

"You look a bit drunk to me," said Fabie.

He sat down, gazing far into the distance, through the wall.

"It was magnificent," he said. "Magnificent." Then he fell silent. Fabie looked at him with a smile.

"Aren't you ashamed of getting drunk at your age?"

"It was magnificent," Brabbant said again. "There were two ministers and three generals. Two and three make five. Two ministers and three generals."

"You never told me you knew so many generals."

"Hadn't I told you I knew two ministers and three generals? It was magnificent. The most wonderful day of my life since my first communion. My mother cried with emotion too. You're stupid when you're young. There were three generals."

"You aren't going to tell me there were three generals at your first communion?"

"No. There were two ministers and three generals. Two and three make five, not counting Tolut, who didn't come."

"You'd better go to bed."

"No. I shan't go to bed. You only go to bed when you're going to die. Tolut told me so. Tolut, he's an old friend of mine, an old childhood friend. And now he sleeps in an armchair so as not to die. *I* shall sleep standing up."

He was speaking with difficulty.

"You shouldn't have drunk so much," said Fabie, worried.

"In front of two generals and three ministers? You must be joking. It wasn't possible, madame, because two and three make five."

He stood up.

"I'm going to sleep standing up so as not to die."

He fell to his knees.

"Amen."

And he began to say some prayers.

"Oh, shit!" said Fabie, "he's completely sozzled."

She took him by the shoulders and dragged him over to a divan and managed to hoist him onto it. Mumbling, he offered no resistance. When he was lying down he fell silent, and then looked at Fabie.

"Fabie."

"So you recognize me?"

"Fabie, I'm going to die."

"What *are* you talking about?"

"And anyway, everyone's going to die."

"Drink doesn't suit you, my poor Antoine."

"Since you want me to sleep lying down, I'll sleep lying down, but because I'm going to sleep lying down, I shall die."

"Don't worry. Go to sleep."

"It was magnificent. Magnificent. There were two ministers and three generals. Two and three make five, not counting Tolut, who was at a funeral because he buries everyone these days, my friend Tolut. There were lots and lots of people and they all admired me because I'm a millionaire now. All the millions I own, I've put them in a big safe under Charlemagne's tomb in Aix-la-Chapelle. That's only part of my fortune because aside from that treasure I own the whole of the Rhineland and the whole of the left bank of the Rhine. The Germans don't suspect it. They're stupid, aren't they?"

"They certainly are."

"They're stupid, but I'm going to die. So I'll tell you what's in my will: I'm leaving the Rhineland to France and my millions to you. Do you understand?"

"Naturally I understand. What would you expect me to do with the Rhineland!"

"You'd give it to France. I'm cleverer than two ministers and three generals. I'm a millionaire. Five hundred million. What will you do with five hundred million?"

"I'll buy you a beautiful tombstone."

"That's very nice. You're a real Paris sparrow, always ready with a joke. I know I can trust you. I can sleep in peace."

Mumbling, he fell asleep.

It's really bad to get drunk at his age, thought Fabie.

The next morning, when she awoke, Brabbant was already up. She called to him. He came in, a shaving brush in his hand, ready to daub his face.

"Good morning, my little Fabie. Did you sleep well?"

"Not badly, and you?"

"Excellent, excellent. You know, last night, it was magnificent."

"You aren't going to tell me there were two ministers and three generals, are you?"

"Why not? Naturally there were two ministers and three generals. Two and three make five, not counting Tolut."

He stammered as he spoke. Fabie looked at him, her eyebrows meeting in concentration.

"Was it you who sent me the umbrellas yesterday?"

"What umbrellas?"

"The two hundred umbrellas from the Bazar de l'Hôtel-de-Ville?"

Brabbant considered the matter, holding his shaving brush in the air like a torch. He smiled.

"I bought you some umbrellas because it's going to rain a lot this winter. My friend Alfred told me so. You know my friend Alfred, the fellow who knows everything, sees everything, foresees everything? He told me it would rain a lot this winter. So I thought that some umbrellas might come in useful for you."

"Two hundred?"

"Yes. I bought you two hundred umbrellas because it's going to rain a lot this winter. My friend Alfred told me so. You know my friend Alfred, the fellow who knows everything, sees everything, foresees everything? He told me it would rain a lot this winter, so I bought you two hundred umbrellas because I thought that some umbrellas might come in useful for you."

Fabie looked at him, terrified.

"This is it," she murmured.

"This is it," Brabbant repeated, like an echo. "I'll go and shave," he added.

Without moving from the spot, he thrust his shaving brush into his mouth. He looked at Fabie triumphantly and then, taking the shaving brush out of his mouth, spat the lather out all around him.

"This is it," he repeated. "This is it, this is it, this is it."

He began to laugh.

"And what's it all about?" he asked, with a knowing look. "Brabbant's going to die. Brabbant's going to die because he went to sleep lying down. If he hadn't lain down, he would have gone on living for hundreds and hundreds of years. But he lay down, so he's going to die. He's going to die and leave the

Rhineland to France and five billion to his little Fabie. Isn't that right, my little Fabie? There's no need to thank me! Five billion, that's the least I can give you. But naturally, the Rhineland to France!"

"I understand, that's only natural. Here—d'you mind if I make a phone call? I don't feel very well. I'd like to see a doctor."

"You don't feel very well. What's the matter with you? Hold on, I'll phone my friend Professor Wullmar."

He went over to the telephone.

"Don't bother, don't bother," Fabie cried.

"We are going to telephone the famous Professor Wullmar."

He picked up the receiver and asked for a number.

"Hallo? Hallo. I would like to speak to Doctor Wullmar. It's Monsieur Brabbant. Yes. Yes. Is that Doctor Wullmar? Hallo, yes. Very well. I'm phoning you because my girlfriend has asked me to phone you. Hallo. Do you understand me? not very well? It's very simple, Doctor, I'm going to die. Do you understand? I'm going to die because I slept lying down. Eh? What joke? You want me to say it again? I'm going to die because I slept lying down. You understand, it's urgent. At the moment I'm with my friend, Mademoiselle Fabienne d'Halincourt, 45 avenue Mozart. It's urgent, you understand. Good-bye, Doctor."

He hung up.

"You see, it was simple. Good old Doctor Wullmar. I'll go and shave."

He made his way to the bathroom, shaving brush in hand.

"Hold on," said Fabie. "Wait till he gets here."

"All the same, I can't receive the famous Professor Wullmar if I haven't shaved."

"It isn't important. You can shave later."

Brabbant looked at her.

"Wait," she repeated. "You can easily wait."

He sat down, legs apart, hands on his knees and holding his shaving brush like a scepter. He remained silent until the bell rang.

Doctor Wullmar came in.

"You see, Doctor," said Brabbant, "this is it."

He looked at him with a smile.

"This is it," he repeated. "It's over. Five billion for Fabie, and the Rhineland for France."

36

ROHEL AND TUQUEDENNE were awaiting their departure.

They had both got their degree in June; then the one left for Le Havre to collect his inheritance and the other for the Rhineland under the lame pretext of perfecting his German. Tuquedenne senior, impressed both by the fall of the mark and by the university qualification finally acquired, had offered to pay for this little trip. Tuquedenne junior lived in Mainz, then in Cologne. He was able to witness various incidents that gave rise to a monetary debacle which became famous in history and which the journalists' reports made known to the entire world. He wrote to Rohel, suggesting that they should meet in Aix-la-Chapelle, but Rohel didn't want to cut short his stay in Dinard, a stay for which his friend almost immediately found a likely explanation.

Tuquedenne returned to Paris towards the middle of September. For about ten days he lived a singularly idle, empty life. He went from cinema to cinema, drank by himself in bars he wouldn't have dared enter in the old days because you can't see from outside what is going on inside. Sometimes he would allow himself to be seduced by a prostituted, frigid female, for which purpose he liquidated his library, in this way spending the rest of his days on the *quais*. He also liquidated all the bits of paper he had accumulated, burning with neither pity nor respite some manuscript works whose puerility now made him blush. He nevertheless picked out some of them and made them into a packet which he fastened with a great blob of sealing wax, like a full stop. Rohel came back at the beginning of October; at their first meeting he introduced him to his girl-friend, Mademoiselle Thérèse Brennuire.

They awaited their departure. The military authorities had already been kind enough to inform them of its exact date and their destination. They waited. These were days without purpose, days without hope. For Tuquedenne they were entirely empty, like a gulf which he—dust—was floating over. For Rohel, the abyss was widening every day and he could clearly see the moment of the fall and the separation. To kill this insubstantial time they "amused themselves" by visiting Paris like the foreigners they believed they had become; or else they went to the races, trying to look like sporting men. Rohel spent his money with elegance, while Tuquedenne found it difficult to come by any.

One day, Thérèse told them that Brabbant had succumbed to senility and was close to death; her father insisted on her visiting him in the clinic because he didn't dare go himself, being much too afraid of his emotions. They offered to accompany her in the performance of her duty. When they got to the nursing home, a lively discussion was taking place between a nurse and an old gentleman who wished to see Brabbant; this he was categorically refused. Monsieur Brabbant's condition called for complete rest. The visitor, who was Tolut, was not surprised by the presence of his niece and two of his former pupils. He immediately began to explain his case, protesting against the tyranny of the medicasters and apothecaries. Thérèse, who wasn't particularly keen on watching Brabbant draw his last breaths, conscientiously asked to see Professor Wullmar. He wasn't there. Finally, an exceedingly youthful doctor informed them that Monsieur Brabbant's condition was unchanged and that no visits were allowed.

They went out. Thérèse excused herself for leaving, but she had to report to her father on the march of events as soon as possible. Tuquedenne and Rohel were left alone with Tolut, who didn't seem disposed to let them go, and who was anyway very little concerned with the activities of his niece.

"It's a great tragedy," said Tolut. "He certainly won't recover, at his age. A man of his merit! Did you know him?"

"A little," said Rohel.

"You used to play billiards with him at the Ludo," said Tuquedenne.

"That's true, that's true. He won't play billiards anymore. Nor will I. I don't play anymore. I no longer have time to enjoy myself. I have too many worries. Ah, I have so many worries, young men! If you only knew!"

"We don't know," said Rohel.

"You couldn't know. Dying doesn't arise at your age."

"That depends," said Tuquedenne.

Tolut, offended, said nothing. Then he changed the subject.

"Well, my friends, so you're graduates now?"

"Since June," Rohel replied.

"That's good, that's very good. My nephew is a graduate, too. Do you know him?"

"A little," Tuquedenne replied.

"And your friend Hublin, has he got his degree too?"

"He gave up. He's in coffee now."

"Really, really. And your friend Cindol?"

An enumeration was threatening. All his former pupils were preparing to march past. Rohel cut this exhibition short.

"Cindol? He's dead."

"He's dead? He was my best pupil. At his age, he's dead!"

"Yes, Monsieur Tolut."

"My friends, I'm going to tell you a secret. *I* am not going to die."

"That's quite possible," said Tuquedenne.

"Yes, isn't it? Do you know why and how?"

They didn't know.

"By not lying down. I sleep sitting up. That's a good idea, isn't it? If I went to sleep lying down, I should die. I know that very well. So I sleep sitting up. I'd told Brabbant this trick but they must have forced him to lie down in their diabolical clinic. So he's going to die. He was a man of merit, believe me."

"And so now you've become immortal, Monsieur Tolut."

"Well, yes! I have to. So long as I haven't discovered the way to leave behind me . . . But it would take too long to explain."

"We're listening, Monsieur Tolut."

"That's good; that's very good, to be willing to learn, all the more so as this question concerns you after all. Aren't you philosophers?"

"Precisely."

"And what do they say about death, philosophers?"

"Some say that philosophy is a preparation for death, others say that the free man doesn't think about it."

"As always, some say yes and others say no," said Tolut.

"There's no contradiction," Tuquedenne remarked.

"And after?" Tolut asked. "After, what do they say about that? Some one thing and others another, don't they?"

"More or less," said Rohel.

"I know, I know. But it's all the same to me. The future life, annihilation, metempsychosis, the whole caboodle, it's all the same to me. But there's one thing I am not indifferent to. Shh! Don't tell anyone! There's one thing I am not indifferent to, shh! and that is to trailing these worries and anxieties with me."

"Do you have so many then, Monsieur Tolut?"

"My life has been a swindle, you know that very well, you know it as well as I do! You know very well that I taught something I was ignorant of, that I dared to teach you something I didn't know."

"What was that; history?"

"History, for example, did I know Charlemagne? And Caesar, did I frequent him? And Napoleon, did he even exist? It's idiotic to talk about what you don't know. And geography! That's the last straw! Have I been to China, to Australia, to Japan? Nothing but lies, everything I taught you, nothing but lies."

"But you know very well, Monsieur Tolut, that geography teachers are not necessarily explorers."

"That's true. Even so, I could have traveled a little."

"Have you never been out of France, Monsieur Tolut?"

"No, never. Ah yes, though, I did once go to London."

"You see, you *have* traveled."

"Yes, but that was after, a long time after. That doesn't count. And what a journey, my young friends! I arrived just in time to see him die. And so you know how he died?—laughing. He was jeering at me! He died laughing. If it weren't for all these things jostling one another in my head, I would die laughing too. What does life do for me? And what do I do in life? Eh? Can you tell me? Of course I'm capable of dying laughing. Only, only, I don't want to die trailing this remorse with me."

"Come on, Monsieur Tolut," said Tuquedenne. "You know very well that all geography teachers are in the same position! And anyway, you were a very good teacher."

"Very good," said Rohel.

"You're very kind, young men, but that's not the point. *I* know my conscience. *You* don't know it, you don't know my conscience. To die laughing, nothing easier! If only I could not trail it with me! It *is* possible. There's a trick. I discovered it, the trick, when I was on my way to the blind man's funeral. Do you want to hear it?"

"That would interest us very much."

"Shh, eh? You leave a ghost behind. After that, you're at peace. The ghost may torment other people, but *you* are at peace. Good riddance!"

"What do you have to do to leave a ghost behind?"

"It's very simple," replied Tolut, looking pleased.

"Which would you prefer, Monsieur Tolut? To be immortal or to leave a ghost behind?"

"The question arises, since you know both tricks," Rohel added.

Tolut shook his head.

"The thing is, no one is ever immortal. One day, you aren't paying attention. You lie down, and you pass on. That's what happened to my friend Brabbant. It's a very good trick but it's so difficult that one fine day you miss it, and that time, that's it. No, no one's immortal. It's never been known."

"Then you'll leave a ghost behind, Monsieur Tolut?"

"I hope it won't torment you."

"That wouldn't be very nice of you, Monsieur Tolut."

"What would be nice of you would be to come to my funeral."

"But of course, Monsieur Tolut, we'll be there without fail."

"Well then, what's to stop me dying laughing?"

Rohel and Tuquedenne couldn't see anything to stop it. Tolut stopped at the curb, his eyes staring at the tips of his cracked bootees.

"His eyes put out," he murmured.

He looked at the two young men.

"It isn't necessary, is it, for me to put my eyes out? That would be too awful, wouldn't it? All the same, I'm not going to put my eyes out."

"Don't do anything of the sort," said Rohel.

"That's good, that's very good."

He gave a funny little cackle.

37

THEN THE OLD MAN made a quaint little sideways jump. A car coming up fast propelled him into a tree. It was a magnificent carom. The corpse lay flattened, face down. People came rushing up from all sides. The skull opened like an overripe orange. People encircled the dead man, chathowling, some cursed the driver. Later, an ambulance arrived.

"We'll have to find out the date of the funeral," said Tuquedenne.

The next day, Thérèse informed them that her father, much affected by these tragic events, had taken to his bed and didn't ever want to leave it. In this way he counted on avoiding the flapping wings by which he felt threatened. They were to meet at nine o'clock at the hospital where they had taken the tiny little corpse of the former teacher.

True to their promise, then, Tuquedenne and Rohel went there at the appointed hour. They were surprised at the number of people who were preparing to form the cortege. They would never have thought that so many people could have known Tolut, or that so many who showed no interest in him when he was alive would have been eager to accompany him once he was dead. It was thus that writers and artists who were on visiting terms with Brennuire felt obliged to come; many colleagues put in an appearance and even a historian, a member of the Institute, not to speak of first cousins and second cousins who had come from their province in some numbers.

"It's very sad," said someone, "that he can't take advantage of his family vault."

"It can't be helped," said someone else, "it's a terrible expense. The railway rates are prohibitive."

Rohel, repeating this conversation to Tuquedenne, announced his intention of offering them a check to pay for the transport of old Tolut, deceased.

"Let the dead bury their dead," Vincent advised him.

The cortege formed, and then began to move. Thérèse walked at its head, a victim to the family. They had insisted on a religious ceremony even though in his time Tolut had been a great champion of the cause of laicism. They made their way, then, towards a church. A priest bombinated in the Latin language; as he had been well paid and was conscientious, he pronounced some suitable words for the occasion, but without great conviction. Then the cortege re-formed and gravely made its way towards the cemetery. Like their neighbors, Rohel and Tuquedenne began to chat.

"Do you think he left a ghost behind him?" Rohel asked.

"In any case, it won't come and torment us," said Tuquedenne. "We're keeping our promise; I hope he'll keep his."

"It's odd, isn't it. That venerable, honest, worthy man had a guilty conscience."

"That often happens, people of experience say so, but they were unnaturally gaga, his qualms about geography."

"Did you understand his story about his trip to London?"

"No. There was someone who died laughing. That frightened him."

"Then there was that story of the one-eyed man being blinded and run over. Do you remember what he asked us before he threw himself under the car?"

"Yes. Maybe we could have asked him to put his eyes out.

His ghost would probably have liked that."

"If Tolut has really pulled it off, he's gallivanting all over the world now."

"I can already see him busy with his charming family," said Tuquedenne.

"He must be at Monsieur Brennuire's bedside."

"Poor fellow."

"How does that suicide affect you?"

"It's like an old skin that I've sloughed off, the corpse of my childhood."

"These things call for a celebration."

"Yes, by a funeral."

"And by a departure. It's a good combination."

"There are things that die together," said Tuquedenne. "After that, a new era begins."

"Our new era is beginning pretty badly. Eighteen months of military slavery."

"Will you desert?"

"No."

Which made them laugh. Some people were shocked, and looked round.

"We're irritating these cattle," said Tuquedenne.

They entered the cemetery. The cortege lumbricated its way between the graves until it reached the hole in which Tolut-corpse was going to putrefy. The priest sang once again. Then there were some little speeches. A gentleman spoke in the name of the former pupils of the Ecole normale supérieure. The member of the Institute spoke in praise of the discreet, conscientious scholar the deceased had been; he even took advantage of this to air his ideas on historical method.

At last the coffin was lowered into the grave and they dispersed, once again shaking the mitts of the members of the family.

"There," said Tuquedenne. "Simple, simple, simple."

"Yes, but they added a few flourishes."

"Even so, it's significant and convincing."

They left the cemetery and took a taxi.

"Are you going to see Thérèse again today?"

"I'm very much afraid not."

"What must be terrifying is the old boy in bed with his blue funk."

"One wonders why so much cowardice. Old men who seem so decent . . ."

"Shall we have a last drink?" Tuquedenne suggested.

"The last? That's true, I'd forgotten. Are you going this afternoon?"

"Yes. A last drink, then?"

They had themselves driven to a café.

"I'm glad they aren't sending you too far away from Paris. Personally, whether I go to Morocco or anywhere else, it won't change anything. It'll be the first time I've been anywhere."

"What do your parents say?"

"Oh! My parents already see me as a corporal."

It was midday. The crowd filled the streets, coming and going, dispersing or conglomerating, circulating or standing still, pouring down the entrances to the métro like a river of bitumen, assaulting the buses like a cloud of locusts; a crowd treading on each other's toes, digging its elbows into each other's ribs, spitting into each other's backs: a grumbling, gloomy, anticfray crowd.

A fine sight for young people.

Alfred

WELL! WHEN EVERYTHING was ready I made my way quite
calmly to Longchamp, which was reopening. I didn't hurry. I
get there during the third race. Naturally I treat myself to the
enclosure, and *Cesare Ranucci* won the third, as was written
in my papers. Then I went over to a booth and put ten francs on
Léonora. And then, after that, I look around me, I listen to what
people are saying, I observe. I felt really sorry to see all those
poor chaps flailing around in the dark and not knowing that
Léonora was going to win. Knowledge is a fine thing, after all:
I didn't even look at the race, I didn't even look at the notice
board. I went up to the window and collected 303 francs. I put
three francs in my pocket and three hundred on *Arlinde*. No
one around me was talking about *Arlinde*. So *Arlinde* started at
sixty-four and a half to one, and 19,650 francs turned up in my
pockets. The public were excited about the long odds, but not
many of them were collecting. None of this impressed me,
because it had been calculated in advance. For the last race,
even so I did go to see how it went. It's a pleasant sight. As I
knew what was going to happen I didn't need to shout or make
my heart beat faster than usual. My horse did what had to be
done for my figures to be correct. *L'Avalanche,* she was called
and *L'Avalanche* represented ten thousand francs for me at
eighteen and two-tenths to one, so that I left with a net profit

of 201,643 francs, just what I wanted, exactly what they took from my father, taking into account the rise in the cost of living and the fall of the franc.

I took the next day off. I entrusted my treasure to a credit institution and after that I went for a nice quiet walk. The day after, I go back to see the manager and I say: "Here I am again." He tells me: "That'll be so much." I give him what he wanted and I went back to my job having fulfilled my destiny, the des-. tiny written by the stars, and now I let people revolve around me in circles, like hares in the shooting gallery in a fair, until someone more skillful pulverizes them.

October is here, the students are back and the leaves are going to fall. One more, one less, they don't count for me any-more. I make the saucers circulate and the tables turn, and I don't interfere in anything that is none of my business. Some people come, others go. There are some who haven't fulfilled their destiny and who imagine that it will last forever, this little life. There are others for whom it's all over, and these we don't see anymore, like Monsieur Tolut, like Monsieur Brabbant, like Monsieur Brennuire.

When the time had come, a car hit him. Of course it was suicide. I foresaw long ago that he would commit suicide, Monsieur Tolut. You only had to look at him, to listen to him. There was no need to observe the planets. And since his little trip abroad, it was actually written on his face that he wouldn't hold out. It's bad to see death the way he saw it, with grimaces, and it's also bad to have something rotting and fermenting inside you. That makes things nasty. He said that geography tormented him. Nonsense. I'm not naïve, or a simpleton. I let him talk. He asked me whether you could know the date of your death. I didn't answer that one. Which made him look cross. It was gnawing at his guts, his conscience was. What a thing it is to think you have one! In the end it led him where it had to lead him. People will say: yes, but he had to die one day or another. True, but there's the way. That Monsieur Tolut, there was nothing for it, he had to die the way he did, lamentably, with that thing he called his professional conscience making his blood curdle. He's finished his little round and someone else has already taken his place.

The earth took possession of Monsieur Brennuire not long afterwards. I'd reckoned him up, the poor old man. He wasn't a day late for the rendezvous I'd fixed for him. The other one followed him soon after. It turned out so that the funerals took place almost one after the other. I didn't go, but the papers talked about them. The better one of the two was Monsieur Brabbant's. There were a lot of people, because he was the administrator of the SIGI, a limited company with a capital of ten million francs and whose name Monsieur Tolut didn't at all like because of the possible pun. All sorts of very respectable people were at Monsieur Brabbant's funeral. It was a great success. People made speeches and there was even what you might call a funeral oration. And then a few days later, the papers reported that he was a crook and that the SIGI was a swindle. What a fuss there was then, especially as it had to do with the Rhineland and the mark. The papers were as pleased as could be and made a meal of it. Naturally they printed his biography and his real name and all his convictions and of course he was just the sort of chap I thought, just a small-time crook who collected measly little convictions here, there and everywhere.

And then, bit by bit they realized that it wasn't so much of a swindle as they had wanted to make out at first and that Monsieur Brabbant had only spent a small part of the money he had collected, that he had even speculated successfully on the rise in the pound (thanks to me, but no one knows anything about that and I'm not going to boast about it; as they say in the papers, I'm a modest man). However, Monsieur Brabbant had actually bought one property, more precisely a little townhouse in the sixteenth arrondissement, where he lived with a young woman who has disappeared. I understand that, that she's disappeared; how right she is, they'd make trouble for her and a lot of good that would do her, afterwards. Coming back to Monsieur Brabbant, he really was the sort of person I said he was, just a small-time crook, and even when he had put together a beautiful big swindle he got practically nothing out of it. A house in Passy and five hundred thousand francs in one year, that's not a lot. Even so, it's better than the little swindles he'd been amusing himself with all his life. And even so, once again, he'd had to wait until he was seventy to become ambitious and have big ideas, and this certainly happened to him because of a woman, no doubt the little chick who's disappeared. After a whole lot of gossip the papers finally stopped talking about her, but that doesn't mean that they've stopped filling all their pages with their filthy printer's ink that makes your hands so dirty.

The third one too, he has fulfilled his destiny. I hadn't done his little reckoning, but it's quite certain that if I had, it would have fitted him like a glove. When he heard that his friend had fallen ill, it upset him. When he heard that his brother-in-law had been run over and killed, he took to his bed. When he heard that his friend had just kicked the bucket, he got the shakes. When he heard that his friend was a crook, he began to breathe his last. When he heard that his money wasn't completely lost, he died of joy. He was a small-minded gentleman, that Brennuire. They finally buried him, like the others. He had fulfilled his destiny in his own way. Everyone has his own way. Poor Brennuire.

No doubt people will wonder how I know all these stories and who described Monsieur Brennuire's emotions to me. Obviously they weren't in the papers, Monsieur Brennuire's emotions. But I heard Professor Wullmar describing them to a gentleman with him whose name I don't yet know. The empty places for the next hecatomb have been filled and the round is starting again. And the seasons are returning, holding each other's hands, and I remain, watching them and turning the handle. That lot had only been coming for three years, there are others for whom it lasts longer, sometimes up to two or three decades. They come for years and years, so that anyone might think it would last forever, but their destiny gets fulfilled. They disappear to get caught up in some other cycle or to get down from their wooden horses.

The dead leaves have fallen into the mud and people are treading them underfoot while they wait in the rain for the tram. I watch them through the window and my breath makes a mist on it. A new year is beginning. There are the regular customers and the new ones, there are old ones and young ones, thin ones and fat ones, civilians and soldiers. There are some who talk politics and others who discuss literature; there are some who want to start a little review and others who catch diseases from women; there are some who imagine they already know everything and others who look as if they don't know anything at all. As for me, I remain here, I serve them cold drinks in summer, hot ones in winter, and spirits in all seasons. I don't interfere in anything and I let everything carry on in its own way. The days go by and the nights go by too and the years and the seasons and you might think that everything would go on revolving like this forever, just as the customers go on coming for their daily coffee or aperitif, but the moment will come when there are no more seasons or years, no more days or nights, when the planets have completed their revolutions, when phenomena have no more periods, when everything will cease to exist. The entire universe will vanish, having fulfilled its destiny, just as here and now men's destiny is being fulfilled.

Notes

My thanks and gratitude to Madame Claude Debon and to the members of the *Séminaire Raymond Queneau,* Paris. Under the guidance of Madame Debon the seminar has met monthly, six times a year, for the last eight years. Some of its members are academics, others are not. All are united in their enthusiasm for Queneau and his work. Each year they choose one aspect of it, or one of his books, to discuss in depth—although most of them already know everything more or less by heart. For my (and your) benefit, this year (1989) they devoted two out of their six sessions to *Les Derniers jours,* in which they were able to give me solutions to almost all the problems that had defeated everyone else. Only once was there something that none of them knew (see note to p. 117, below).

It helps to remember that Queneau was a native of Le Havre. As he said in his autobiographical "novel" in verse, *Chêne et chien,* written (when he was 34) in 1937, the year after the publication of *Les Derniers jours:*

> Je naquis au Havre un vingt et un février
> en mil neuf cent et trois

It also helps to remember that in *Les Derniers jours,* Queneau was writing about his student years in Paris (1920-1923) some twelve or thirteen years later.

*

p. 4   *couch grass:* a Queneau in-joke. *Le Chiendent* is the title of his first book, published in 1933, three years before *Les Derniers jours.* Apart from its primary meaning, the expression "Voilà le chiendent" is Hamlet's "Ay, there's the rub," and the word is made up of *chien* (dog) and *dent* (tooth). Dogs have always had much significance in Queneau's mythology.

p. 4   The Lozenge: "La Pastille." Queneau liked to make multiple puns and allusions. There is a make of cough syrup, cough lozenges, etc., called Sirop de Tolut, Pastilles de Tolut. But: *pastille* is also a slang word for what we would politely call the anus. And an even less polite French expression for the above-mentioned part of the body is "trou du cul." One French friend has suggested that the joke might also well be: *Tolut* rhymes with *trou du cul, trou du cul* = *pastille.*

p. 6 "You know what they say about the French": that the French know nothing about their own geography, always ask for more bread, and all have the Legion of Honor.

p. 9 This chapter can be precisely dated. Apollinaire died on November 9, 1918, and was buried on the day of the First World War Armistice, November 11. Ironically, as his funeral procession was going by, the happy Parisian crowds were shouting: "Down with Guillaume." They were, of course, referring to Kaiser Wilhelm. Few of them had heard of Guillaume Apollinaire.

p. 16 It seems that the rue de Kabul (or Caboul) never actually existed. Apart from this one instance, all the streets Queneau mentions are topographically exact.

pp. 16-19 *Un sabord* is a porthole. *Un tambour* is a drum. *Mille sabords!* is the old seamen's (and pirates') exclamation: Shiver my timbers!

p. 20 " 'Ah, how *daily* life is' ": Jules Laforgue.

p. 23 "a housemaster": a *maître d'internat,* or *pion* (see later), is someone, usually still a student, who supervises boarding-school children. *Maîtres d'internat* are badly paid, badly treated, and usually much despised.

p. 31 PCN: physics, chemistry and natural sciences—courses taken in the first two years of a degree in medicine.

p. 32 A *demi* is not a small glass of beer, but a large one (half a liter). A *bock* is a small glass (a quarter of a liter).

p. 34 "homais": from Monsieur Homais, the provincial apothecary in Flaubert's *Madame Bovary,* "type of the self-satisfied country busybody, who never opens his mouth without making a speech, is ready to settle the affairs of the world at any moment. . ." (*Oxford Companion to French Literature*).

p. 35   Landru: Henri Desiré Landru (Paris, 1869–Versailles, 1922), charged in 1919 with the murder of ten women and one boy. According to the prosecution, he promised marriage to all the women, but killed them and burned their bodies in his kitchen stove. There was only circumstantial evidence against him—teeth and burned bones were found in his villa at Gambais (Seine-et-Oise), and the women's names were found in a notebook of his. Landru admitted having stolen from them but denied having murdered them. The rest of his story is told later by Alfred, Messrs. Brabbant and Tolut, et al. Charlie Chaplin's film *Monsieur Verdoux* was based on the Landru case.

p. 59   Queneau enjoyed making puns on his name. Hence *queneau-kout,* for *knock out* (more or less). And, a little farther down, Carpentier is *k'no-ktout.* (Queneau wrote: *queneau-coutte,* and *mis k'no-coutte.*)

p. 59   It seems that Carpentier really did own (or run) a saucepan factory.

p. 91   Cardan: Gerolamo Cardan (Pavia, 1501–Rome, 1576), doctor, mathematician and philosopher.

p. 91   Bayle: Pierre Bayle, French writer (Le Carla, 1647–Rotterdam, 1706). Taught history and philosophy. *Dictionnaire historique et critique,* 1696-97.

p. 93   *pneu:* short for *pneumatique:* "A letter sent by pneumatic despatch or tube." Only in Paris, though. Guaranteed to arrive in probably less than an hour. Alas, they no longer exist. (Why?)

p. 96   Suze is probably referring to one particular poet who frequented the Rotonde, but nobody can suggest which one.

p. 97   "painting; neither knew much about it": Queneau later became a connoisseur and collector of modern paintings. He was friendly with many painters and often wrote introductions to their exhibition catalogues.

p. 115   the Nord-Sud métro line (now line number 4) took the artists of Montmartre to visit the artists of Montparnasse, and vice versa. For this reason, Pierre Reverdy called his avant-garde review *Nord-Sud.* It flourished from 1916 to

1918, published Apollinaire, Max Jacob, Breton, Soupault, et al., and championed cubism. Reverdy's review existed in friendly rivalry with Pierre Albert-Birot's equally avant-garde review, *SIC* (1916–19).

p. 116 "the stupid nineteenth century": dixit Léon Daudet.

p. 117 "curled up": Queneau wrote *se trondela*. None of the seminar aficionados had any idea what this meant. You can imagine the lively discussion that went on as to what Rohel might possibly have done before falling asleep. Finally, though without much hope, it occurred to me to consult Maurice Rheims's *Dictionnaire des mots sauvages*. There I found the word, with the quotation from *Les Derniers jours,* and Queneau's explanation of it. He says it is a port-manteau word, a combination of the way a gun dog curls up *en rond,* and a *tendelet* (an awning) that one rolls up (*enroule*). He is surprised not to find *se trondeler* in any French dictionary, because it was current usage in Le Havre during his childhood.

p. 126 "incarcerated in the Vatican cellars": this is in fact part of the plot of Gide's *Les Caves du Vatican* (one of the books Tuquedenne is reading in chap. 22). It was first published in 1922.

p. 129 "makes *hallebarde* rhyme with *miséricorde*": Brabbant must have cast a fleeting glance at Alfred Jarry's 1903 poem "Bardes et cordes" (Bards and Ropes). But, as the title suggests, Jarry did *not* consider the two words to rhyme. His poem consists of ten verses, each of two lines. Each alternate line ends in *-arde* and *-orde*.

p. 143 "reading . . . *Barnabooth,* also in the original": a joke. The original language of *A. O. Barnabooth* (by Valery Larbaud) is French.

p. 143 "the establishment on the hill": the Sorbonne.

p. 144 "He made pessimism his profession of faith": Queneau once asked me whether I was an optimist or a pessimist. Without thinking, I immediately answered: "An optimist." He then asked me: "How do you know?"

p. 155 "To whom could he have confided his misgivings?": poor Tolut! He doesn't realize that he has already confided his misgivings to both Alfred and Rohel.

p. 161 The Carpentier–Siki match was fixed; Siki was supposed to take a dive, but changed his mind by the third round and went on to defeat Carpentier—making Brabbant's bet all the more remarkable.

p. 175 *Fantômas:* character created in 1911 by Marcel Allain and Pierre Souvestre. Fantômas is the technician of the perfect crime, and he always escapes from his sworn enemy, Inspector Juve. The Fantômas series is regarded as a classic of the genre.

p. 177 A citron: a Citroën, of course.

p. 211 *ci-gît:* here lies . . .

p. 226 Alfred's last chapter is a good example of Queneau's fondness for changing his tenses back and forth, maybe even several times within one sentence. If one really wants to analyze this practice, a subtle reason for it can always be found.

BARBARA WRIGHT

DALKEY ARCHIVE PAPERBACKS

FICTION: AMERICAN

BARNES, DJUNA. *Ladies Almanack*	9.95
BARNES, DJUNA. *Ryder*	11.95
BARTH, JOHN. *LETTERS*	14.95
BARTH, JOHN. *Sabbatical*	12.95
CHARYN, JEROME. *The Tar Baby*	10.95
COOVER, ROBERT. *A Night at the Movies*	9.95
CRAWFORD, STANLEY. *Some Instructions*	11.95
DAITCH, SUSAN. *Storytown*	12.95
DOWELL, COLEMAN. *Island People*	12.95
DOWELL, COLEMAN. *Too Much Flesh and Jabez*	9.95
DUCORNET, RIKKI. *The Fountains of Neptune*	10.95
DUCORNET, RIKKI. *The Jade Cabinet*	9.95
DUCORNET, RIKKI. *Phosphor in Dreamland*	12.95
DUCORNET, RIKKI. *The Stain*	11.95
EASTLAKE, WILLIAM. *Lyric of the Circle Heart*	14.95
FAIRBANKS, LAUREN. *Sister Carrie*	10.95
GASS, WILLIAM H. *Willie Masters' Lonesome Wife*	9.95
GORDON, KAREN ELIZABETH. *The Red Shoes*	12.95
KURYLUK, EWA. *Century 21*	12.95
MARKSON, DAVID. *Reader's Block*	12.95
MARKSON, DAVID. *Springer's Progress*	9.95
MARKSON, DAVID. *Wittgenstein's Mistress*	11.95
MASO, CAROLE. *AVA*	12.95
McELROY, JOSEPH. *Women and Men*	15.95
MERRILL, JAMES. *The (Diblos) Notebook*	9.95
NOLLEDO, WILFRIDO D. *But for the Lovers*	12.95
SEESE, JUNE AKERS. *Is This What Other Women Feel Too?*	9.95
SEESE, JUNE AKERS. *What Waiting Really Means*	7.95
SORRENTINO, GILBERT. *Aberration of Starlight*	9.95
SORRENTINO, GILBERT. *Imaginative Qualities of Actual Things*	11.95
SORRENTINO, GILBERT. *Mulligan Stew*	13.95
SORRENTINO, GILBERT. *Splendide-Hôtel*	5.95
SORRENTINO, GILBERT. *Steelwork*	9.95
SORRENTINO, GILBERT. *Under the Shadow*	9.95
STEIN, GERTRUDE. *The Making of Americans*	16.95
STEIN, GERTRUDE. *A Novel of Thank You*	9.95
STEPHENS, MICHAEL. *Season at Coole*	7.95
WOOLF, DOUGLAS. *Wall to Wall*	7.95

DALKEY ARCHIVE PAPERBACKS

YOUNG, MARGUERITE. *Miss MacIntosh, My Darling*   2-vol. set, 30.00
ZUKOFSKY, LOUIS. *Collected Fiction*   9.95
ZWIREN, SCOTT. *God Head*   10.95

FICTION: BRITISH
BROOKE-ROSE, CHRISTINE. *Amalgamemnon*   9.95
CHARTERIS, HUGO. *The Tide Is Right*   9.95
FIRBANK, RONALD. *Complete Short Stories*   9.95
GALLOWAY, JANICE. *Foreign Parts*   12.95
GALLOWAY, JANICE. *The Trick Is to Keep Breathing*   11.95
HUXLEY, ALDOUS. *Point Counter Point*   13.95
MOORE, OLIVE. *Spleen*   10.95
MOSLEY, NICHOLAS. *Accident*   9.95
MOSLEY, NICHOLAS. *Impossible Object*   9.95
MOSLEY, NICHOLAS. *Judith*   10.95
MOSLEY, NICHOLAS. *Natalie Natalia*   12.95

FICTION: FRENCH
BUTOR, MICHEL. *Portrait of the Artist as a Young Ape*   10.95
CÉLINE, LOUIS-FERDINAND. *North*   13.95
CREVEL, RENÉ. *Putting My Foot in It*   9.95
ERNAUX, ANNIE. *Cleaned Out*   10.95
GRAINVILLE, PATRICK. *The Cave of Heaven*   10.95
NAVARRE, YVES. *Our Share of Time*   9.95
QUENEAU, RAYMOND. *The Last Days*   11.95
QUENEAU, RAYMOND. *Pierrot Mon Ami*   9.95
ROUBAUD, JACQUES. *The Great Fire of London*   12.95
ROUBAUD, JACQUES. *The Plurality of Worlds of Lewis*   9.95
ROUBAUD, JACQUES. *The Princess Hoppy*   9.95
SIMON, CLAUDE. *The Invitation*   9.95

FICTION: GERMAN
SCHMIDT, ARNO. *Collected Stories*   13.50
SCHMIDT, ARNO. *Nobodaddy's Children*   13.95

FICTION: IRISH
CUSACK, RALPH. *Cadenza*   7.95
MAC LOCHLAINN, ALF. *The Corpus in the Library*   11.95
MACLOCHLAINN, ALF. *Out of Focus*   5.95

DALKEY ARCHIVE PAPERBACKS

O'BRIEN, FLANN. *The Dalkey Archive*   9.95
O'BRIEN, FLANN. *The Hard Life*   11.95
O'BRIEN, FLANN. *The Poor Mouth*   10.95

FICTION: LATIN AMERICAN and SPANISH
CAMPOS, JULIETA. *The Fear of Losing Eurydice*   8.95
LINS, OSMAN. *The Queen of the Prisons of Greece*   12.95
PASO, FERNANDO DEL. *Palinuro of Mexico*   14.95
RÍOS, JULIÁN. *Poundemonium*   13.50
SARDUY, SEVERO. *Cobra* and *Maitreya*   13.95
TUSQUETS, ESTHER. *Stranded*   9.95
VALENZUELA, LUISA. *He Who Searches*   8.00

POETRY
ANSEN, ALAN. *Contact Highs: Selected Poems 1957-1987*   11.95
BURNS, GERALD. *Shorter Poems*   9.95
FAIRBANKS, LAUREN. *Muzzle Thyself*   9.95
GISCOMBE, C. S. *Here*   9.95
MARKSON, DAVID. *Collected Poems*   9.95
THEROUX, ALEXANDER. *The Lollipop Trollops*   10.95

NONFICTION
FORD, FORD MADOX. *The March of Literature*   16.95
GREEN, GEOFFREY, ET AL. *The Vineland Papers*   14.95
MATHEWS, HARRY. *20 Lines a Day*   8.95
MOORE, STEVEN. *Ronald Firbank: An Annotated Bibliography*   30.00
ROUDIEZ, LEON S. *French Fiction Revisited*   14.95
SHKLOVSKY, VIKTOR. *Theory of Prose*   14.95
WEST, PAUL. *Words for a Deaf Daughter* and *Gala*   12.95
WYLIE, PHILIP. *Generation of Vipers*   13.95
YOUNG, MARGUERITE. *Angel in the Forest*   13.95